FUNERAL GIRL

EMMA K. OHLAND

Carolrhoda LAB
MINNEAPOLIS

Carolrhoda Lab®
An imprint of Lerner Publishing Group, Inc.
241 First Avenue North
Minneapolis, MN 55401 USA

For reading levels and more information, look up this title at
www.lernerbooks.com.

Design elements by: Fractal/Shutterstock.com; Rodina Olena/Shutterstock.com;
Duda Vasilii/Shutterstock.com; sommthink/Shutterstock.com.

Main body text set in Janson Text LT Std.
Typeface provided by Adobe Systems.

Library of Congress Cataloging-in-Publication Data

Names: Ohland, Emma K., author.
Title: Funeral girl / Emma K. Ohland.
Description: Minneapolis : Carolrhoda Lab, [2022] | Audience: Ages 13–18. |
    Audience: Grades 10–12. | Summary: "When Georgia revives the spirit of a
    recently deceased classmate at her family's funeral home, she's forced to sort out
    her complex feelings about grief and mortality" —Provided by publisher.
Identifiers: LCCN 2021048671 (print) | LCCN 2021048672 (ebook) |
    ISBN 9781728458007 | ISBN 9781728460734 (ebook)
Subjects: CYAC: Ghosts—Fiction. | Grief—Fiction. | Death—Fiction. | Funeral
    homes—Fiction. | Family-owned business enterprises—Fiction. | LCGFT:
    Novels.
Classification: LCC PZ7.1.O4425 Fu 2022 (print) | LCC PZ7.1.O4425 (ebook) |
    DDC [Fic]—dc23

LC record available at https://lccn.loc.gov/2021048671
LC ebook record available at https://lccn.loc.gov/2021048672

Manufactured in the United States of America
1-50828-50167-3/8/2022

Dear Reader,
This book includes discussions of dying, corpses, grief, depression, and anxiety. If any of these topics aren't productive for you to engage with in this moment, please feel free to set this book aside.

TO CARSON,
SINCE FOREVER, FOR FOREVER

CHAPTER 1

The dead woman's name was Betty. She was eighty-three when she died from a heart attack alone in the room of her nursing home. There were only seven people at her funeral, if you included me and the pastor. And I wouldn't exactly say we counted since we were getting paid.

I stood at the back of the chapel in one of my many black dresses and one of my many pairs of black Mary Janes. It was pretty much the uniform. I had a good view of the back of the heads of the five women who attended, and I stood right in line with Pastor Hugh Wilson as he gave his eulogy. Three of the women were rather young, and they accompanied two older ladies, both in wheelchairs. I'd overheard the younger women talking before the funeral. They were nurses from Betty's nursing home. I assumed they had dragged the older ladies with them because, judging by the angles of their heads, they had fallen asleep.

I'd seen plenty of small funerals in my lifetime. Small usually meant fifteen to twenty people, close friends and family who wanted an intimate celebration of life. Betty's funeral wasn't just small, it was empty. You'd expect the quietest person at a funeral to be the dead body, but today, the congregation took the cake.

On the dais beside Betty's British-style coffin, a photograph of her younger self rested on an easel. The large print was adorned with a frame of fake white roses provided by Richter Funeral Home. The image matched the one printed on the card stock in my hands. Betty's memorial pamphlets. Mom had unknowingly printed far too many.

Hugh spent only ten minutes talking about what a wonderful, kind, and God-loving woman Betty had been. He told a quick story from her childhood, explained her work in the community, and said that she lived a quiet life with her late husband. He proceeded to list the usual funeral-safe adjectives, as if he was reading from a funeral-themed Mad Lib where he switched up the names of people and places but stuck to the same descriptors. Kind. Generous. Loving. If the person was lucky, heroic. At the end, he'd usually mention refreshments being served in the viewing room or a reception being held after at (noun, location). But this time, he just bowed his head and pocketed his handheld Bible.

The funeral was over practically before it started. The nurses stood up and rolled the older women down the aisle past me without a moment's hesitation. They gave their obligatory thank-yous, telling me that it had been a lovely service, but I heard one of the older ladies complaining about the temperature and how long they'd been there. I thanked them for coming and shuffled the extra pamphlets in my hands. I'd have to toss them in recycling after this.

Then, all that was left in the room was a teenage girl, a preacher, and a dead body. Sounded like the start to one of the jokes Dad liked to tell.

Hugh stepped off the dais toward me, prepared to start a conversation. I groaned internally.

2

Because of Somerton's unfortunately small size, Hugh was one of only three religious leaders who regularly officiated for us. Sometimes other officiants were brought from elsewhere in the county upon request, especially if the funeral was secular, but Hugh spent the most time around Richter. He'd known me since I was little, and because he and my twin brother, Peter, got along so well, he tried to be buddies with me too. Dad always said it was important to start making connections now for when Peter and I ran the funeral home. But I didn't enjoy the small talk that required.

So, instead of engaging, I walked right past him, pretending I was about to start cleanup. Thankfully, he got the message and exited through the glass chapel doors.

Now all that remained in the chapel was a teenage girl and a dead body. Sounded more like the start of a horror movie.

I drew the curtains on the glass doors, twisted the lock, and turned to face the coffin. It loomed in front of me, thick and glossy.

I pocketed one of the pamphlets and set the others down on one of the benches, keeping my eyes locked on the casket. The dais was three steps up and Betty's casket rested on a wooden bier, so I could only see the tip of her nose from down here.

When I took those steps, I was able to stand above the coffin. It was our most basic casket, made of veneer with a white cotton lining. We suggested this one to those on a tighter budget. Whenever a client requested the cheapest option, Mom would hand them the green pamphlet from the coffee table. The red pamphlet was our deluxe package for those privileged enough to be buried in bronze and velvet.

I ran my hands along the fabric, feeling the fibers beneath my fingers. My hands lingered close to Betty's arm, which was clothed in a navy-blue suit. That was Mom's job in body prep if the clients didn't provide an outfit. Dad did the rest.

Betty was as white as the lining, and I felt cold standing near her. Her face in particular was whiter than the rest of her body thanks to all the powder, and her skin was pulled and molded to make her look younger than she was, less human than she was. She looked as if she was made of wax instead of skin due to the embalming fluid that had replaced the blood inside her cheeks. Those cheeks were coated with a thick layer of makeup and the sockets of her eyes stuffed with molds to keep shape. Staring at her sent a feeling of familiarity coursing through my veins that stiffened me like the embalming fluid.

Dad dressed up the bodies to appear presentable to attendees at an open-casket funeral. I never understood in what world this mannequin-like visage was presentable to any audience. If you looked at the picture printed out on the memorial pamphlets or the easel, you'd barely be able to tell they were the same woman. No one could see the incisions in her legs or arms or neck used to drain her blood.

I continued to run my hands along the cotton, back and forth. I was nervous, knew I was stalling. I did this every time.

I couldn't take my eyes off her face. She looked so much like someone I could have known. There weren't any neurons firing in her brain anymore. None of what lay before me could possibly be Betty, but I tried to picture what she would have looked like without molded eyes or plastered cheeks. I couldn't reconcile the body's plastic face with her gentle features in the photo.

Thinking about Betty alive but seeing her dead triggered my breaths to start shaking with my hands, and I gripped the side of the coffin more tightly, like it was the only thing keeping me upright. Sometimes I could swallow away the anxiety

4

and just do it—other times it felt like this. Like it was going to win. Like it controlled my breathing instead of me.

But I wanted to do this, maybe I needed to do this. I felt for my breaths and I took them back. Made them slow. Reminded myself they were mine. And with a deep exhale, I removed my hands from the coffin, my fingers leaving prints pressed into the lining. I reached toward what was once Elizabeth Ann Cooper's cheek, and my finger met her skin.

In an instant, wearing that same navy-blue pantsuit but looking far more lifelike, Betty stood next to me. Her head moved around the room, her back arched, and she blinked as if to wake herself up from a dream.

"Hi, Betty," I said, leaning down a bit to catch myself in her line of view. I still hadn't perfected initiating these conversations.

Our eyes met, hers a deep blue that felt so real, and she squinted at me. "Am I late for bingo?" she asked.

While in reality she was probably very late for bingo, I couldn't bring myself to break her spirit.

"No, you won't miss it, don't worry," I said.

"Is Nancy going to be there?"

These interactions always went differently. Some people knew immediately where they were. Others were completely confused or thought they were right back where they had been before they died. There was no pattern, no way to predict what would happen. I tried to calculate exactly where on this spectrum Betty fell because she looked at me like she knew, but she spoke like she didn't.

"Um . . . I don't know. How do you feel, Betty?" I'd done this so many times, but I hadn't gotten better at it.

"I'm still mad at Nancy," she replied with a scoff. "Is she

5

going to be at bingo? Because if she is, I think I'll go back to my room and watch *State Fair*. I am not in the mood."

I tried to contain a smile. "Do you know where you are?"

She peered around, wrinkling her nose, forgetting about her feud with Nancy for a moment. "No," she said, the anger in her voice lifting. "This isn't the bingo room. This . . ." She paused. "Well, this isn't home at all."

I wished I could come into these conversations with a strategy, but instead I had to take each moment as it came. At this point I had two options. I could be blatant—cut to the chase, tell them where they were and ask them what they wanted—but that was always risky. There'd been a few freak-outs, which were understandable but hard for me to deal with. I always tried my best to comfort people, but there's only so much you can do to help someone who's just realized they're dead. A few times, people had gotten so out of control that I'd had to touch them again before I made any progress. I was always shocked at how many people handled the news calmly, but I had no way of knowing how Betty would react. Every ghost was different.

The second option was also a gamble. If I withheld the truth, going along with a ghost's assumption that they were still alive, they were more likely to remain calm but less likely to give me any answers.

"Where are we?" Betty asked.

Since I didn't have much time, I decided to go the direct route. "We're at your funeral."

Betty's eyes widened and her posture stiffened. "What? What happened?" Her eyes suddenly found the photo of her between the flowers, and she stepped toward the casket to see her body lying motionless. Her hands shot to her mouth to catch a gasp.

"You had a heart attack. Your funeral just ended. You're okay." I held out my hand in a comforting gesture but knew if I tried to place it on her, it would pass through her like she was made of air.

"*Okay?* I'm dead!" She threw up her hands. "And I am in the ugliest pantsuit!"

"Not my mom's best choice," I admitted.

"Well," she huffed. "How was my funeral?"

"It was . . . fine," I said, rather unconvincingly. I wasn't about to send her to her grave knowing it had been so empty. But I also couldn't lie.

"Nancy didn't come, did she? She probably gave me the heart attack. I always knew she had it out for me. It was the look she would give me, you know? That evil gleam in her eyes."

"It was natural, Betty," I clarified, desperately wanting to know more about this drama between the two of them but also wanting to get down to business.

"Did they do an autopsy to confirm that?"

"Betty." I held out my hand, trying to steady her with the gesture alone. "I wanted to ask you a few questions before I send you . . ." I stopped. I shouldn't have said that last bit. I bit my tongue as if that would pull the words back in, but her eyes narrowed, telling me she'd caught them.

"Are you an angel?" Betty asked, her look suspicious now. "Do you send me off to the next life?"

"Um. Kind of?" I'd thought about what this was over and over without a conclusive answer. After three years and ghost after ghost, I still didn't know what I was.

"So, am I going to Heaven?"

Oof. That was the big question. And every time I was asked, I was more and more uncertain. Aside from the random facts Hugh had spewed in his eulogy, I had no idea what Betty had done in her lifetime. I didn't know if her actions would lead her to Heaven, Hell, or another place no one knew about, or if I would tap her again and send her into some unknowable nothingness without consciousness. I could talk to the dead, not see beyond death. Instead of explaining my spiral of an answer, I said, "I hope so."

"Will I get to see Wilmer?" she asked.

"Was Wilmer your husband?"

"Yes. He left us years ago. It hasn't been the same without him. I visit his grave every week. He needs to know I never forgot him. Does he know? Has he been okay without me?" She clutched at her heart like it was actually beating beneath her palm.

She was talking like I had confirmed I was an angel. But at least she was calm, she was giving me answers. So I said, "He's waiting for you."

I wasn't certain of the morality of saying it. It both deeply unsettled me and warmed some piece of me. I wanted her to have a glimmer of hope. I wanted that glimmer of hope. But I wasn't sure if it was real.

"Oh, then please, please let me see him." Tears filled her eyes and fell down her cheeks without leaving a trail on her foundation.

"But first, do you have any final requests, Betty? Anything I could do for you?"

She thought about it for a moment, wiping the tears away from her cheeks. "Getting to be with Wilmer is all I could ask for," she said.

"Are you sure? Do you have any children? Or other loved ones who should have something or know something? Do you have any, I don't know, unfinished business?"

"I just want to be with Wilmer," she repeated.

I twisted my left hand around my right wrist. I'd tapped her hoping there was some final wish I could help her with. Seeing Wilmer wasn't a wish I knew I could grant. I wanted something else, something tangible, a way I could make her death mean something. But then I felt another ache, remembering that Grandma had been glad she'd get to see Grandpa.

The best I could do was to tap Betty again. Hopefully that meant seeing Wilmer, just as I hoped Grandma was with Grandpa.

"All right," I sighed. "It was nice to meet you, Betty."

"Thank you," she said.

There was nothing to thank me for. I returned to the coffin, reached out reluctantly, and tapped her body's cold cheek. Her apparition disappeared. My finger lingered above her skin as I stared at the place on the dais where she'd once stood. The room once again silent.

"Georgia, is the room already clean?"

I practically jumped from my own skin. The chapel doors were shaking. I was shaking along with them, my heart pounding in my throat. I cursed myself for cutting it so close.

"Why is it locked?" It was Peter trying to get in for cleanup duty.

I jumped down from the dais and rushed to open the door.

"Sorry," I said, kicking the stand to keep the door propped open and avoiding eye contact with my brother.

"Why was the door locked?" he repeated, eyeing me suspiciously just as Betty had.

"Jeez, Pete. It's not like I was summoning demons in here or anything. I just accidentally locked it." My heart was still pounding, and I was trying to keep it out of my voice. I didn't prefer to chat with the ghosts after the funeral for this very reason, but I hadn't gotten a chance alone with Betty beforehand. Peter eyeing me, arms crossed, was a reminder of the risk. "What?" I snapped.

"Just here for cleanup," he said, shrugging and pushing past me. "Looks like you haven't even started."

"Hey, it's your job this time."

Peter and I were the only two children of Greg and Andrea Richter. Since Richter Funeral Home was a family business, it would someday be ours. Ever since we were twelve, we'd been helping run the funerals as practice for our future career.

Peter looked exactly like my parents. They all had tanned white skin, perfectly straight noses, and dark thick hair, while I had stringy dirty-blond hair, a hooked nose covered in freckles, and the complexion of one of the palest white corpses. Despite my resemblance to the dead, Peter was the one who was all about the family business. Peter had been an aspiring mortician since day one. He was also a perfect student, a star football player, and one of the most adored people in school. We shared a womb but that's where it stopped. Each of his skills was a brick forming a path that could lead him straight out of Somerton, but for some reason, he wanted to stay.

"Mom says she's ordering pizza. Go tell her what kind you want."

"Just no meat," I said, grabbing the pamphlets off the bench.

"Tell her that." He started flicking off the lights.

"She knows that."

Peter walked up the dais and removed the picture from the easel, placed the flowers in the corner, and grabbed the lid of Betty's coffin. I took one last look at Betty's nose before Peter closed the lid. It felt like he was doing that to her, shutting her in there for all eternity, and I was letting it happen. She'd be buried and forgotten. I doubted Peter even knew her name.

And I hoped with all my might that wherever she was, she was with Wilmer.

When the workday was over, I settled in the tiny living room upstairs, reading on the couch in front of the unlit fireplace, while Mom, Dad, and Peter crowded into the kitchen and opened the pizza. The smell wafted through the apartment.

"Georgia, do you want sausage or pepperoni?" Mom asked.

"Did you not get cheese?"

"Nope. Just these."

I stared at her and closed my book, but she didn't realize anything was off.

"We have breadsticks if you're not feeling pizza," Dad said.

"I'll be right back." I sighed and walked down the hall to my bedroom. Morty, our Siamese cat, was enjoying a nap on my pillows. I bent down and reached underneath the bed, shifting a few boxes until I finally grabbed my large pink binder. It held hundreds of sheets of scrapbook paper with already worn edges. About seventy pages were filled out, the rest waiting to be.

I brought the binder to my desk and turned on my lamp, flipping to the next available page. It was on the right side. Alexander Wheeler, who had come through Richter last week, was on the left. His pamphlet was taped neatly in the corner and my handwriting filled the rest of that page. What he'd told me, what I'd learned in his eulogy, and what his final request was.

I'd talked to him before the funeral, though not for long because he knew right away and panicked. But he instantly had a final wish: tell his wife the combination to his safe. He said there was something special in it for her and his kids. He didn't tell me what. Afterward, I wrote the combination on a sticky note, stuck it inside a memorial pamphlet, and made sure it ended up in her hands. That was my go-to strategy for relaying simple pieces of information to the living, seeing as having the undertaker's kid approach a funeral guest with information from beyond the grave would raise suspicion.

I placed Betty's pamphlet in the center of the next page, now her page, and taped it at the corners. I filled in what I knew about her: Wilmer, her enjoyment of bingo and *State Fair*, her hatred of Nancy. I also added what Hugh had said: she grew up in Vermont, was the first in her family to go to college. But there was a lot that I didn't know—what she'd studied, where she'd traveled, what her hobbies were, what her dreams were. Too much of her page was left empty.

I'd had more time to talk with Jonathan. Had more time with Louise before him and Edgar before her. Their pages were full of little details. They'd all had final requests. I wished I had more to write about Betty. I wished I had spoken to her before her funeral instead of after. Now it was too late. No one would know more. Betty's name would be lost in the wind and no one would even try to grab it.

There was a gentle knock at my door, and I closed my scrapbook.

"Are you going to join us for dinner?" Mom called from the other side of the door.

"Not tonight."

I could feel the defeat sliding through the crack between the door and the frame, but Mom just said, "Okay," and I heard her walk away.

I leaned back in my chair and remembered all the times we'd ordered pizza and my parents had put meat on it. I'd been a vegetarian since I was five. I knew Mom and Dad were busy, but I was tired of constantly having to remind them about something so simple.

I flipped my scrapbook open to the first page, from four years ago. The pamphlet was taped to the left side of the page, and on the right was a photo of Grandma and me building a snowman when I was in first grade. He'd stood in Richter's front yard for two long weeks, and we'd go out every day after school to feed him carrots to keep him strong. I remember finding it morbid that his diet consisted of his own body parts, but Grandma assured me this was normal for snowpeople.

I grabbed all the pages in my hand and dragged my thumb along the edges, creating a little breeze on my face as I flipped through the paper. Whenever I revisited these profiles, a fresh grief cropped up. I missed these people. Many of them had been wonderful and kind. I wished I could have known them for longer. Every time that feeling twinged at my heart, I repeated their names and what I'd learned about them, determined to keep them alive in the one way I could.

I flipped through the pages again and again and again, repeating the names and reciting details and remembering their final requests until it was way past dark.

CHAPTER 2

I used to read the newspaper every morning, starting with the obituaries. The newspaper was a ritual in our family. At breakfast, Mom and Dad would sip their coffee and flip through the pages, handing them to us when they were done. Peter always reached for the sports first, but it was the records of the dead that always captured my attention. Mom had to write obituaries for some of the people who passed through here, so I always checked to see if Richter Funeral Home was attached to any of the names and if I recognized anyone's face.

The morning after Betty's funeral, Mom was sitting across from me reading the local news section, and Peter was scribbling away at homework he'd clearly forgotten about and would still manage a perfect grade on. Dad was already downstairs working because he'd received a death call in the middle of the night. I'd recently stopped reading the obituaries every morning because I wanted one moment in my day that didn't feature death. But today, I found myself drawn to those names and words again.

"Did you notice the turnout at the Cooper funeral?" I asked, sitting down and grabbing for the obituaries. Peter looked up at me, then eyed the pages in my hand. I read the ages under all the pictures and ignored him.

"Yeah, it was pretty small," Mom said.

"Mom," I said. "Small is like twenty people. Betty's funeral was *empty*. It was so sad."

Mom raised her brow at me over her sip of coffee. "Betty?"

Whoops. Usually, in the business, we refer to the deceased by their title and last name or by their full name to maintain a business relationship.

Instead of acknowledging Mom's surprise, I said hastily, "Isn't it sad? I mean, she lived this full life, but because she wasn't, I dunno, particularly likable to the people in her nursing home or because she didn't have any children or whatever the case was"—I didn't tell her about Nancy or Wilmer or the fact that she indeed did not have children—"she's just going to be buried six feet under, pushing up daisies while maggots eat at her body and she rots until she's nothing but bones."

"She's going to be cremated," Mom said, blinking at me.

I dropped the paper onto the table. "You know what I mean."

"Yes, Georgia, I know what you mean. As is life."

I tensed. I hated those throwaway statements. "Do you get any information on what she wants done with her ashes?"

"What is your interest in Mrs. Cooper?" Peter said. He punctuated the question by folding his arms on the table and leaning toward me. I wanted him to go back to ignoring me like usual.

"Is it a crime to try and learn the business?" I shot back.

Peter rolled his eyes and returned to his homework.

"We don't get to decide where her ashes are laid or how her body is taken care of. You know that, Georgia," Mom reminded me. The words "taken care of" implied a kind and gentle process, but her tone made it meaningless.

"Right. She tells you what she wants in her will, yeah?"

"Not always. But Mrs. Cooper did, yes. She stated in her will that she wanted to be cremated. I'm not sure if she stated

15

what she wants done with her ashes. If she has family, then they can do with them as they will. Since we aren't a crematorium, we won't be dealing with that aspect. You already know this."

"Mom, she didn't have a family." It came out angrier than it sounded in my head. I sank back in my chair and lowered my voice. "That's what Hugh said."

I'd caught Mom off guard. "Why such an interest all of a sudden, G? Usually you're reluctant to talk to us about this stuff and now you're mad at me for not getting into the details with you?"

"Her funeral was sad. I was just curious."

"It's fine to be curious, but it's not like you."

"Sorry. Never mind." Then an idea occurred to me. I pulled out my phone and Googled *Wilmer Cooper, Somerton, Lionel County, Indiana.* "I'm heading to school."

"Half an hour early?" Peter said skeptically, but I grabbed my backpack from the couch and ran down the steps of our apartment before Mom's suspicions could grow.

"Have a good day!" Dad called over to me from the office, and I waved my arm before exiting Richter. I didn't look behind me when I closed the door.

School was a few blocks over east, and like Peter said, it didn't start for another thirty minutes, so that's why I headed off in the opposite direction.

Two blocks from the funeral home was Hugh's church, one of three in town. Somerton was not religiously diverse— or diverse in any sense of the word for that matter—so all the churches were Christian. I didn't know much about the denominations since my family wasn't religious, and I hadn't even set foot inside a church. I only knew what I saw inside Richter's chapel.

Right behind the stone church was a small cemetery that housed no more than fifty graves. A Gothic fence marked the perimeter, and a stone path led up to the entrance. I opened the creaky metal gate and stepped in. Most of the headstones were worn and falling over because this was an older cemetery and hadn't been used lately. In the far corner, however, were a few newer granite headstones.

I headed toward that corner, passing the old headstones along the way. Most of them had moss growing on them, some had been tipped over by time and weather, and the ones that had completely fallen made my heart lurch. There was one in particular that drew my attention. A large tree branch lay across it, and since there were no trees above, I gathered it had fallen victim to some kids playing games here at night. I removed the branch to discover moss completely growing across the name. I knelt down and grabbed a stone to brush it off. *Shirley A. Jackson 1912–1925. Loving daughter.*

Shirley had died when she was three years younger than I was now. I bit my lip as that familiar chill crept down my arms. It was the sting of how scared that girl must have been, how thirteen years wasn't close to enough time. I wished I knew what she looked like.

Take a deep breath. Another. Another. I tried to release the tension in my limbs. Tried to blink away the bad thoughts. That was futile, but at least I could slow them for the moment.

It didn't take me long to find Wilmer. A rotting bouquet of flowers lay on the plot, and I imagined Betty coming here to visit him every week. He'd died five years ago. I felt that tightening again as I imagined living five years without the person you'd spent nearly all your life with, like what Mom would do if Dad died.

Next to Wilmer's grave was an empty plot and no headstone. I hoped that would be where Betty would rest—that somewhere in her will she'd stated a wish to have her ashes spread in the plot next to him. I took a seat on the grass across from his grave and wondered what their life had been like until I had to leave for school.

Sure, I lived in a funeral home, but there was no place more lifeless than Somerton High School. It smelled more like bleach and death than our body freezer did, and it was colder too.

More often than not, I entered school with headphones in and head down, to avoid looks from my classmates while also protecting my eyes from the harsh fluorescent lights that drained the color from everyone's faces. I preferred to look at people through the wax on the green-tinted floor. Peter was the one who knew everyone here. I mean, I *knew* everyone—it was hard not to when you'd gone to the same school with the same seventy kids your whole life—but Peter was friends with everyone. As soon as he entered the building his buddies would run up to him, and they'd talk about this and laugh about that. When we were in middle school, I'd been a part of that. When he and I were best friends. But eventually, it became cool for Peter to live in a funeral home and menacing for me to.

In the sophomore hallway, surrounded by clumps of chatting students, I flung my locker open to pile my books into my backpack.

"Did you hear?" a girl asked loudly enough to overpower my music. I turned around and pulled an earbud out, thinking she was speaking to me. Once I realized it was just Bailey talking to Lane next to my locker, I returned my attention to Spotify.

Backpack full, I slid down my locker to sit on the floor and pulled my phone out to check the time. Even though I'd stopped by the cemetery, I still had almost ten minutes before the warning bell. Maybe it wasn't timing that had made me leave.

"You look like death," a different voice said. I pulled out both earphones, knowing who it was this time. Amy Chen. The only person who would run up to me when I entered the school.

"You make that joke far too often for it to be funny," I said.

"The joke will never die."

"Literally stop." I made sure they could see the overly dramatic roll of my eyes.

Amy gave a curtsy and tossed their hair. They were wearing a new outfit: mixed patterns of home-sewn cloth overalls and an oversized T-shirt. They had sewn lace to the straps of the overalls to really mark it as an Amy Chen original. Amy sewed and designed their own outfits and planned on running their own fashion boutique. They were one of the few Asian students at Somerton High, the only Chinese American, and the only out enby, so they always said if they were going to stand out, they were going to do it on their own terms.

Amy sat next to me against the lockers, adjusting the straps of their overalls like they were still testing out the fit. "So why haven't you been responding to my texts lately? I see your phone still works."

I shoved my phone into my pocket and decided to keep my hand there with it. "We had two funerals this week and I had to work both, so I needed to do all my homework last night. You know our science lab is due today."

Amy nodded, solemn, still waiting.

"But I'm sorry. Mom and Dad kept me really busy." Everything I said was true, but not technically true when put together.

I could see that this wasn't going to slide with Amy. I'd been consistently busy with Richter since middle school, when Mom and Dad officially hired Peter and me as assistants, but I'd still always made time for Amy. We'd both been close with Peter, and when everything happened, Amy was there for me. They stuck by me, always talked when I needed them to and stayed quiet when I needed that. They were truly the most supportive friend someone could have. But it always got harder for me to give my energy to them right after I'd woken a ghost.

I felt awful about it, and I almost made a pun about ghosting them to lighten the mood—Amy always appreciated puns—but I decided that one was too risky. They didn't know about the ghosts.

"Just, when I text, can you at least text that you're busy and can't text right now?" they said.

"Yeah, for sure."

We were interrupted by a gasp from down the hall. "Oh my god!"

Both my and Amy's necks craned to find the source, and we discovered a girl who had her hand over her mouth in horror. I couldn't see what she was horrified about. Nothing around her seemed particularly off.

"Why hasn't the warning bell rung yet?" Amy was looking at their phone, and the time read 8:03.

I jumped when the intercom came on, and Amy laughed at me. In response, I shoved their shoulder, but we both froze when Principal Wendell's voice sounded over the intercom.

"Students will not be reporting to their first-period class. Instead, all students will go to the gym and find a seat in the stands for a mandatory assembly. Thank you." The intercom clicked off.

Immediately, everyone started moving toward the gym.

"Do we have a pep rally today?" Amy asked, hopping up from the ground to offer a hand to me.

I shouldered my bag and shrugged. "Maybe it's got something to do with fall break coming up?" It was the Thursday before break, but that didn't usually warrant a school-wide assembly.

"It's about last night," a guy behind us said.

"What happened last night?" I turned around to ask.

"There was a car accident."

My muscles seized up and chills attacked my skin. Tightness all over.

I shuffled into the gym quietly with everyone else, and Amy and I found seats on the bleachers. I looked around for Pete but couldn't spot him.

All the teachers and staff were standing in the middle of the court. Wendell was waiting at the roll-in podium, watching all the students gathering onto the bleachers.

"Quickly, please," he said into the mic. "Find a seat and be quiet." Usually Wendell's approach to student interactions was all, *Hey, I'm hip with the kids. I know memes.* I had never heard him sound so serious before.

I studied the teachers' faces. Many of them held tissues to their eyes, others stood with stone visages. Wendell fell somewhere in the middle, clearly upset but not quite crying. I saw Mrs. Berry sobbing.

"God," Amy whispered as it started to sink in.

I scanned the bleachers, trying to figure out who was missing. This was a small school, with fewer than a hundred students in each graduating class, but with everyone crowded together like this it was impossible to pinpoint who was unaccounted for.

Had I seen Peter since breakfast? Just when I was starting to panic, I spotted him walking up the bleachers to take a seat in the back row with Eileen Smith. Of course Peter was fine, but I couldn't help that thought creeping up the back of my neck.

The gym was quieter than it usually was when we were summoned. At pep rallies the noise of the band and cheerleaders would echo off the walls to the point where I couldn't hear myself think. But right now I could hear all my thoughts far too loudly.

"As many of you might have heard . . ." Wendell began. Complete silence blanketed the gym. Anyone who still wasn't seated stopped dead in their tracks. "There was an accident last night."

The students who hadn't realized gasped.

"Milo D'Angelo didn't survive."

My brain blurred, my hands started sweating. Milo.

"It is a terrible loss, and we all ache and grieve," Wendell continued, pushing past the catch in his throat. "We were lucky to have Milo here at Somerton High for the time that we did." I had never seen him cry before.

Wendell kept talking, but I couldn't hear him anymore. The buzzing in my ears and the whispers of students kept me from hearing anything other than Milo's name.

Milo was in my grade. He had Mrs. Berry's English class with me. I hardly spoke to him. I remembered he liked to draw. He was white with shaggy, dark hair. What color were his eyes? When was the last time I'd seen him?

Just like that, he was gone.

I could feel his absence in a way I had never felt anything before. It was more than I'd ever felt his presence.

I could hear Wendell again all of a sudden; he was asking for us all to bow our heads in a moment of silence to remember Milo.

"Bet it was suicide," a kid behind us said. That kid was Liam Macek, so I didn't find what came out of his mouth particularly unexpected.

Amy instantly turned around. "Do not go around spouting that shit."

"I'm just saying. 'Accident' sounds like a cover-up to me. Plus, he was a weird kid." Liam shrugged. His buddies nodded in agreement.

"Well," Amy hissed, "why don't you stop being a disrespectful dick and shut up." I could feel the heat of Amy's words even as they faced forward and shuddered in frustration. It wasn't their greatest comeback.

"Jesus, girls are so sensitive."

"I'm not a girl," they hissed again, then turned to me with a look of fury.

I wanted to back Amy up. I wanted to snap at Liam, but I couldn't quite control any motion in my body. My foot kept tapping against the metal. I knew I was annoying the other kids in our row of bleachers, but there was a disconnect between my brain telling my leg to stop and my leg actually listening. Amy put their hand on my back in an attempt to calm me, but their touch instead made me feel more claustrophobic.

I pictured English class with Berry, seeing myself sitting in the middle and Milo in the middle back, or maybe the middle left. I couldn't remember exactly where he sat. He never said a word in class. I hardly ever thought about him. But now I needed to conjure every memory I could. Desperation clawed through my mind as I came up empty.

Then the assembly came to an end. Principal Wendell told us to resume classes like normal. I doubted he meant it like *that*, but it still felt insulting.

Amy pulled me up and walked with my hand in theirs down the bleachers.

His name kept repeating itself in my head, over and over.

Milo.

◊

For the rest of the day, I felt like school was being held in a completely different building. Everyone was in shock. At the start of each class, every teacher said a few words about how much Milo would be missed. Then it was back to the scheduled lesson plan, but nobody could concentrate.

Mrs. Berry took it the hardest. Her eyes were red and her cheeks were puffy the entire period. She forgot to have us turn in our papers. I wondered if she'd been close with Milo.

I wondered if any of us had.

◊

Amy wanted to walk me home. I asked them not to. They did anyway. They wanted to talk about how horrible Milo's death was and how different the rest of the semester would be. But I couldn't talk. My tongue felt like a metal plate in my mouth and my thoughts were running too fast for me to catch one and form it into words. Eventually, Amy stopped trying, and we walked silently the rest of the way, their arm around my shoulders.

At Richter, I went straight to my room and opened my laptop. I googled Milo's name. Articles from the local news sites described last night's events.

At 10:12 p.m., I'd been in bed, asleep and safe. At 10:12 p.m., Milo had been walking home—from where, I wish I knew. At 10:12 p.m., Milo had moments until the collision and only two more hours left to live. Someone—a drunk driver, probably—going far above the speed limit had hit him and driven away; the police hadn't located the person responsible. Milo was rushed to the hospital, underwent emergency surgeries, and didn't make it. At 12:15 in the morning at the county hospital, Milo was declared dead.

He was my age. In my grade. We had been in class together just yesterday and every other day this year. One thought kept permeating the chaos in my head. It could have been me.

I opened a new tab and logged on to my rarely-used social media profile. I searched and clicked Milo's name, which brought me to his page. We were "friends."

A photo of Milo smiled at me from the screen. I realized I hadn't really been able to picture his face clearly before. All I remembered was his dark shaggy hair, but I hadn't remembered his tan skin, round face, or dark eyes—or how big a smile he had. I hadn't really ever looked at Milo D'Angelo, and the more I looked at him now, the scarier I found the fact that he was no longer alive.

I clicked through his older profile photos. They were a mixture of pictures of himself, photos of anime characters, and drawings I didn't recognize. One was a photo of him from maybe fifth grade. He was wearing a soccer jersey, and both his parents stood beside him. They were all smiling, one happy

25

family. I remembered when he was in soccer because I'd also played soccer. We'd played on the same team.

I clicked back to his profile and scrolled down to read recent comments people had posted: my classmates sending their love and prayers.

Tommy Collins: *Love ya man, gonna miss ya like a brother.* Had Tommy ever talked to Milo? Pretty sure Tommy made fun of kids like Milo.

Hudson Pierce: *Hope you're resting in peace, homeboy.* I didn't even think anyone used that word anymore.

Hannah Bryant: *I didn't know you very well, but it will be so strange not having you there anymore. Love and prayers to you and your family.* That felt more appropriate.

Other students wrote about what a great guy Milo was, what fun they had together. The only specific example I saw of these "fun times" was a comment about a sleepover Milo and Charlie Alan had back in fifth grade.

Half these kids didn't know Milo. I suspected no one at school really knew Milo. He was quiet and reserved. Most people would see him in the hall and label him the weird, quiet, greasy kid who liked anime. Yet all of a sudden everyone had been best friends with him.

I clicked out of the tab and shut my laptop. I sat at my desk for a while, staring outside the window at the trees and the pavement below.

The wind continued to blow the leaves, the sun would set soon enough, and there was one fewer person in the world to see it.

CHAPTER 3

Richter Funeral Home always caught the eye, but I wasn't sure it was for the right reasons. Main Street was rich with foliage that changed colors perfectly with the seasons, and all the houses had homegrown gardens that marked the street as the most picturesque in Somerton. But then you arrived in front of Richter on the corner lot at the end of the block.

The trees that had once framed the property had been removed so people could see the sign in the front yard: *Welcome to Richter Funeral Home.* The funeral home itself was a large, looming house made from a combination of white siding and tan brick. There was a wicker swing on a porch that wrapped most of the house's perimeter—perfect for summer days. There was a garden too, and windows framed by frilly curtains that sparkled in the sunlight to invite visitors.

Richter Funeral Home fell into the uncanny valley of houses. It was almost believable, almost lovely, but something about it would make your skin crawl.

Maybe it was the uncomfortably large size. Or the way the porch was never used on those summer days but the wicker swing always gently swayed. And maybe it was the way that porch ended at a large garage door behind the house, where the vans and hearses arrived with their presents. And the gardens were a lie, masking all the death behind the door with the beauty of life.

Upon entering Richter, you were greeted with baby-pink floral wallpaper and red carpeting straight out of the '70s. On the walls were paintings by unnamed artists that no one actually looked at. Fake flowers rested on random tables, taunting us mortals. There were perfectly comfortable chairs that were impossible to ever feel comfortable in while you waited for the inevitable. If you cried, the sound was absorbed by the thick carpet and the cluttered walls.

To the right of the entrance was the sitting room, where Mom would meet with clients. The Richters wanted you to feel comfortable, to forget why you were really here with them today, so there was coffee and hot chocolate to sip on. There was a table with what seemed like regular magazines. But a closer look revealed they were listings of the funeral packages Richter offered. If you saw something that interested you, you'd be encouraged to visit the display room featuring Richter's most popular selections so you could take a coffin for a test run.

To the left was a long hallway that felt like it would never end as it led you to the two visitation rooms and the chapel. Straight ahead was where all the secrets lived—the office, the display room, the preparation rooms, the reposing room, and the door to the basement embalming room. But any direction you took, you could never go back.

When you walked through Richter, whatever your business was, you had no idea what was going on beneath the dull red carpet. Or at least you tried to forget.

Dad worked down in the embalming room, and Mom did the admin work and filed all the papers. Peter helped Dad downstairs, but I hadn't set foot down there in years. I helped

28

Mom with paperwork. Peter and I played usher. We put up. We tore down. I turned on the music during wakes to help muffle the sounds of mourning. It had become my routine.

For me, though, what made this place so uncanny was the fact that it was once a home. My grandparents had purchased it from a large, wealthy family about fifty years ago. The rooms that were once lived in were converted for the exact opposite purpose. Even the apartment upstairs, where I'd grown up, felt lifeless.

Though it was no longer a home for living, it was still the only place I'd ever lived. It was tied up with my entire identity. I'd always been the mortician's daughter, the future undertaker, the weird girl who lived with corpses. Richter wasn't just my last name; it was a fate I couldn't escape.

◊

The first thing I noticed at school the next day was Milo's decorated locker. Fake flowers were taped around a picture of him, which I recognized as his profile picture. The display looked like an imitation of the setup we did at funerals. Cards were propped up in front of his locker, and unlit candles crept out to the middle of the hallway and in front of neighboring lockers.

I couldn't peel my eyes off the shrine. I wanted to read the cards on the floor and light the candles, but I also wanted to turn around and walk home without having to deal with the day.

Usually Amy and I sat at my locker for a few minutes before the warning bell, but I didn't feel like talking to them right now. Instead, I went straight to first period.

Milo was trailing me everywhere I went. I heard his name twice walking to class, and I entered Mrs. Berry's room to find another shrine on his desk in the back. That same photo smiled at me, and I felt my throat get tight. I kept my eyes off it as I took my seat in front of it.

Milo had sat right behind me this entire semester and it had never fully registered. I mean, I remembered now. I'd seen him every day. But I couldn't summon that memory until he was missing from it.

Everyone walking into class wore somber faces, but when the morning bell rang, Mrs. Berry didn't make any mention of Milo or the shrine in her back row. I wondered if someone had done this in every classroom on Milo's schedule. She picked up where we'd left off with *The Great Gatsby* despite no one having done their reading the night before. In a case of terrible timing, we'd just gotten to the part about Myrtle. I don't know if Mrs. Berry wanted to use it as a jumping-off point to talk about what happened or what, but everyone just sat in uncomfortable silence.

It got colder as the day went on. Eventually, I couldn't avoid Amy anymore because we had speech class together right before lunch. When they asked me where I'd been that morning, I lied and said I'd come to school late. I ate lunch with them, and we tried to talk about normal things. Amy was sharing Tumblr posts, but when I wasn't receptive to that, they started talking about their plans for their future in fashion.

Usually, I was happy to daydream with Amy about when we would both finally escape Somerton, but today I couldn't. My mind was back in Mrs. Berry's room, sitting in front of the shrine. At Milo's locker, reading the notes from classmates. In my room, looking at Milo's profile on my computer screen, clicking through his photos and reading old posts. On the bleachers, frozen to the metal, heart pounding, brain scream-ing. It was with wherever his body currently was—cold, absent, pale, alone, dead. Amy couldn't find me in any of those places because I was hiding there.

My last class of the day was algebra. Peter and Eileen were in it too. Three years ago, that would have meant all of us sitting near each other, doing homework together, and walking home from school after. Now, it meant ignoring each other while they took seats together across the room from me. I inevitably had to deal with Peter at Richter, but there were no expectations for me to hang out with him at school. And I never had to interact with Eileen anymore.

When the final bell of the day rang and our teacher told us to enjoy fall break, I was released from public school's grip out into the chilly air. Finally being alone was what I needed. But Peter must have known that because he ran up behind me, calling my name.

"Are you doing okay?" he asked.

"I'm fine," I said, annoyed that he'd ruined the last few minutes I could spend ignoring his existence.

"I just . . . I heard you crying last night."

"Oh," I said, suddenly worried that if he'd heard last night, he must have been able to hear all the other nights.

"I was stressed about a test today," I said, which was half true. I'd had a history test, but I wasn't stressed about it. I hoped that would be enough to get him to stop talking to me.

"I feel that," Peter said. Right. Mr. Perfect Grades. Then, out of the blue: "Were you close with Milo?"

My lip twitched, but I didn't answer him. I didn't know how to approach actually talking about Milo. As much as I'd been thinking about him, his name hadn't escaped my lips once.

"I guess I wouldn't know, honestly," Peter hedged. His voice was sad. "I don't know you all that well anymore."

31

I wanted to snidely ask why he thought that was, but his mention of Milo had triggered a spiral, and I couldn't stop picturing a cold, dead body, bleeding on the road, lifeless on a hospital bed.

"Okay," he said, his shoulders falling. "Eileen says hi."

I hadn't spoken to Eileen in years, and I resented that Peter was still friends with her after what she'd done—that he had the audacity to bring her up. But I couldn't stop thinking about Milo long enough to be mad at them. I couldn't process any new feelings in the same space where Milo's profile picture was burned into me.

We walked the rest of the way home in silence. I chewed on my lip the whole time, a bad habit I had developed after Grandma died. In my peripheral vision, I noticed Peter occasionally glancing from his phone at me, but I avoided eye contact. I made it up the stairs to Richter first. Peter went downstairs to help Dad in the embalming room. I stayed in my room until 5:30. Call time.

◊

When Dad was done preparing the body for a viewing, he would bring it up from the basement to a private reposing room in the back while the visitation room was being set up. This was where the body lay in the coffin and where Dad would ask the family's approval of his work before giving them time alone to mourn. That was often when I talked to them—after Dad dropped the body off and before the family arrived. I usually had about thirty minutes, and I could either lock the room's main door for privacy or escape out the side door if I got interrupted. But no one had ever walked in on me. Peter the previous day was the closest anyone had come.

When Dad left the room this time, I sneaked in after him.

The man's name was Theodore Bower. He was older and from the town over. He'd died of natural causes, according to his obituary. He'd been a lawyer, and the funeral was set to be full because he had a giant family who loved him, including his husband, their four kids, and nearly a dozen grandchildren. There was so much I could learn about him, about his full and long life. But when I got there, when I locked the doors and approached his open coffin, something stopped me.

It didn't feel the same. As I stared down at him, my fingers running along the seam of the coffin where linen met mahogany, the usual desperation didn't surface. Instead, when I looked at Theodore's face, I couldn't stop thinking about Milo. About the full life that Milo wouldn't get to live. He'd never have kids like Theodore. Never have a career like Theodore. I suddenly didn't know what I would ask Theodore's ghost because the questions that came into my head weren't for him. I didn't want to know what Theodore's job was like, I wanted to know what Milo's would have been. I didn't want to know about Theodore's family, I wanted to know about Milo's. I wanted to know Milo's final request.

I tried to force my hand to reach out and tap Theodore, but it wouldn't listen. It made me feel sick to my stomach. I couldn't do it.

I left the room knowing I was giving up my only chance.

Running a Richter funeral was very systematic. With slight adjustments here and there, at the core, they were all essentially the same. Funerals usually happened in the mornings and wakes or visitations happened in the evenings, though that wasn't a hard-and-fast rule. The rare evening funerals were often especially creepy, though, because death felt more real at night.

Almost every funeral had a visitation first—generally either the night before or the morning of the service—when the family and friends of whoever was lying dead in the casket could view the body (if it was open casket) and greet other mourners. Peter and I would stand off to the side and make sure everything ran smoothly: we monitored the music and refreshments, directed people looking for the bathrooms, et cetera. Mom and Dad were around too, but they often mingled. I'd observe the grieving, listening to conversations and learning what I could about the deceased. By the time I was thirteen, I thought I understood what it was to grieve, I'd seen it so much in front of my eyes. But nothing could've prepared me for when Grandma died.

After the visitation, I ushered people into the chapel for the service and handed out the memorial program, which might feature a photo of the deceased along with a poem or a verse from scripture. Our funerals came with a range of available modifications, but there were two main options for the service: religious or secular. If religious, the officiant would give a sermon and say a few words as if they actually knew the dead. If secular, they'd just say a few words as if they actually knew the dead. Family and friends might share stories. Peter manned the tech if a slideshow of photos had been arranged, and he adjusted the many lights in the chapel to fit the mood. For never having attended church, we did a fair job of imitating various forms of it.

Afterward, there was often a reception. This could be held in one of our visitation parlors, but more often than not it happened at a more enjoyable location since the body didn't have to be there. And since the reception was about celebrating life, why would anyone want to be surrounded by the reminder of death? Of course, in some cases, like Betty's, there wouldn't be a reception at all.

Richter's part of the process ended once we cleaned up the rooms and moved the body to the crematory or transported it to be buried. Richter didn't have an incinerator, even though that wasn't uncommon.

I'd tried not to let the process become monotonous. I'd tried to make every single funeral count, but that was impossible. It was like a math equation that I was taught to plug into and chug out. It became habit, and you'd lose track of why you were even doing it. You adjusted the variables depending on the dead person, you regurgitated the same words to the grieving, and you came out the other side with another funeral under your belt.

And that was exactly how tonight's funeral went. Theodore was lucky enough to get a full chapel and a slideshow of his life. With every picture that came up of him smiling, holding his kids or his grandkids, I found myself looking at his eyes, then down at his body in the coffin, feeling the disconnect. I was angry at myself for not speaking to him earlier. I also couldn't help contrasting his service with Betty's. It was refreshing to see how many people loved him, but it was unfair that Betty didn't get that.

And through the whole event, I couldn't stop thinking about Milo.

By the time Peter and I were done cleaning up, it was almost 9:00 p.m.

"Great start to fall break, eh?" Peter said. We were in the

front sitting room because we were too tired to even walk up the stairs to the apartment. This room was like our second, more uncanny living room. The couches hadn't been replaced since Grandpa had run the place. They smelled musty, and the floral print screamed to be let free.

"I'm exhausted," Peter groaned when I didn't respond. He was leaning his forehead on one hand and scrolling through his phone on the other.

I had no idea why he was suddenly speaking to me so much. But I reached out for the newspaper on the coffee table, scrambled around with all of Richter's pamphlets, to show him I wasn't going to entertain it.

There was Milo's obituary attached to that same damn picture. That picture defined his memory.

I could feel Peter's gaze on me. It always felt like he was watching me lately. I turned my head to let him know I knew, but he didn't turn away. His head was still on his hand, but his brows were raised.

"Warren's party is on Wednesday," he said.

"So?"

Warren's party was called the Fall Break Extravaganza or something. His parents were out of town every fall break, but the party was infamous enough that they had to know about what their sons did with the place when they left—they just didn't care. Everyone at our high school went every year because it was the only exciting thing that ever happened in Somerton.

"I'm going to go. I decided why not," Peter said. "You should come." He smiled and finally lifted his head from his hand.

I scoffed. "No."

"Why not?"

"Um, I have better things to do."

"Like what? Mope around Richter all day?"

I tightened my grip on the paper. He closed his eyes and sighed. "Sorry," he said. "That wasn't necessary."

I stood up from the couch, done with having to interact with him for the day or at all ever, but Peter stood up too.

"Wait, I'm sorry," he said.

I stared straight at the wall. He'd still said what he'd said.

"I'll go, you can stay," he said, pocketing his phone and grabbing his jacket from the back of the chair.

I watched as he trudged toward the apartment door. I could hear the steps creak when he ran up to the apartment.

Then Dad came up from the embalming room and locked the basement door behind him. He always said he locked it to keep visitors out, but he'd only started doing it after the night he and Mom found me down there.

"Mom's making dinner," he said. "I'm going to finish up some paperwork, but why don't you go help her?"

"Okay." I didn't really want to, but I didn't want to fight him on it either. Plus, I didn't like to be around him when he'd just embalmed a body, which was a lot of the time.

He went into the office, and I grabbed the obituaries section and tucked it into the pocket of my dress.

Upstairs I found Mom pouring a pot of spaghetti into a strainer, the steam fogging up her glasses. Peter was sitting on the couch petting Morty. The apartment was so small that we were always in each other's space.

"Go change, guys. Dinner is almost ready," Mom said.

Peter and I changed out of our funeral clothes. Dad came upstairs, having finished his paperwork. Mom set the plates on the table and we all sat down to pretend like we were a normal family having a normal dinner.

But we couldn't have a normal dinner, because we could never not talk about funerals.

"You know, we had a student die when we were in high school," Dad said when we'd barely taken a bite of our food.

I hadn't thought I'd have to talk about Milo with them. But clearly they'd heard. Everyone had heard by now.

"She was a freshman when your mom and I were seniors, so it was a little different."

"It's weird," Peter said. "I didn't know him well, but . . ." Peter caught me stabbing my pasta and stopped talking. I was spreading it around my plate, putting it on my fork and dipping it off, doing basically everything except eating it. I did not want to be having this conversation.

"Did you know him, Georgia?" Mom asked. "The D'Angelo boy?"

I shrugged. Everything I was feeling made it seem as if I had. I wished I had. He was stuck in my head like I had.

"Well, we should be getting him tomorrow morning," Dad said.

My head shot up. I didn't know how I hadn't realized that. I'd been so hyper-focused on the dying part that I hadn't thought any further ahead. Of course he'd be here. His body would live two stories down from me. And if he was here . . .

"His dad called today to begin the arrangements," Mom said. "His mom should be meeting with us in the next few days for the details. The funeral is next Saturday because I think they have to wait for his grandparents to get into town."

I was frozen in my seat again. I felt like I was back on the bleachers. My hand gripped my fork more tightly.

"I bet I'm not allowed to help with the embalming process for that, yeah? Since he was a student?" Peter asked. Typical of him to turn Milo's death into business.

I stood up before Dad could answer. "I'm not hungry anymore." I put my full plate of pasta in the sink and went to my room.

Curled up on my bed with the lights off, I stared at Milo's obituary on my desk. Milo would be here tomorrow. My father's hands would pump the last remaining bit of life from his body and fill him with chemicals, making him look fake, as different from that profile picture as possible.

I cried, not thinking about whether Peter could hear me. I let the tears fall down my cheeks, past my ears, to land on my bed. When I needed to scream, though, I did it into my pillow.

I was angry that I had been so obsessed with Milo that I couldn't talk to Theodore. I hadn't even grabbed a pamphlet for my scrapbook. But that wasn't why I was crying. It was because Milo's story was my worst fear, and him arriving at Richter only made it more real.

CHAPTER 4

Saturday morning greeted me with the dreary rain that was too common in Somerton this time of year. But it also brought the rumble of the garage door opening. I hopped out of bed as soon as I felt it. This was the only moment I was ever thankful that my window had a view of the parking lot behind Richter, where the hearses arrived.

I wondered how Milo had spent his Saturday mornings, if he was the type to sleep in or wake up before the sun. I didn't have to wonder how he was spending this one.

I watched as the van pulled into the garage. In a surge of what felt wrongly like excitement, I quickly threw on a hoodie and ran downstairs.

◊

I didn't know what to call what I did. I didn't know if it was talking to ghosts, waking the dead, resurrection, necromancy, or none or all of the above. I didn't know why I had it or what all the rules were. But I did know one thing. I knew when it started.

It was when my grandma died. She was the first one I talked to.

Dad's parents owned Richter Funeral Home before us. Dad grew up in the apartment where we lived. Peter's room had been his, while mine had belonged to his brother, Michael. Grandpa was the undertaker, and Grandma ran the books and did all the talking because Grandpa hated people, at least when they were alive. He said that was why he became a mortician—the dead never expected anything from him.

The family history got messy when Grandpa Richter died. Peter and I weren't even born yet, so I'd only heard stories. Uncle Michael apparently had hated Grandpa and the business all along, and he disowned the family—leaving Dad, a newly married twenty-something, to inherit Richter and take care of his grieving mother. We didn't put the sob story on the back of our pamphlets. We kept it simple with a "Family owned since 1957."

Grandma had been too heartbroken to work, so Mom took over admin for Richter. Grandma retired and lived with us and watched Peter and me when we were born. She hid her hurt well, because I couldn't remember a single moment when she'd been anything less than stoic. She taught me piano and read practically every book at the library aloud with me. She told me her own stories about growing up in Somerton that I never believed were real because they were too exciting to take place in this dull town. But she always assured me they were true and that one day I'd have my own tales to tell.

The summer before seventh grade was perfect. Peter and I had the best friend group: us, Amy, and Eileen. We were inseparable, spending practically every evening after school together. We would film movie trailers for our favorite books and stay up all night playing board games and ride our bikes around town like life was eternal.

In late July, Grandma caught pneumonia. Despite what she made me believe, she hadn't been whole for a long time, so the pneumonia easily took the rest of her. When she was gone, she left a void in Richter, and all that had been happy only hurt.

Peter was the strong twin. He wasn't as close to her as I was. I never saw him cry once. He was quiet and composed, like Mom and Dad. I was mad at Peter for not being more upset. I was mad at my parents for not holding me while I cried, but I didn't want anyone to see me cry.

After eight years of lessons with Grandma, I quit playing piano because it hurt too much to touch the keys. I grew distant with Peter and Eileen because I couldn't pretend to be happy around them. Amy had lost their grandma when they were younger, so they understood what it was like. Plus, that was around the time Amy realized they were nonbinary, which was around the same time I was starting to understand my asexuality, so we bonded over those self-discoveries. Our differences from other people became our closeness, and we started to fit together more than we did with anyone else. And after what Eileen did, when Amy defended me and Peter didn't, we reached a breaking point.

The first time I fully realized I'd die, I was six and we'd just adopted Morty. I was instantly struck with the dread that one day he'd die, Grandma would die, my parents would die, and I'd die too. It was an all-consuming thought, but Mom and Dad told me I didn't have to worry about that for a long time because it was so far away. And I held on to that, thinking it was true. Because even though I was surrounded by dead people every day, I'd never actually experienced loss. It was something separate. Something I saw but didn't know.

When Grandma died, it was suddenly closer than it ever

had been before. So I started to think a lot more about death. Wondering what happened after the heart stopped pulsing blood inside the flesh. I researched different gentle or grue-some ways bodies can be disposed of and gained a vocabulary of medical terms related to terminal illnesses. I started to look at everything living and recategorize it as not-yet-dead. I started trying to stay awake out of fear of not waking up in the morn-ing. I started falling asleep to the terrifying thought that it would be me one day.

A few days after Grandma's death, I was lying in bed in pure terror. I think it was the anticipation of her funeral that triggered it. I could feel the gravity pulling me into the bed, knowing that it would inevitably pull me into the ground and the darkness I lay in now would one day be eternal, and I had zero control over when that would happen. I hypothesized it would be like before I was ever born, but that didn't quite make sense because that was before I *was* and *knew* and this would be after, and that inherently made it scarier. I tried picturing an afterlife, but then the thought of being conscious for all eternity nearly scared me more than simple oblivion. The terror turned to weird fascination as I remembered all the images I'd come across during my research. And that's how I ended up crawling out of bed and sneaking downstairs. Everyone else was asleep, which I had come to think of as a certain kind of death.

I avoided the last step because it creaked. When my feet felt the fibers of the red carpet, I knew I was officially in Richter territory.

The fact that our embalming room was located in the basement definitely added to the creepiness factor. The door at the top of the steps was kept closed at all times with a sign that read *No Smoking—Fire Hazard* right beneath the one that read *Authorized Personnel Only: Alarm Will Sound.* We wouldn't want anyone to see a dead body in a funeral home, now would we?

The alarm was a lie, so I turned the cold handle. I still remember how small I felt looking down the concrete steps into the dark. I'd been down there before, but never alone.

The floor of the embalming room was the same cold concrete, but despite the darkness I knew when I had made it down the steps. I could smell the bleach before turning on the lights, and when I flipped the switch, the dim fluorescent glow confirmed it. The room was a mix between a laboratory and a hospital. There were kitchen counters and cabinets lining one blue-tiled wall, and machinery pushed up against the other. In the middle of the room was a metal table where the dead bodies lay helpless as Dad poked and prodded and filled them with preservatives. The only window was a small hopper window in the corner near the ceiling, but it had been locked and covered up after two little kids got caught trying to peer in. So, no natural light. Not even during the day.

Directly opposite the staircase was a large metal door. The closer you walked to it, the colder it got. The door to the body freezer. When you opened it, you saw the drawers, four by three, lining the wall. I'd never gone into the freezer before. I'd seen Dad walk in to slide open a drawer and wheel a body out, but I'd never felt the rush of the cold air or known what it felt like to open one of the drawers and slide a body out with my own hands.

I summoned whatever courage Grandma might have left me and opened the door. It was dark, and the dim light from above the embalming table wasn't quite reaching it. I could feel the cold. I could smell the cleaner. I felt the wall for another switch.

When the light came on, I instantly saw my reflection in the shining steel across from me. As I stepped forward, my reflection grew bigger until it became deformed by the angles of the drawers.

I grabbed the handle of the drawer that held my reflection and pulled. This one was empty, so I was relieved.

My hand was shaking but not from the cold. I closed the drawer. I could have bailed. I could have swallowed my anger and my fear and turned off the lights and gone to sleep. I would have never known what I could do. But the sickly fascination was taking over. The need to stare, to know, to let the obsessive thoughts win. So I didn't go upstairs. I instead pulled open another drawer and saw the dead body of my grandma.

She was a lump in the dark underneath a white sheet. Her toes weren't sticking out like in the movies. All her flesh was covered, but that was without a doubt her body right in front of me.

I tugged at the drawer, which was heavier than I'd thought it would be. The lump slid out toward me smoothly. I folded the sheet back at her feet because I couldn't bring myself to look at her face yet. There was a tag attached to her big toe with her name: *Tabitha Richter.*

I felt as cold as the room. Seeing her name confirmed that my grandma was actually dead, gone, empty. I was terrified of what seeing her face might do.

Thankfully, when I pulled the sheet off her face, her eyes were closed. Her skin was pale, and it almost looked like her wrinkles had softened with death. She didn't have the same rosy cheeks, and she'd never make that bright smile again. I didn't know then that her smile had been hiding pain. All I knew was that I wanted desperately to see it again.

45

Of course, the tears fell, and the sobs overtook me. I felt like my heart was tightening and expanding so rapidly it would decide to finally burst from my chest. This was final. It was the words *The End* personified. Her end. Our end.

I fell to the floor, melting into myself and bursting from myself simultaneously until the equilibrium of those two forces settled into numbness. The emotion of that moment would forever remain in my body.

I don't know how long I stayed on the ground beside the slowly decaying body of Tabitha Richter, but eventually, I pushed myself upright to face it. I stared at her face until my eyes lost focus. I stared at her flesh like I had stared at my wall every night for the last few days. I was in disbelief.

I blinked and again actually looked at her. My exhaustion was getting the better of me, so I decided to let this be goodbye.

"I love you," I told her, feeling the tightness fighting to control me again. I took a deep breath and reached to touch her cheek. I wanted to know what a dead body felt like, what my body would someday feel like, because despite having seen corpses my whole life, I'd never actually laid a finger on one. I thought touching her would make it more real and less real at the same time. My hand rested on her cheek, and I didn't want to ever move.

"Georgia?"

I instinctively leapt back. My hand retracted to my side, and I slammed against the wall, one of the handles of the drawers digging painfully into my ribs. A naked woman, with rosy cheeks and a soft smile, stood in the doorway to the freezer.

I screamed so loudly that every ounce of my pain escaped. The scream echoed in the embalming room and rang in my ears and rose up the stairs and shook my body. I was staring at

Grandma standing before me, as impossibly alive as ever. Her hand shot to her mouth, but she stepped toward me. I dodged away from her reach until I was pressed into the corner, looking back and forth at her bodies—the one breathless and prostrate under a sheet, and the one breathing and beating, alive.

"What are you doing in the freezer?" she asked, looking around. "Are you okay?" She took another step toward me, and another scream pulsed with the cold.

My arms guarded my head and I fell to the ground with heaving sobs.

"Shhhhh," she said. She didn't understand. My head was buried in my lap and I was willing her to go away, to go away, to go away. I knew I was seeing things. I was tired and sad, and I'd been reading so much about death that it must've flipped something in my brain. Even as I tried to rationalize, the violent, loud sobs kept coming and she kept telling me to be quiet and that everything was okay, but hearing her voice the exact way it had sounded before she died only made the situation worse.

She reached out a hand, ready to stroke my hair. I couldn't back any farther into the corner, but where her fingers should've met my hair, they instead went straight through my head.

Even though I didn't feel anything, I cried out again, pressing into the wall until my whole body ached, repeating to myself that this couldn't be real. Grandma withdrew her hand and stepped back, staring in confusion.

"Georgia!" This time, the voice was Mom's. She and Dad came pounding down the steps in their pajamas with terrified eyes.

"What is going on?" Grandma's ghost asked. I hated hearing her voice even though it was the one that used to tell me stories and sing to me. I didn't want the thing in front of me to speak. She moved out of the way for Dad and Mom to come into the freezer, and they rushed past her without a glance.

"What the fuck are you doing down here?" Dad yelled.

Mom leaned down and wrapped her arms around me, berating my dad for yelling. I was still sobbing uncontrollably, unable to properly catch a breath. I looked up at my grandmother, the one Mom and Dad apparently didn't see.

"Jesus Christ," Dad said, clearly seeing the dead one. He slid Grandma's corpse back into the chamber and slammed the door. "What were you thinking?"

The ghost just stood, staring at her son yelling, her daughter-in-law hugging her hysterical granddaughter.

"What's going on?" Then it was Peter calling from the top of the steps, peering down at the scene.

"Go back to bed," Dad shouted up at him, but I'm pretty sure he stayed awhile.

Mom sat down and pulled me onto her lap. I had never felt so protected by her arms. "It's okay, sweetie," she whispered in my ear. We rocked back and forth together while the ghost continued to stare. I looked up at my grandmother through my tears, trying to process the fact that Mom and Dad were in that room, completely unaware of her presence. The ghost wouldn't go away no matter how many times I tried to blink her there.

"She's hysterical," Dad said. Yeah, and I was hallucinating.

"She's having a panic attack," Mom snapped. "We need to get her back to bed."

Dad looked angry and maybe a bit hurt, but his voice had lowered. He ran his hand through his hair before helping us off the ground.

Mom led a hysterical, panicking, hallucinating daughter out of the freezer and up the steps. Dad turned off the lights and locked the ghost of Grandma in the freezer room. I looked back to see Grandma's sad eyes as the door shut.

Mom tucked me into bed that night. She sat with me and said she was sorry. She said she knew it was hard to lose Grandma. It was the first time I had seen her cry about it.

Mom eventually left when she thought I had fallen asleep. I hadn't even closed my eyes because I was too afraid of the image of my grandmother burned on the back of my lids.

When I was alone, I went to my door and put my ear against it to listen to what Mom and Dad were saying in the living room. They were whispering.

"She okay?" Dad asked.

"She's clearly taking this hard," Mom said.

"I know, I just can't have her going down there like that. There's dangerous stuff down there."

"She's grieving, Greg."

One thing watching funeral attendees grieve didn't teach me was how much of grief was physical pain.

I couldn't hear Dad's response because he suddenly got quieter. Both their voices turned to whispers, and I gave up trying to hear them. I could tell they were worried it would happen again and that they didn't know what to do about it if it did. I was worried it could happen again too, but our *it*s were different. I didn't tell them what I'd seen because I hardly wanted to admit it to myself. I don't think I slept at all that night. I knew the ghost was two stories below, trapped in the cold chamber.

I never saw Grandma's ghost again. I hadn't known yet that I needed to touch her physical body a second time to send her spirit away, so I don't know if her ghost ever dissipated or found her way to another world or something. I assumed she escaped from the freezer one of the times Dad opened the door, but

I never saw her wandering around Richter. I hoped her spirit had found peace somehow, but the fear that I'd doomed her to a life in some kind of purgatory lurked in my chest, slowly devouring me.

Lying in bed that night, I wasn't even sure if it would or could ever happen again. I hoped not. But it did. Because even after condemning Grandma to that fate, my curiosity won.

Dad kept the door to the basement locked from that point forward. He didn't want me having any more episodes and potentially hurting myself or damaging something in the embalming room. I didn't want to go down there again anyway. I only set foot in the basement one other time, when my father taught me to embalm a body.

CHAPTER 5

Milo's name was everywhere: in the paper, on every social media app I opened, out of everyone's mouths at school. He was in my head, he was in the air, and now his body was in the same building as me, right beneath my feet. He was so close I . . . well, I could touch him.

I ran downstairs after seeing the garage doors open, but I wasn't sure what I was planning on doing. Everyone was awake, and Milo wasn't in a convenient location. I decided I would have to wait until that night. Downstairs I found Dad leaning on the doorframe of the office.

"The D'Angelo boy arrived," Dad said, not noticing me yet.

"I have a meeting with his parents today to finalize some of the details," Mom replied. This was the business side of things.

My heart was pounding in my throat as I thought about how close I was to him. Soon I could wake him, I could ask him my questions. Hear his final request. I assumed it would have something to do with how he died. He would probably want me to help find whoever did it. The terror of becoming a part of that gurgled in my stomach. I didn't know how I could pull that off—or anything about how investigations worked for that matter. I'd be in over my head. But the need to speak to him, to understand the inscrutable, won.

Dad probably heard my heavy breathing. "Hey, G," he said. "What're you doing? You're off duty today."

"I don't have any big plans." I shrugged, trying to be as casual as possible. "Can I help out?"

"Is that Georgia I hear? Offering to help?" Mom had gotten out from behind her desk to join Dad at the office threshold. She was smiling like she was kidding, but she was also right. Usually I only begrudgingly accepted the work they had me do for pay. But I figured that if I offered up my services willingly, I'd have an easier time reaching Milo.

"I don't have plans," I repeated, but I could feel the nerves slipping into my words.

"You'll have plenty of time to work here when you run the place," Dad said, and I might have visibly shuddered. "Text Amy—I'm sure they'd love to see you. Or go join Peter and Eileen. I think they went to get ice cream or something."

Amy. I hadn't responded to their texts from last night. And there was no way I was going to go insert myself into Peter's excursion with Eileen. Mom and Dad were always trying to get me to hang out with them again, but they didn't know.

I wanted to stay and try to get close to Milo, but I felt awful that I'd been ignoring Amy, and I hadn't hung out with them in a while. That would be a way to kill time until tonight too.

"Okay, I'll text Amy."

I walked into the front room. Against the wall, across from one of the pink camelback sofas, was a black metal coffin. I paused for a moment before sitting down, thinking Milo was lying there. But it was empty. It was common to see coffins lying around the place, whether we'd gotten a shipment in or Dad was doing some rearranging in the display room, and I usually never thought about it.

I looked at my phone and saw about twenty texts from Amy.

Amy: hey!! Happy fall break!!!

Amy: Do you know some schools only get like two days for fall break? What kind of torture is that? Guess that's one good thing about Somerton! Go Buffalos!

Amy: oh damn you have a funeral right? Sorry for the spam text back when you can!!

Amy: Georgia?

Amy: okay G you usually text by now

Amy: are you dead??

Amy: thankfully if you are, you're in the right place!

Amy: TEXT BACK!

Amy: Did you hear about the vigil??

The texts went on, and I honestly just sort of scanned through them. I got the gist, so I drafted a response.

Me: I'm sorry!! The funeral was huge last night, and I was exhausted so I passed out . . . what vigil?

Amy responded almost immediately. I imagined them staring at their phone all night, waiting for me to respond.

Amy: It's totally okay, G. Wanna meet up today? I'm out running errands with Mom this morning, but after that I'm free.

Amy: Oh and Milo's.

Just as I was sending a response, the urgency of learning more details about the vigil making my thumbs fumble across the keyboard, the front door opened.

During business hours, the front door to Richter was unlocked for ordinary business reasons. It was another thing I was used to—seeing strangers alive and dead coming through the place where I lived. But this time, the bell above the door caught me by surprise, and I stared at the woman who walked in.

Even if I hadn't heard Mom say she was coming, I would have known who she was immediately. She had brown, curly hair tied back into a bun. Her nose was pointed like Milo's, and her cheeks were covered in freckles like Milo's, her skin tan like his. Her hand was firmly grasping the strap of her purse as if that strap was the only thing left that she could hang on to, and her shoulders hunched because her entire concept of gravity had shifted. I noticed her beauty, but I also recognized the pain.

"Mrs. D'Angelo," Mom said, walking out from the office and holding out her hand.

"Jen," Milo's mom said, letting go of that grasp on her purse and landing her hand in Mom's.

"Jen," Mom repeated with a nod. "I'm Andrea. Let's take a seat in here." Mom motioned toward the sitting room, right across from the room where I was. She shot me a glance that obviously meant *leave* because we weren't allowed to participate in client meetings.

Then Milo's mom looked over at me. I gave her a weak smile. Her face was puffy and red. I got up from the couch to leave, and she wouldn't take her eyes off me, even as she turned her body to follow Mom. And even after she took a seat in front of the pamphlets, she looked to me again. Her gaze followed me until I was out of her sightline. I leaned against the wall to listen.

"I want to start by offering my condolences," Mom said. "I understand this will be a tough process, and we don't want to make you uncomfortable in any way. Our job is to help you through this. If you ever have any questions or concerns, or if you just need some time and we have to stop our meeting, I completely understand."

I barely heard Milo's mom whisper a weak "Thank you."

There was a moment of silence. I suspected it was because Mrs. D'Angelo was crying.

After a few more moments, Mom asked, "Do you have any requests or priorities for the service? We'll work around what you want and need."

"We . . . we really need to keep it as cheap as possible. But we also want to give our Milo the best. He deserves the best."

Mom grabbed the green pamphlet and used it as a visual guide to her spiel.

The rest of the meeting was mostly logistical. Mrs. D'Angelo never asked to pause. She hardly said anything at all. I couldn't imagine what it felt like to be her. I'd lost Grandma, and that was bad enough. I wondered if Mrs. D'Angelo knew that the body of her son was right beneath her feet, naked and covered in a sheet that had covered the bodies of so many before him. I wondered if she'd seen his dead body. I wondered when I'd get to. I let all these thoughts race around my head until I decided I shouldn't be listening. I texted Amy.

Me: Yeah sure. Where?

◊

We met at Café Dante, a little coffee shop on Somerton's main square. The square was actually a semicircle since Somerton didn't have enough businesses to fill in the geometry of downtown. The café was only five blocks from Richter, so I walked there right away and grabbed us a table by the window.

From there I had a view of the bookstore where I used to spend a lot of my time with Amy and Eileen. I hadn't been back since that summer. Next to the bookshop was a locally-owned restaurant called Lucky's. My family used to go there after soccer games when Grandma was still alive and able to share a booth seat with me. It had been open since she was a kid, so it was one of her favorite restaurants. Somerton didn't have many chains. We had a McDonald's out toward the highway, and we were rumored to be getting a Starbucks, but that rumor was more than five years old. We were lucky to even have a public library.

All the buildings on the square looked appropriately businesslike. No one would have ever mistaken them for houses. They weren't trying to be something they weren't.

Amy took a seat across from me, and I tried to smile at them as they shook off their jacket. Usually I was excited to see Amy, but sitting here felt like an obligation. I wanted to be present, but I couldn't be.

"So happy it's fall break, so pissed I have a paper to write. I mean, what part of 'break' don't teachers understand? I wish I was in Berry's class with you instead of Lebbing's," Amy said.

"No, you really don't. We're reading *Gatsby*, right?" They nodded in response. "Well, we conveniently got to the part where Myrtle is run over by the car. I think Berry thought it would encourage discourse."

Amy gasped. "No way! That's so messed up."

I nodded.

"No, but like, we don't need to apply our experience to Fitzgerald right now to understand a greater meaning or whatever. We need to grieve. I'm going to go get us coffee. The usual?"

I nodded and they walked up to the counter to order. I watched Amy happily talking to one of our favorite baristas, and I thought about their use of "we." It felt wrong to apply grief to the whole student body. Grief was what I'd seen in

Milo's mom that morning, not the sad faces of the students in the hallway. Was anyone who didn't know Milo well enough allowed to grieve for him? Wasn't that just called sadness? But sadness wasn't quite right to describe what I felt every time I thought about Milo.

"And the vigil is happening on Monday," Amy said when they returned with the coffee as if our conversation had never paused. "Want to go?"

"Who's going?" I asked, taking a sip of my scalding cappuccino.

"The whole school, probably," they said. "Maybe the whole town. Even my mom got an invite, but she's working then, so I'll just go with you."

"Where is it?"

"The church on Third," Amy said.

"Who's organizing it?"

"G, I don't know everything. I just saw it online."

I didn't respond because I could sense the slight annoyance in their tone. Amy knew me way better than I gave them credit for because they said, "You're off."

I kept sliding the sleeve of my cup up and down to tap it on the wooden table, and I was avoiding eye contact with them, so that had probably given it away.

"It's the whole Milo thing," I said quietly. We had been talking about him at a reasonable volume before, but the second I came even close to saying what was in my head I felt the need to whisper.

"Yeah, G, I know." Amy held their hand out across the table for me to take. I actually hesitated, even though their touch always made me feel safe. Because they didn't really know. I grabbed it anyway. "You want to talk about it?" they asked.

I looked out the window without looking at anything in particular. "I *want* to want to."

"You don't have to," Amy clarified. "Just, if you need to, I'm here." Amy was always there, so why couldn't I get there too? I missed when being with them felt entirely natural and I didn't second-guess everything.

We held hands for a bit, and I kept looking out the window, letting all the Milo thoughts swim around my brain. I wished I could release the thoughts from my head and place them on the other side of that window. I'd be able to examine them closely, view all the intricacies and maybe finally understand, ask them why they were there in the first place. I'd put a barrier between those thoughts and me, and they wouldn't be able to break back through. I'd turn to Amy, and I'd be able to smile and enjoy my time with them without feeling like everything was hazy. Milo at my house, his mom's face, the force of his body slamming against the car, wondering what bones broke and what he looked like after. I couldn't get those thoughts to leave.

"He's at Richter," I said. I had to say it before I let my brain stop me.

"Who?"

"Milo," I said in an exhale, so soft that only I could hear it. But Amy read my lips and widened their eyes.

"Whoa. That's got to be weird," they said.

I nodded and thought about telling Amy what Milo being at Richter meant for me. Not about the ghost part, but that I was scared. That I was stuck in this spiral of thinking about his death and my death and the inevitable universe's death. But I couldn't say it. I didn't want to put that on them, and I was afraid of what they would think. Amy was indifferent to most things Richter-related, which usually meant they were the perfect person to be around. They never dug me deeper by loving or hating the funeral home. But that meant I didn't know how they'd react if everything came spilling out. If they'd even get it.

"Oh, crap," Amy whispered, looking at something behind me. I turned around to see what was up. In walked Eileen and my brother.

We locked eyes before I could turn around and pretend I didn't know they were there. Instead of pretending they didn't see us either, they made their way over.

"Hey, guys," Peter said.

"Hey," I said. Amy stayed silent, releasing my hand and clasping their own together in their lap.

Eileen gave me a big, bright smile, and I remembered how I used to feel jealous of how beautiful she was. She still had the same dark black skin and corkscrew black curls she'd had when we were younger. But now she was taller, more athletic, and even better at makeup than she used to be. For a while, Eileen and I were closer than Amy and I were. I used to spend so much time with her, and now I couldn't even stand to look at her.

"Hey, Georgia," Eileen said.

I wanted to bury my face in my hands and groan, releasing all the awkward.

"Hi," I said instead.

"We're going to see a movie later. Do you guys want to come?" Eileen asked. If it had been Peter asking, I would have assumed this was a pity invite, the obligatory *she's my sister* invite. I would have assumed Mom and Dad had texted him and pressured him to ask me. But it was Eileen asking, and I didn't know how to read that.

"I . . . um. . . no thanks." I didn't even offer up a rain check.

Eileen nodded, and her smile gently faded. Peter looked at Eileen, then at me. I looked at Amy like they could help me get out of this.

"I guess we should go order?" Peter said.

"Yeah, okay . . . See you around," Eileen said and followed Peter toward the counter.

"What. On. Earth?" Amy asked.

I shook my head. I had no idea why they'd speak to me at all, let alone invite me to hang out. "Can we leave?" I asked.

"Please."

Amy walked me back to Richter even though they had brought their bike and could've gotten home way faster. When we got to the corner of Main, they asked if I wanted them to come in. I didn't even have to answer for them to know.

"I'm always here, G," Amy said, giving me a quick hug. "Just a text away."

And instead of reaching out when they were even closer than that, I watched them climb on their bike and ride home.

I checked my phone to see the time, but I'd only managed to use up an hour. I didn't have a funeral to run, there was no homework over break, and I was too antsy to read.

I knew I couldn't wait until after Milo's funeral to wake him; it needed to be tonight. I went to my room and set a timer for 2:30 in the morning, then curled up on the bed with Morty while the images cycled through my head. Milo's mom. Milo's body downstairs. Eileen's sad smile. Amy reaching out a hand and me practically shoving them away. At least Peter wasn't home, so he wouldn't hear me cry.

CHAPTER 6

I didn't sleep at all that night. The anticipation kept me from even blinking for too long. It was 2:00 a.m., and my family was usually asleep by midnight, but I wanted to make sure they were as deep as they could go.

I hadn't changed my clothes. For some reason, I wanted to be presentable to Milo. He saw me half asleep in leggings and a T-shirt almost every day at school, but I felt this moment deserved a little more effort. Jeans instead of leggings. A sweater to keep warm in the freezer room.

I had never been so nervous. I was nervous to talk to Milo, but I was also nervous to go downstairs for the first time in so long.

I grabbed a pair of shoes, preparing for the cold concrete flooring of the basement, and turned my phone's flashlight on. It led me to the main staircase, and I crept down them, avoiding the creaky one.

The shadows of the funeral home were darker than usual as they hid within each other.

I knew where Dad kept the key, so I grabbed it from the drawer in the office and took it to the basement door. Unlocking it was the first time I wondered if this was a bad idea. I'd been thinking of this moment every second that day. But now that it was right in front of me, I couldn't imagine anything good coming from this. I didn't know what I would say to Milo. I couldn't remember any of the questions I had for him. I didn't know why I cared so much. But it was the exact thought of turning around and walking upstairs that propelled me down to the basement. I had to. It was the only thing that could help silence it all.

More shadows welcomed me. I didn't turn on the light so that I wouldn't have to confront the room as a whole. I used the illumination from my phone to guide my weak legs forward, until I was standing in front of the freezer room door. As I stood on the concrete, I wondered how much blood had been spilled on it, down the drain over by the embalming table. But I tried not to think about the machinery that hid in the darkness, the names and uses of which Dad had drilled into my head.

I held the light up to the handle and pulled the freezer door open before giving myself enough time to rethink it. I stepped into the coldness, knowing he was here.

I stood in the exact spot where it had started three years ago.

The start of this inexplicable power. The start of being afraid of everything ending, of noticing how time moved both horrifyingly quickly and painfully slowly.

The freezer room was bigger than I remembered, but I felt trapped between the walls. I flicked the light on, and I instantly saw my reflection in the steel. I was taller than I'd been last time; my head reached the top row of drawers, but I still saw the same scared girl looking back at me.

I pulled one of the drawers open. It was empty. After another two tries, I finally came to the drawer I'd avoided. The one where Grandma had been. Sure enough, opening that door revealed two feet covered beneath a sheet.

My breath caught, and I took a step back, staring at the lump. I had so obsessively pictured his mutilated body lying on the road. But there it was right in front of me, whole, and I was terrified of seeing it. It was Milo, it was Grandma, it was Betty, it was me. The panic spiked. I grabbed at the hair near my scalp and tugged, as if I could pull the thoughts out through my pores to spill over the floor. I tapped my foot until it became a stomp, smashing the thoughts lying there on the floor until those death thoughts were dead themselves. I bit my lip till I tasted iron.

Breathed. Dropped my hands. Breathed. Looked up and caught my reflection.

I pulled the drawer out toward me, pulled at the sheet to reveal Milo's head. I suddenly felt like seeing anything else would be a total violation.

There he was, his tan skin paled. His dark, shaggy hair had been pulled away from his face, so I could examine his features fully. This was Milo, plain as could be, but he was also just a slab of meat on a table. Bodies after death and before burial were in their own state of purgatory. The body wasn't the same boy who stared through my computer screen or through the frame on his desk at school. But it was. I couldn't make sense of it.

I didn't want him to be here. I wanted him to be walking through the school hallways. I wanted him to be at home with his parents.

I reached out and touched him right on the nose.

An image of Milo's living, breathing self appeared on the other side of the drawer. There was no consistency to where around me the ghosts landed when I woke them, but I had never had a ghost appear staring me right in the eyes.

In a quick motion I grabbed the sheet off his body, making sure to keep my hand away from flesh. Closing my eyes to avoid seeing more of the corpse, I slid it back in the drawer, then threw the sheet over his spirit-self.

He didn't seem to register what was happening. It was like he was still asleep with eyes wide open.

His skin had returned to its natural complexion, and his hair was no longer being pulled toward the back of his head by gravity. Now he was the same boy who'd sat behind me in Berry's class, who'd been captured in those photographs.

But he wasn't.

I could tell he was finally coming around when he spat the words "What the fuck?"

"Hey, Milo" was all I could manage to say. My heart was knocking to be let out.

"Where am I?" He sounded angry and confused and defeated. He looked down at the sheet draped over his shoulders, around the room, right at me. His eyes were alive. I hadn't ever looked at him like this before, and I hated that it had to be after he died. I couldn't tell if he recognized me.

"What do you remember?" I asked.

He scrunched his face. "I was . . . I was walking home from Lucky's."

"Anything after that?"

I saw the moment in his eyes. He looked to the drawer where his dead body lay. "Was that me?" So he had noticed it after all.

"Yes and no, I suppose."

He pressed himself against the wall. "Is this a fucking joke?"

"No," I said. "I'm sorry. You were hit by a car on Wednesday night."

He nodded toward the drawer. "Show me."

"Milo—"

"Georgia, If I'm dead, I should get to see my body."

He knew who I was.

His logic sounded fair enough to me, so I closed my eyes and pulled his body from the drawer, keeping my hand on the metal rim to make sure not to touch his skin again. I wasn't sure if I could wake someone up twice. I'd never tried. I didn't want to risk it.

I couldn't see his reaction to his corpse, but I heard his breathing get heavy, and he started saying "Oh my god" over and over. I heard him fall to the floor. I heard him crying.

I slid the drawer shut again and opened my eyes to see him curled into a ball on the concrete, the sheet wrapped around him like he wanted it to be a warm blanket. This was what I must have looked like when I saw my grandma's ghost, except he was seeing his own dead body. He wasn't even lucky enough to see the embalmed made-up version at his funeral. This was the real, raw thing, and I had done that to him.

I let him cry. I took a seat against the wall across from him, and I waited.

"Why is this happening?" he asked. Another question I asked myself too often: why anyone has to die, why some people die sooner than they should. But then I realized he was asking about the two of us having this conversation right here.

"Um." I didn't know the answer to that either, but I could do my best. "I can talk to ghosts."

He actually laughed. "Guess that makes sense," he said. "Since I am, apparently, a ghost now. And we're talking. Wait, are you also dead?"

"No, I'm just a weirdo with the ability to talk to the dead."

"Right. Your family owns Richter Funeral Home."

I nodded.

"So, I assume that's where I am right now."

I nodded again.

"Jesus." He grabbed at his hair. Then he lowered his hands and sobbed into them. I looked away, but I couldn't un-hear it.

I didn't know how to stop him, whether or not I should stop him. I had things I wanted to talk to him about and ask him, but this moment wasn't mine.

I didn't know what I'd been expecting. That he'd be one of the ghosts who wasn't bothered by his own death, who was just happy to have one last person to talk to? That I'd be able to easily ask him all my burning questions, learn every intricate detail about his life before sending him to whatever comes after? Like he was my captive audience, a robot ready to receive input and produce output for my personal gain.

I'm not sure how long he cried, how long I sat there in my own silence surrounded by his sobs. I finally decided it was too long. I had done this to him, and I had the power to stop it.

"I'm sorry," I said. "I'm really sorry. This was a complete mistake." I was furious at myself for thinking this was okay. All this pain was because of me. Putting ghosts through this was selfish.

Milo looked up through his reddened face and tears. His chest was heaving, and he was trying to get one good breath. Because of me.

"I never should've done this," I said and reached for the handle of the drawer to end it once and for all.

"Wait, stop!" He almost shouted it. My hand froze. He clutched the white sheet at his chest as he stood up. "What happens"—he nodded toward where his body lay—"when you touch me again?"

"I really don't know. On my end, you just disappear. I'm not sure where you go."

He took a shuddering breath and looked at me with pure

terror on his face. "Please don't," he said. "I don't . . . I don't want to die again."

I had never thought about it like that before. That I, by waking these people up, was causing them to die twice. Did that make me a killer?

He was looking at me still, pleading.

I didn't know what had happened to my grandma's ghost. I didn't know what would happen if I kept someone awake on purpose. No ghost had ever begged me to do it before.

"I have to," I said, because I thought I did.

"But aren't you like some sort of medium? You can talk to ghosts—can't you keep me awake? Did you not wake me up for a reason?"

I gulped. "I guess I did."

"Then please don't send me back."

I dropped my hand to my side and sighed. If I were given the chance to be a ghost instead of traveling into the inevitable unknown, I knew pretty well which choice I'd make.

"Thank you," he said.

I didn't know if it was the right choice. But I wanted him to stay, and he wanted to stay, so that had to count for something.

"So why did you wake me up?" he asked.

"Well. I wanted to ask you some questions. Talk to you. Get to know you. Maybe fulfill whatever final request you have." I shrugged like waking up a former classmate from the dead and sitting and talking in her father's personal morgue was super casual. I couldn't quite bring myself to explain that he was the first person my age to come through Richter and that I'd been obsessively picturing his death for days and that I was stuck in a spiral I thought only he could help me escape from.

"My final request, huh?" Milo looked down at his hands,

retreating into himself. That posture was so familiar, and I suddenly could vividly picture passing him in the halls or walking into Berry's class to find him leaning over his desk scribbling on paper. "I've never thought about that before. I didn't really think I would die before I was, like, at least eighty-five."

I smiled a little. Even with all my thoughts about death, I'd still always seen myself living to be an old lady like Grandma. But ever since I'd heard about Milo, I pictured suddenly dying young. I pictured being the one getting hit by a car and dying at 12:15 a.m. I pictured it all ending at any moment.

"I guess," he said, "I guess I can think of a final request."

My posture straightened. "Yeah?"

"Is there any way I could wear clothes? This sheet is soft and all, and it really fits the ghost aesthetic, but I'd be more comfortable in actual clothes if I'm going to stick around."

I hadn't even thought about the logistics of keeping Milo awake. Could he wear clothes? Where would he sleep? Where could he go?

"Uh, sure. Wait here a second." I stepped out of the freezer room, leaving Milo behind, and I took a deep breath of warmer air. The kind of deep breath that's supposed to calm your nerves and clear your head. It didn't do either of those things.

Clothes. Housing. How was any of this going to work?

I flicked the lights on and went to the closet where Dad kept the sheets and towels and latex gloves and jaw wires and eye molds. I grabbed an extra sheet and went back to the freezer.

"I already have one of those, but thanks," he said.

"This one's for your body," I told him. "You might want to look away. It's up to you."

"I'd never seen a dead body before," he remarked. "Never thought my first would be my own."

It was hard to imagine never having seen one because I'd seen so many. By the time I was a toddler, I'd probably been around more dead bodies than living ones. Dead bodies were my normal, yet they never felt normal to me.

I pressed my chin to my chest so I wouldn't see Milo's corpse when I pulled the drawer out. I didn't know if Milo decided to look, but a moment later the body was covered in a fresh sheet and back in the freezer.

"Since you can hold the sheet, I assume you can wear clothes. My brother is about your size. I can bring you something of his," I said.

"Do I have to stay in this room?" Milo asked.

"Oh. No." I'd left Grandma down here. I couldn't do that to Milo. "You can—I guess you can come to my room."

I wasn't sure how far Milo's spirit could travel from his body, but I figured any place within Richter was safe, since I'd talked to plenty of ghosts in the chapel and the reposing room.

I shut off all the lights and closed the freezer room door behind us, letting my phone flashlight guide us up the steps. Milo was following me closely, but neither of us said a word.

When we reached the apartment, I moved extra slowly and kept my breath quieter than usual. I know my family wouldn't see Milo if they woke up, but I didn't want to explain where I was coming from. We finally reached my room.

"Wait here," I told him again, trusting that he wouldn't move. I went to Peter's room and prayed he wouldn't stir. I grabbed a pair of old jeans and a sweatshirt I knew he never wore. When I returned to my room, I placed them on the bed in front of Milo and turned my back. "I won't look."

"Okay," Milo said and got dressed. "You sure Peter won't miss these?"

"I'm sure."

"Okay, I'm decent."

I turned. He was in my room, wearing my brother's clothes and folding up the white sheet, looking like he had never died. And I had no idea where to go from here.

"Thanks for this," he said. "I hope your parents won't mind."

"They won't see you. I'm the only one who can." I flashed back to me screaming on the floor of the cold chamber, Mom and Dad rushing past Ghost Grandma, completely unaware of her presence.

I threw the sheet into my closet and took a seat on the bed. Milo took a seat next to me.

"The clothes weren't really your final request, were they?" I asked.

"Oh, no. I was kidding about that. There is something else."

After striking out twice—first with Betty not having a request and then with my not having the guts to wake Theodore—I was ready.

"Is it about how you died?" I asked. "Do you want me to try to find out who . . . killed you?"

He pondered that for a moment. And then he laughed. "You know ninety percent of these don't get solved?" He seemed way more casual about it than I would ever be. "No offense, Georgia, but I don't think you're going to track down the driver who hit me."

"Oh. Okay." I was relieved, but I was also at a loss. If that wasn't his final request . . .

"There's something more important," he said.

I wanted to know what was more important—what this boy wanted more than anything in the world.

"It's my parents. I know they're having a really hard time

right now. They were having a hard time before I died, so this has messed everything up even more. Can you check on them?"

"Check on your parents?" I thought about Mrs. D'Angelo in Richter, planning her son's funeral.

"Yeah. Make sure they're okay for me. Tell them I loved them very much and that I wish I could have been better."

"Sure," I said, though I wondered what he meant by that.

"So," Milo said, breaking a three-second silence that felt like an eternity. "What do we do now?"

I looked at my phone to see it was almost four in the morning. "Do ghosts sleep?" I asked him.

"You tell me. You have more experience with this sort of thing."

"I don't, actually. I've never spoken to a ghost for more than like thirty minutes."

"Well, I guess we could try."

I grabbed a pile of blankets and some pillows and formed a makeshift bed on the floor next to me. I climbed into my bed and he climbed into his.

"See you in the morning," he said.

"Can't wait," I replied. I placed my hands on my stomach and looked up at the ceiling, mentally creating shapes in the darkness and tracking the constellations of my glow-in-the-dark stars. Ghost Milo lay next to me while his dead body lay two stories down. I was in the same room as the boy who had been hit by the car, who'd sat behind me in Berry's class, who wanted me to go check on his parents who were grieving for him right now.

What had I done?

CHAPTER 7

When Peter and I were thirteen, Dad decided it was time to teach us how to embalm a body. It had been barely two weeks since Grandma died. We'd held her funeral at Richter, and we'd spread her ashes in the gardens and on the plot next to Grandpa. I'd watched when Dad tossed the ashes over the plot and so many of them flew away on the wind. I'd imagined they had escaped to go and save Grandma's ghost.

Dad said it was time for us to start learning the details of running the business, but I also suspected it was his morbid way of teaching me how to cope.

So one Saturday afternoon he took Peter and me down to the basement, outfitting us with lab coats to keep our clothes clean and to keep everything up to code.

Peter sat on the edge of his stool, eager to learn the names of all the tools and to finally know each step of the process. I felt no enthusiasm. I was nervous to be back down in the embalming room, to watch Dad literally manhandle a dead body, and to see how into it Peter was.

I kept staring at the door to the body freezer, wondering if Grandma was still trapped in there, pounding against the door, screaming to be let out.

"Today, kids," Dad said theatrically, "I will be teaching

you one of the most valuable life lessons in the world. Along with changing a tire and learning to do taxes, knowing how to embalm a body is critical."

Peter laughed with Dad.

"My father never taught me how. He was always down here while Michael and I wandered around upstairs entertaining ourselves, so you guys are lucky to see this in action. I learned all this for the first time in mortuary school, but I want you to build these key skills early since you two will run this place one day."

I rolled my eyes at the millionth mention of my inevitable future, but I was surprised that Dad had mentioned Michael. Michael was a different kind of ghost in Richter. We only ever heard about him as a part of distant memories, and if we tried to ask about him, Dad pretended he didn't hear us.

As I watched Dad preparing the embalming fluids, I thought that Michael had been smart to leave.

"The first thing you'll need is, of course, a body." He stood up from his rolling stool and walked into the cold chamber. A moment later he returned with a body on top of the rolling bed. He lined up the bed with the table, on the opposite side from where Peter and I sat. When Dad slid the sheet-covered lump off the rolling bed and onto the table, the body came right at us.

Standing across the table from us, Dad unfolded the sheet in the big reveal of his act.

Peter and I were staring at the body of a middle-aged white man. He had no idea that his corpse would be used to teach two thirteen-year-olds how to drain his blood and stick synthetic liquid into his veins.

"Coooool," Peter said, dragging the word out to really emphasize his awe. It was just a dead body, something he'd seen a million times before. But we'd never seen a body in preparation up close before.

"What was his name?" I looked at his blue lips, at the vein that ran the length of his neck and disappeared at his chest. I kept my hands firmly planted under my legs even though I was wearing gloves. I didn't want my hand to come anywhere near him.

"Oscar Fitz," Dad said. Oscar Fitz later became page 2 in my binder, right after Grandma.

"How did he die?" I asked.

"Aneurism," Dad said casually. Then he officially began his lesson. "The first step is to make sure you have the right body, and then check that body for vitals. We learn this in mortuary school. It's just an extra precaution to prevent premature burial. It might seem silly, but it's a vital step. Ha. Get it? Vital? Anyway, I'm sure you've both heard the horror stories in the business. There's that famous memoir *Wait Wait I Wasn't Dead*, it's a great read." Dad had wanted to keep that as a coffee table book in the front room, but Mom immediately shot down the idea.

I stared at Oscar Fitz, certain that he was dead without needing to feel for a pulse. No alive person looked like that.

"Then we have to wash the body and shave it." With his gloved hands, Dad grabbed a plastic package and tore open the top to reveal a sanitary sponge. "This is another sanitation precaution. We're dealing with a dead body here."

He couldn't have made that any clearer.

"Then we set the face. In this case, we'll use a photo of this guy when he was alive to make the features look as realistic and presentable as possible." Dad propped the photo on his side table. I'd seen plenty of dead bodies after the embalming process, and I was of the firm belief that no matter how hard any mortician tried, no surgical or cosmetic work could make a dead body presentable.

Dad used eye caps to keep Oscar's lids closed and a wire to shape the jaw and keep his mouth from hanging open. He mentioned that depending on the condition of a body, an entire facial reconstruction could sometimes be necessary.

"Then, the most exciting part," Dad said.

"What is it?" Peter asked. I tried to sit even harder on my hands.

"We use this machine here," Dad said, pointing to one of the metal objects by the counter. It was on wheels, so he pulled it toward us. "It's called a centrifugal pump. It allows us to drain the bodily fluids and replace them with the embalming fluid. We do this through arteries. The machine here mimics the beating of the heart."

I wished I could hop off my chair and go upstairs to my room, or just anywhere other than right here.

"Where does the blood go?" Peter said.

"Just down the drain through this sink," Dad explained.

The blood literally was sent into the sewer. Dad discarded it like it meant nothing.

I realized that this exact process was what Dad had done to Grandma. How could he have done this to his own mother? Just the thought of draining the blood from Mom while she lay lifeless on a metal table in front of me made me want to throw up.

Dad made an incision and inserted the tubes into the heart. I watched as the plastic machine met the plastic skin of Oscar Fitz. Peter hopped off his chair to get a better look.

"It's best if, as the pump drains and refills the body, we massage the arms and legs to prevent blood clots and rigor mortis. Or should I say, Richter mortis." Dad began to demon-strate while laughing at another terrible pun.

Peter chuckled too.

Dad continued. "The embalming process takes anywhere from one to three hours, so you could be doing this awhile. You can help me with this part." Peter put his gloved hands on Oscar's left arm and mimicked Dad as he massaged the other arm.

I heard the noise of the pump and stared at Oscar's cold skin. The sound of the blood going down the drain reminded me of a slurping noise, like the drain was excited to pull the blood into it. I wanted to plug my ears.

"Georgia, you can take the legs," Dad said, moving his arm toward Oscar's stomach.

I stayed on my stool and shook my head. "No thanks."

"Come on, Georgia, you learn best from doing."

"It's kinda fun," Peter said, smiling and increasing his movements.

"I said no!" I jumped up off the stool, my hands still behind me. "I don't want to help."

Dad sighed and wiped his brow with his wrist. "Fine. Go help your mother."

I glared at Peter, furious at his enthusiasm. I glared at my father, furious that this was his job, treating the dead with dis-respect and making jokes all the while. I wanted to yell at them. But I just turned on my heels and stomped upstairs. Walk-ing up the steps, I felt simultaneously sick to my stomach and fascinated.

At dinner that night Peter talked about how much he'd learned, and Dad made some comment about how I didn't enjoy it. I kept my mouth as firmly closed as Oscar's had been. I couldn't eat a bite. My head was reeling with resentment for my family and sickening images of drained blood and stiff limbs and empty corpses. I decided I would never forgive my father for that day.

I created my scrapbook that night, pasting Grandma's pamphlet onto the first page, along with the picture of her and me building a snowman. I started Oscar's page but waited until his funeral to get a pamphlet. Oscar was the second one I woke.

I was so desperate to know if I'd hallucinated Grandma, so curious about what I was able to do. When I tapped Oscar and he too appeared right in front of me, I had to admit it was real.

I didn't tell Oscar he was dead. He was as clueless as Grandma had been. He asked who I was, where he was, what had happened, but I couldn't give him any answers. I was still trying to process it all, trying to understand why it was happening, but I was calmer that time. Oscar was only awake for about five minutes because he was the first one I tapped again. I wanted to figure out the rules to my power. And when he disappeared, it was confirmation that had I just touched Grandma's body again, I could have ended it.

Since I hadn't asked him anything, I padded his page in my scrapbook with information I learned from his eulogy.

That night, I stayed up late researching embalming techniques and procedures, watching online tutorials and reading (albeit false) stories about people waking up on the embalming table, body embalming mishaps, body embalming "with pictures!" I knew for sure I never wanted to be embalmed. But I couldn't peel my eyes away from my laptop, and I bookmarked some of the most fascinating websites. I created a secret folder in my browser to save all the links about death. And I created a place inside me where all my fears about death would secretly live.

CHAPTER 8

Soon enough, Milo's body would be put through exactly what Oscar's had been. Dad would massage his arms and legs until the blood slipped out of his veins and slurped down the drain like it meant nothing. He would be disinfected as if he was no different from morgue counters, and his jaw would be wired shut and his eyelids glued closed. He'd be stuffed, dolled up, and placed on display because for some reason people needed a tangible reminder that he was in fact dead.

I hadn't known if ghosts could sleep or not, but Milo was able to. I woke up before him and looked down at him under the blanket. He was so still that if not for the color of life beneath his skin, I might've thought this body was no different than the dead one below us.

There was a knock on my door, and my heart thudded. "Yeah?" I called sleepily, reminding myself that the owner of the knock wouldn't be able to see Milo on my floor.

Mom opened the door. "Morning, sunshine. Why are all your blankets on the floor?"

Telling her "I had a restless night" was thankfully believable.

"I'm sorry." She frowned. "Well, I was going to ask if you'd be willing to do some chores around the apartment today.

Peter is going to help your dad with some things downstairs. Maybe it'll be a good change of pace after a rough night."

"Yeah, I can."

"Thank you. I left a list on the counter. I'll be downstairs most of the day too." She smiled, but she couldn't erase the remnants of her previous expression before closing the door.

The moment the latch clicked, Milo's eyes shot open. And there I was, officially faced with last night's decision. He was here, he was awake, and he wasn't going away.

"How did you sleep?" I asked awkwardly.

He stared at the ceiling before answering. "I forgot for a moment. I feel like I'm alive."

I felt like he was too.

"You'd think maybe being a ghost would feel hazy, or like a dream, or you'd have this total understanding of the limitations of your existence. But you don't. At least not me." He sat up and leaned on his knees. "I feel real." He held out his hands in front of his face, examining his palms and then the backs, wiggling his fingers. "Solid," he said, grabbing at the blankets, running his hands along the carpet. "I feel things when I touch them. But I can't just do anything, right? There must be limitations."

"I don't know, Milo. Like I told you, I've never woken up a ghost for longer than half an hour."

"So that must mean I'm different."

"I know as little about being a ghost as you do."

"Right," he sighed. "I wonder what a ghost's day-to-day looks like."

I had no idea how to handle this. All I wanted to do was talk to him, ask him questions, even if he didn't have answers to any of them. Like why this had happened to him and how

I was supposed to come to terms with it one day happening to me? I needed to ask.

"Do I float around and haunt people by moving chairs and making lights flicker? Well, I guess I can't float. I feel as weighed down by gravity as ever. Maybe more so."

Just then, Morty slinked out from under my bed. He blinked at Milo like he knew he was there.

"Hey," Milo said, reaching out to pet him. But his hand went right through. Morty didn't even flinch. Neither did Milo. "Is that what happens when I touch you?" he asked me.

I nodded. That rule I knew. It was always strange to watch it happen because it didn't look ghostly. There was no flickering, nothing see-through, but there was also no concreteness to it. It was like when you blink and see a darkness but it's gone before you can even process it. Those moments asked me to accept it as fact without demanding it make sense.

"I guess I'm not as real as I feel," he said.

Morty yawned and jumped up onto my bed to rub his head on my arm, a natural collision of two living beings.

"Maybe you can't touch living things, but you seem to be able to touch everything else," I said.

"Yeah. I guess now the question is, what do I do with that?"

I wasn't sure, but I felt like I had to offer a suggestion. "Would you like to do chores with me?"

"I guess there's nothing like chores to make you feel like a fully alive teenager, huh?"

I told him to wait in my room while I showered. The entire time, I kept thinking how unbelievable this situation was. This was what I'd wanted, to see him right in front of me, to reverse what had happened. Being alone for those few minutes allowed

me to remember why it mattered so much to me. I knew everything I needed to ask him, and suddenly I felt excited that he
was here, awake, able to talk to me.

I quickly dried off and got dressed, running back to my
room with damp hair.

Milo was standing at the window, staring down at the parking lot where, in a week's time, his family would park their car
to attend his funeral. I wasn't sure if Milo was thinking about
that, but I sure was.

"Come on," I said. "I have to clean the kitchen first."

He looked at me, his eyes saying something that I couldn't
read. He followed me into the kitchen.

Milo walked up to the dishwasher, his brows knit. He
picked up a bowl, held it for a few moments to really contemplate the weight of it, then placed it in the cabinet.

"Huh," he said.

"You don't have to do my chores for me," I told him. "That's
not what I meant."

"Just wanted to see if I could. I mean, what else am I supposed to do?"

"You can just keep me company."

Milo took a seat at the kitchen table, and as I turned to grab
another dish, I realized the bowl he'd just put away had returned
to its spot in the dishwasher. I did a double take, checking the
cabinet, blinking. It was like it had never moved.

"What's that look?" Milo asked.

"The bowl you put away . . . it's back in the dishwasher."

"You saw me move it, though, right?"

I nodded.

He scrunched his nose. "So, what, I can interact with things,
but I can't actually change anything about them for real?"

"I guess." It made sense in a way. He wasn't physically here, even though he seemed to be.

We could have done this for a while, testing what Milo could and couldn't do. I only knew the tip of the ghost iceberg.

Now was the time for me to ask him some of my burning questions, but before I took the chance, Milo broke the silence. "You grew up here?"

"Yeah." I put another cup in the cabinet. "My dad grew up here too."

"What's that like? Living in a funeral home?"

I swallowed the lump in my throat. People asked me that all the time. Friends, extended family, literally anyone who found out about Richter. Usually I'd shrug and say it was fine, it was the only life I'd ever known. When I was younger, that was true, but after Grandma died, that answer became camouflage.

"Like," Milo went on, "what are the logistics of it? Is downstairs your house, or is just this part your house? You know what I mean? Like how many living rooms would you say you have? Just the one up here or . . . ?"

No one had ever asked me that kind of question before. They usually wanted to know how the dead bodies were involved.

"I kind of think of this part as my house. Downstairs is the funeral home." I didn't tell him that Peter and I used to play downstairs, climbing into empty coffins or tying each other into the body lifts for fun. I didn't say that we didn't own a normal car but instead an old hearse we didn't use for work anymore. And I didn't mention that we used to host our birthday parties and family Christmas in the downstairs sitting room because our apartment was so tiny. All that would have just complicated the answer.

Milo nodded and looked around. "Well, it's really, really nice." I wasn't sure what apartment he saw around him, but it surely couldn't be the one attached to Richter Funeral Home.

"You don't have to lie to be nice," I said.

Very little about this cramped space had changed since Dad was born. We hadn't given it a paint job or redone the flooring or tried to make it our own in any way. The most we did was get a new couch. The worst part was the white speckled wallpaper on the ceiling. Yes. The ceiling.

"No, I mean it. It's nice. Clean, tidy. Older, but in like an antique way instead of a rundown way," he said.

"Um, thanks." He obviously hadn't noticed the peeling paint at the trim and door handles. Strange how people can look at the same thing and see it in completely different ways.

"So, what did I miss in Berry's class?" He said it like he was telling a joke. It was clear his thoughts had drifted back from our lovely apartment toward his ghostliness, and I couldn't blame him for that.

"Well, Berry was really upset. Everyone was. There was a shrine for you by your locker and at your desk in every class. Berry cried at the assembly when Principal Wendell told everyone what happened." I paused, unsure if he needed or wanted to hear all this right now.

"People . . . a shrine?" He brushed his hair behind his ear. "Wow. Just wow. They cared enough to do that?"

I had stopped cleaning the kitchen at this point and was leaning against the counter, watching Milo stare out the kitchen window toward the sky. "Yeah. And there's a vigil for you tomorrow. You should see all the stuff people are posting online."

He raised his brows, so I pulled up his profile on my phone and placed it in front of him on the table. He made an attempt to scroll, but the screen display didn't respond to his finger. Another limit.

I took a seat next to him and scrolled for him, showing him the posts from our classmates expressing how much they missed him. A reminder to him of all the friendships he'd apparently had.

"Ha!" He sat back in his seat. "Hudson Pierce? He bullied me in middle school." Milo crossed his arms and looked up at the ceiling. "*Homeboy*," he scoffed, a bit of a laugh.

"I'm sorry," I said. "What an ass."

Milo lowered his head to make eye contact with me. "Yeah. I can still hear the stuff he said to me. Like my brain recorded it for me to replay forever."

I hadn't remembered that Milo had been bullied, but now that he brought it up, I thought I could picture Hudson pushing Milo around.

"Do you remember in seventh grade?" That was all Milo gave me, as if I should know exactly what he was talking about.

I shook my head.

"Right after PE one day, Hudson grabbed one of my notebooks out of my hand and ripped it right in half. The strength was impressive actually. Anyway, you and your friend Amy saw it and came up to him, and Amy smacked him in the arm with one half of the notebook. She was pretty badass."

"They," I corrected.

"Right, thanks. They gave me the notebook back and told me I was a good artist. No one had ever told me that before."

As soon as he said it, the entire memory came back to me. Amy and I had seen Hudson tormenting Milo. I remembered feeling sick of Hudson. But I also remembered how mad I'd felt in general. It had only been a few months since Grandma died and everything went down with Peter and Eileen. I was made up of anger. If Amy hadn't gone over and smacked Hudson, I think I would have.

"I forgot about that," I said. I couldn't believe the memory hadn't surfaced until now.

"Well, it meant a lot. What Amy said was the only thing that kept me from sobbing right in the hallway. I went and did it in the bathroom instead. So, thanks."

"It was all Amy."

"I know, but you were there with them. I felt like you were quietly backing them up. I wanted to thank you both then, but you left really quickly."

I remembered that too. After Amy smacked him, Hudson had looked at me and said, "You don't need to force your body-guard on me." It was months after Amy had defended me, so the fact that people still remembered what happened stung. I ran to the bathroom and Amy followed. Somehow, Amy didn't get in any trouble. I guess Hudson decided not to tell.

"Plus," Milo said, "I knew you were dealing with your own stuff at the time."

Even to this day people remembered. Luckily my phone buzzed and Milo pushed it toward me so we could drop the subject.

I thought it was Amy and their sixth sense of knowing when someone was talking about them. But it was a message from Mom asking me to bring her some paperwork that she'd left on the counter. I glanced around and spotted the papers next to the microwave. I grabbed them—and noticed Milo's name printed in bold toward the top.

Milo noticed too. He stiffened, and all the color drained from his face.

I gulped. "Stay here," I said. "I'll be right back."

Halfway down the steps, I heard Mom talking to someone. I stopped at the edge of the railing to listen.

"She couldn't make it," a man said.

"No, no, I totally understand," Mom said.

"It's been hard."

"I can't even imagine." Mom's voice was warm and comforting.

"That's my dad." Milo's voice sounded in my ear from behind. I jumped, almost tipping forward down the stairs, and turned.

"I told you to wait in the apartment," I whispered.

"Georgia, is that you?" Mom called.

"Stay here," I whispered again, holding my hand out to keep him there. I worried that if he saw his dad, he'd decide to leave with him. But he didn't move. He stood stiff, eerily corpse-like. I jogged down the steps and turned the corner to the front room.

"Were you talking to someone?" Mom asked as I handed her the papers and looked at the man sitting across from her.

"Just myself." I summoned a halfhearted smile. Milo's father was tall, even with him sitting down I could tell. He had dark hair like Milo and a scruffy beard that clearly hadn't been tended to in days. His eyes were red, tired, sad. But unlike Milo's mom when I had seen her, he offered me a weak smile.

"This is my daughter, Georgia," Mom said. "Thank you for the papers, G."

Milo's dad nodded at me, and Mom grabbed a pen, placing the papers on the table between them.

I lingered for a second longer, trying to find the resemblances between Mr. D'Angelo and his son, but Mom shot me her usual warning look, so I left and ran back up the steps.

Milo hadn't moved an inch. "What did he say?"

"He didn't say anything. Please, can we go back upstairs?"

Milo listened this time and I followed him to the living room. We both took a seat on the couch, across from the fireplace.

Milo's expression was blank, and we sat in silence while I let him process and while I let my heartbeat slow.

"You said yesterday that you wanted to help me fulfill that final wish," he said, staring at the floor. "I'm serious about wanting you to make sure my parents are okay." His eyes met mine. A shiver ran down my spine.

"Okay. I will," I said.

"Please." The color ran back to his face. His brow knit and his lips started to quiver. I could tell there was something serious lingering on his lips, but I didn't want to ask what it was. It reminded me of when he'd begged me to keep him awake.

"I will," I repeated. "I promise."

CHAPTER 9

M ilo wanted to go with me to see his parents, but I thought
that was risky.

"I don't know if you can leave Richter," I told him. "I don't
know how far away from your body you can be without—something else happening."

"Like what?"

"I have no idea! Maybe you would, like, disintegrate or
something. I don't know the rules. I just don't think you should
risk it."

So he agreed to wait in my room while I went.

It was weird to suddenly be so far from him. I worried that maybe he had to be close to me to keep existing.
Maybe that's what happened to Grandma. But it wasn't like
I could stay in my room forever. And I'd made a promise.
Plus, fulfilling final requests was the whole purpose of this,
wasn't it?

On my way to the front door, I ran into Dad as he came
up from the basement. He was wearing his lab coat like he'd
forgotten to take it off, and he had that look that he wore after
every embalming—a little tired, but mostly exhilarated. There
was only one body it could be.

I instantly hated him for doing that to Milo. I wanted to

scream at him and hear him apologize for every single body he'd worked on. For enjoying it. For showing me how. But instead, I walked by him without a word.

There would be even less of Milo D'Angelo in that body now. No more blood. Just formaldehyde. I wasn't sure how I could face his parents knowing what their son's body had been through.

They lived much closer to Richter than I'd realized. This whole time, every single day, Milo had been only blocks from me. I recognized the house when I saw it: a small white bungalow with a screen porch at the front. The screen door was blowing open and shut in the wind, half hanging off the hinges, making a slamming noise every time it met the frame. The siding was peeling off, and there were shingles missing from the roof. The lawn looked like it hadn't been mowed in months, and half the grass was yellowing. A Jeep waited in the driveway, like it knew Milo was gone. I'd walked by this house every day on the way to school and never once wondered who lived behind the door.

Standing across the street, I had no idea how this conversation would go. Milo had rushed me out of the door before I could plan the conversation in my head or ask him for more guidance. Did I just ask his parents outright if they were okay? Of course they weren't okay. What did he mean by okay? I should have taken the risk and brought him with me. He could've fed me the right lines to say.

I took a deep breath and tried to rehearse quickly. "Hi, you probably remember me. My family owns Richter Funeral Home. I've been talking to the ghost of your dead son and he wanted me to check up on you. How ya doin'?"

This was ridiculous.

So I walked up to their house with the same feeling I'd had moments before tugging Milo's body out from the locker. I didn't know if I should knock on the screen door or the one inside the porch. After a moment's hesitation, I walked up the steps and closed the screen behind me. When I peered through the window at the front door, the house looked dark and empty. Maybe they weren't even home, and this wouldn't mean anything. No one would answer and I would get to walk away. I could tell Milo I checked on them. He wouldn't know.

But I would. Especially after seeing how desperately he needed me to do this, I had to. For him.

I rang the doorbell and heard it on the other side of the wall. I tightened my fists at my legs, shifted on my heels, and waited.

From inside, I could see the shadow of a woman growing as she walked toward the door. She flipped a light on and looked directly at me from the illuminated room. I smiled weakly, waiting for her to let me in but also wanting her to turn me away. For a moment, she just stared, and I was convinced that was all she would do until finally she opened the door.

The strong smell of cigarettes hit me, and I caught my breath. Mrs. D'Angelo's features seemed to droop more than when I'd seen her at Richter, the circles under her eyes were darker and bigger than before.

"Can I help you?" She looked confused and maybe angry.

"Hi." Great start. I shifted on my feet again. "Um . . . I'm Georgia Richter," I said. "My family owns Richter Funeral Home."

"I recognize you from the other day." Her voice was matter of fact.

"Yeah. Um . . ." Words were completely escaping me. I had never felt so blank.

"Is this about funeral arrangements?" she asked.

That would have been the perfect excuse. I could've told them Mom sent me and made up something about finalizing information. I could have brought some fake paperwork and asked them to sign it. It would have been quick, an excuse to make sure they were okay and nothing else. It would have ended there.

But no, I'd shown up with no plan whatsoever.

I was overcome with nerves. I wasn't thinking that clearly, and the words "Milo asked me to . . ." blurted from my mouth before I could stop them.

I cursed myself. I was usually so careful, but being here made my brain all fuzzy.

"You knew Milo?" she asked, going rigid.

"I . . ." I didn't know what to say. The verb tense confused me. I hadn't known him when he was alive, but I knew him now. Of course I couldn't tell his mom that.

"Come in," she said without waiting for a response. She stepped aside and placed a hand on my shoulder to guide me. The cigarette smell became stronger when I stepped in, and I noticed how empty the house felt. Not that it was physically empty—in fact, the room was filled with stuff: the coffee table covered in empty soda cans, clothes strewn around the room, an ashtray still lingering with smoke. I instantly noticed the cluster of flower bouquets by the couch. There must've been nearly thirty of them, each with a little card attached. Despite all this, the house was empty of Milo.

Milo's dad was standing in the doorway to the kitchen. "You're Georgia, right?" he asked. He was even taller than I had guessed when I saw him sitting on the couch at Richter.

"Yes, sir," I said. I couldn't believe I was standing in Milo's living room. In his house.

"Milo never mentioned you," his mom said. In response to her husband's confused look, Mrs. D'Angelo said, "Georgia was Milo's friend."

Mr. D'Angelo dropped his arms from in front of his chest. "Really?"

"I—" I started, trying to figure out a way to explain myself.

"Milo never mentioned much of anything to us," Mrs. D'Angelo said. "Sorry, how rude of me, have a seat." She gestured to the couch and kicked several bouquets out of the way, one of them toppling over. She ignored it and sat down. I took a seat on the other end of the couch. Mr. D'Angelo stood behind his wife.

"Milo was really quiet," Mr. D'Angelo said. "Pretty private. We're sorry we didn't know about you is our point, I think." He looked at his wife to confirm, and she nodded.

"No. Don't be sorry." I shook my head too vigorously "I shouldn't have intruded . . . I just wanted to give you my condolences."

"Thank you," Mr. D'Angelo said. Mrs. D'Angelo started to cry, dabbing her cheeks with her sleeve.

"Were you close?" she asked, trying to breathe through the tears.

If I said no, they'd ask me why I was there and then they'd make me leave. And Milo and I did have a kind of closeness now. Just not the kind implied by her question. "Kind of."

She took a deep, unsteady breath. Mr. D'Angelo stood stone cold.

"I wanted to make sure you were okay, I guess."

That made Mrs. D'Angelo start sobbing.

"Thank you," Mr. D'Angelo said. "It has been really hard." He came around the side of the couch and sat next to his wife, wrapping his arms around her.

One would think the funeral home girl would be prepared for a situation like this, but as I watched their grief pouring out of them, flooding the room, I was suspended in it. There was a distance between me and the mourners who came through Richter. This was so much more personal, here in the D'Angelos' home.

Milo asked me to make sure they were okay, but of course they weren't okay. And Milo hadn't told me how to make them okay.

"It's been so hard," Mrs. D'Angelo repeated through a sob.

I realized I should seem sadder. I dipped my head and nodded. "Yeah." I managed to remember why I was here, what I was supposed to be saying. "He really loved you both."

Mrs. D'Angelo's sobs grew louder, the agony echoing around me. I knew I needed to get out. I'd done what I could. I'd told them he loved them. That was my job.

"Thank you for letting me meet you officially. I should probably be going," I said, starting to stand.

"No!" Mrs. D'Angelo reached out for me, and I instinctively planted myself back down on the couch before she could actually grab my wrist. "Sorry, just . . ." She sniffed and wiped her face. "We would love for you to stay and tell us more about Milo. Did he have any other friends?"

I shifted my shoulders, as if the discomfort was located somewhere in my muscles.

"So many people have sent notes and flowers and cards, it makes it seem like Milo was the most popular kid in school," Mrs. D'Angelo said. At the moment, he was probably the most popular person in Somerton. But not for a reason anyone would want to be.

I didn't know how to tell her that her son hadn't actually been.

"You said he loved us?" Mrs. D'Angelo asked.

"Jen, of course he did," Mr. D'Angelo said.

"All he ever expressed was resentment," she told her husband, throwing out her hands. He shook his head. "He worked almost thirty hours a week because of us, Frank. He worked himself nearly literally to death to help pay our bills, and you didn't see resentment?"

This conversation absolutely did not belong to me anymore. But I couldn't bring myself to leave now. I hadn't known Milo had a job, let alone that he worked so much. I wanted to know more.

"And then some evil, thoughtless, horrible human being hit him and left him to die! And we will never get to talk to him again. We will never get to know him any more." She sobbed. She was talking to her husband, but it felt like her anger was directed at me.

I had intruded enough. I had done what Milo asked. So why was it so hard to stand up?

"I'm so sorry. I really should go. Thank you." I stood up and headed toward the door, but Mrs. D'Angelo jumped up from the couch to follow me.

"Please," she said, stepping out onto the front porch with me. "Can't you stay a little longer?"

"I'm sorry. I have to go."

Her shoulders dropped in defeat, and she nodded. "Okay."

"We hope you'll come to the vigil tomorrow," Mr. D'Angelo said, still lingering in the musty house.

"Yeah, I'll be there," I said. "Um, take care." I turned and left. I walked across the street quickly, feeling their eyes on the back of my head. I couldn't believe I had made up such a lie.

Just after I turned the corner and was out of sight of the D'Angelo house, my phone buzzed.

Amy: Can we talk?

I stared at the text as I kept walking. I knew I was being a bad friend. I knew I hadn't been communicating well with them, that I was pulling back. And I knew they'd be mad. But every thought was permeated by Milo, and I wasn't ready to talk to Amy about that. I hated myself for it, but I pocketed my phone and turned toward home. I closed my eyes, felt the October breeze burn my cheeks, and prepared to go tell Milo what had happened. But after only a few steps, I changed direction. When I needed to think, I always went to the same place.

The small graveyard where Wilmer was buried wasn't the only cemetery in Somerton. On the edge of town, about two miles away from Richter, was a much larger rowed cemetery. It was where Grandma and Grandpa's headstones were. When I was younger, I used to come all the time and walk the periphery. One time, I went through and tried to memorize every name. I memorized seventy-five of them. When I was having trouble falling asleep, I'd try to recite them all in order because reciting the names from my scrapbook was too easy.

Interspersed among the graves were trees that blocked the sunlight. Some plots had small plaques hidden in the grass, while others boasted large gravestones with elaborate carvings. There was one mausoleum with a stone angel watching from above. All the plots were lined in rows perfect for a walk.

I liked to follow a similar path every time, starting at the

95

southmost corner and making my way up through the rows, eyeing each individual headstone. Some days I would skip this route and walk straight to Grandma's plot: row thirty-seven, column nine. Other days I wouldn't let myself look at it.

This time, I started my route and began forming a script of what I was going to tell Milo. I had done what he asked. "Make sure they're okay" had to have meant reassuring them that he loved them—not to *make* them okay. Nobody could do that after a situation like this. But it still wasn't going to be easy for him to hear how fragile they were, and I wasn't sure how to break news like that.

Then, in thinking about how hard it is to tell people things, I thought about Amy. I was shutting out the one person who cared the most. But even when we'd met for coffee, I couldn't get out of my head enough to enjoy that time. I didn't know how to express what was going on, how to tell them why being with other people was so hard, or how to explain the deep fear and debilitating spirals and how Milo played into them. I didn't even fully understand it myself, so how could I make them understand? The thought of even trying was almost more overwhelming than the thoughts themselves.

I kicked a rock down a row of headstones weathering with age. I was in the older part of the cemetery now. At the end was the plot of Leanne Wilson, 1900–1950. I had trouble remembering most dates, but I could always picture Leanne's because it was a perfect fifty years—although I had no way of knowing if those years had actually been perfect. There was a large branch on her plot, right beneath one of the trees. I removed it and tossed it toward the fence line. Nature didn't care about Leanne or any of the other headstones it destroyed, not just in Somerton but everywhere.

We held funerals at Richter and built these beautiful graves and carved everlasting words to remember. But eventually, it would all be forgotten. I didn't know who Leanne Wilson was. I couldn't say who most of the people in this cemetery were. Because those left with the memories die too, and the grass grows over them and trees fall on top of them and time passes to erase them until there's no one to remember. We all inevitably forget.

CHAPTER 10

Milo was still in my room when I got home. He was sitting at my desk, his back to me. As I walked in, I noticed him leaning over a piece of paper from one of my notebooks, scribbling with one of my pencils.

I closed the door behind me, and the sound of the click made him look.

"What's up?" I asked, leaning over to see what he was drawing. I assumed he was drawing. The artist couldn't be stopped.

"Sketching," he confirmed, swiveling the chair to face me.

I remembered all his notebooks, probably covered in doodles and sketches in place of notes. If you glanced at him in class, it looked like he was writing diligently, but he was scribbling another one of his ideas to life.

"How were they?" he asked.

"I told them I was there to make sure they were okay . . . but they're not. They're hurting."

His shoulders slumped. "I need to see them myself."

"They won't see you, though."

"I know, but maybe they'll sense my presence somehow. Maybe that'll help."

I took a seat on my bed. Morty was sleeping on the pillows,

but he got up to come cuddle me. "They'll be here for the funeral on Saturday."

"That's in a week. What do I do for a week? There's no one here who would be fun to haunt."

Morty mewed as if offended.

"You could draw," I suggested.

He turned back toward the desk to look at his paper. "I guess."

"I'm sorry, Milo. I feel like I—"

He interrupted me, holding the paper out to me. "Do you like it?"

"Other side," I said, seeing only a blank page.

"What? No." He twisted the page toward him to check. "It's on that side."

I got up from my bed and stepped closer, thinking I couldn't make out the faint markings. But when my face was only a foot from the paper, I still saw nothing.

"What is it?" I asked him.

"It's a dragon," he said. "Well, it's actually a Vagabond. That's what I call them. They're like dragons but they travel between worlds. There are seven different dimensions in their world, and they're the only ones that can move among them, except for one dragon rider who can ride them through the dimensions. I have, like, a comic thing going." He shrugged like it was no big deal, but it sounded cool and really fleshed out. The only problem was there wasn't a scratch on the paper.

"You don't like it?"

"No, it's not that. I—I don't see anything. There's nothing on the page."

Milo knit his brow and turned toward the desk again. With the pencil, he scratched the lead violently across the page from corner to corner several times.

"Now?" He held it up to me with urgency. The paper was still clear, not even a dent from the pencil's pressure.

I shook my head. He slammed the paper down on the desk, probably remembering the proximity of his dead body.

I grabbed the pencil and drew a faint line. It instantly appeared before us.

Milo couldn't create anything new.

"I want to be an illustrator. Wanted." He grabbed the paper from me and slid it into my notebook.

"I'm so sorry," I said. It sounded like I was expressing sympathy about his predicament, but I was really apologizing for waking him up. I sat down on the floor, my back against my bedframe. "Tell me more about the Vagabonds. Why are they the only ones who travel? What makes the one guy able to and why can't anyone else move between worlds?"

"It was just a comic. I wanted to get it published, but it was dumb."

"Not dumb," I said. "Really cool."

"Nah." He used his feet to swivel the chair back and forth, his eyes down at his lap. "My dream was for people to finally see my drawings. Not look at them—plenty of people looked at them—but to finally *see* them."

"Who's the main character?" I asked.

He looked up at me. "You don't actually care. You don't have to try to make me feel better."

I wasn't really into comic books or graphic novels, and I didn't know much about art. I left that up to Amy, with their understanding of patterns and colors and what looked good and what didn't. But I actually cared about what Milo was telling me. It felt refreshing to hear someone talk about something they were that passionate about.

"No, for real, I'm curious," I told him.

Milo perked up, and he proceeded to tell me all about the world he'd created. He laughed, smiled, used his hands to emphasize. I was excited because he was excited. For that moment, we lived in his comic world with the Vagabonds. Earth was in the fifth dimension, he clarified, the most unstable dimension for the Vagabonds to enter. And while we lived in that dimension, he and I completely forgot he was dead. I forgot that a kid in my grade had been killed in an accident. I forgot that I lived in a funeral home, that my grandma was dead, that I would die. I remembered how I'd once felt with Eileen, Peter, and Amy. By the time Milo finished his summary, I really wanted to read the comic.

But when Milo asked me, "What do you like to do?" the moment faded. Everything swelled into the front of my head again.

"What do you mean?" By now he and I were both sitting on the floor together.

"What do you mean what do I mean? What kind of stuff do you like to do?"

I understood the literal meaning of the question, but it made me feel stuck. "I . . . I don't know." I looked around my room as if I could spot an answer.

"Come on," Milo said, shifting slightly closer to me. There was a crooked grin on his face. He clearly was still caught up in the moment I had just exited.

"All I do is work in the funeral home," I told him. "I don't do any extracurriculars. I have to help my family because they can't afford to pay anyone else. A funeral home isn't actually as booming a business as you might imagine. So I don't have time for sports or anything."

"Peter plays football, doesn't he?"

"Well, yeah. I guess I used to play piano."

"Used to?"

"I stopped when my grandma died."

"Why?"

I thought about it for a moment, remembering how warm it'd made me feel to run my hands along the keys and feel the music beat inside me. It sounded cliché, but it had transported me to another world. I remembered Grandma sitting on the bench next to me when I was first learning. She would adjust my hands to fix their positioning and remind me to keep my back straight. At the end of each lesson, we would play "Heart and Soul" together and would try and see how fast we could play it before our hands cramped. She would laugh because it was ridiculous. In those moments, I felt safe. But it was hard to look back at that and not suspect that her smile was a facade.

"It hurts now," I said. "My grandma played with me."

"Oh. So do you like it?" he asked.

"Piano?"

"Sorry, I meant working at your funeral home."

No one had ever asked me that before. "It's not mine. And . . . not really."

"Why not?"

I had imagined waking Milo up as my opportunity to ask him all my questions, but it was starting to feel like he was here to interview me. "I don't like being surrounded by a constant reminder of my mortality, I suppose."

"Fair enough," he said, deflating a bit. He was now with me in our new moment. "So, why do you wake up ghosts?"

"What?"

"I don't think my questions are that confusing, Georgia."
He was right, but they kept catching me off guard.

"I guess I like knowing their stories. I've always watched
the funerals, and you hear about what the person was like from
the officiant or their family. When I was a kid, I used to create
complex backstories for the dead people who came through.
I would construct their entire lives in my head and have these
conversations with them. But there's nothing like talking to
them for yourself, and after I found out I could, of course I
wanted to. It felt like, for a brief moment, I could reverse death.
And it's nice knowing if there's anything I can do for them.
I must have this weird power for a reason. Like the final request
thing. I know it's cheesy—"

"Your thing isn't cheesy," he said.

"But it's not my *thing*. I don't have a thing."

"People downplay the stuff they're passionate about because
they're embarrassed to be judged for it. Like I did with my comics. I don't really think it's dumb, I'm worried others will."

Instead of trying to form a response, I let my thoughts drift
back to Milo's house, to watching his parents, to wishing he'd
been there to tell me what to say so I could truly complete his
final request. That's when an idea hit me.

"Wait!" I almost shouted. "You can't write anything, right?
But I can."

"I guess," he said, unsure where this was going.

"I could write a letter for you. To give your parents."

His eyes filled with life. "That's brilliant. I'll dictate it, and
you transcribe it and then deliver it to them. Say you found it in
my desk or my locker or something." He seized another piece
of paper and a pen.

I couldn't believe I hadn't ever thought of it before, really.

I could've done this for every single ghost. Instead of trying to get slices of information or pieces of an incomplete puzzle, I could write down exactly what they wanted the world to hear. And especially after seeing the D'Angelos, I knew nothing would be as good as their son's own words. I whispered an apology into the air for the ghosts I hadn't done this for, then grabbed the paper and pen.

"It'll be in my handwriting," I said, suddenly hesitant.

"My parents don't know your handwriting."

"But they know yours. They'll know you didn't write it. And what if they trace the note back to me?" I didn't want to get in trouble for falsifying a letter from a dead boy.

"You can type it," he said. "It'll be my words, saying things only my parents and I could know, so they won't question it."

"Okay," I agreed. It wasn't false if it was his words, I reasoned. I took a seat at my desk and opened up a blank document on my laptop, resting my hands on the keyboard. "Ready when you are."

Milo cleared his throat. "Dear Mom and Dad," he started.

When I tried to type the words, nothing appeared on the screen. I hit some random keys to check that my keyboard was working, but they showed up instantly on the page. I tried typing Milo's words again, but they wouldn't form.

Through the eerie tingling in my spine, I knew what was happening, even if it didn't make sense. I'd written on sticky notes for the dead before. Wasn't this the same thing?

I knew it wasn't, though. This was too intimate. It wasn't just a piece of factual information like I'd relayed before. This was emotion straight from Milo's soul.

Milo could interact with the world, but nothing he said or did would stick. His words were ghosts too.

Milo peered over my shoulder, seeing only random letters I'd typed experimentally. I didn't need to explain. I tried one more time so that he could see me hitting each key: D E A R . . . leaving nothing behind.

"I really am dead, aren't I?" he said, taking a seat on the floor. I joined him.

"Is there . . . anything else we could try?" I asked.

He squinted at me. "You take this really seriously, don't you?"

"I guess. I mean, trying to help is important to me. I can wake ghosts for a reason, right?"

"See? Your thing." He looked pleased with himself. "You said you work a lot at Richter?"

I nodded. Clearly he didn't want to just sit and contemplate his deadness. But it felt strange to shift the subject, even slightly.

"I had a job. I worked like thirty hours a week during school and forty-five during the summer," he said.

I wanted to go back a step, to talk about how awful it was that he now existed in emptiness, but since Milo was volunteering information about himself without any prompting, I started focusing on that.

"Where?" I asked him, pushing away the other thoughts.

"Lucky's. I didn't do any extracurriculars either. Hell, I barely did my homework. I went straight from school to Lucky's, and I was so exhausted afterward that I would go home and draw until I fell asleep. And repeat. What a life."

I'd never seen Milo at Lucky's. "Did you like it?"

"Yeah. I loved my manager. He and I were really close. It was a great job, but it was a lot of work. A lot of time."

"Did you . . . like your life?"

That seemed to catch him off guard, and it caught me off guard too.

He thought for a moment. "It was hard. My mom's on disability, and my dad had to drop out of college not long after she got pregnant with me. He had to get a job to support us, and then he lost his scholarship when his grades tanked. From the time I was old enough to work I helped make money to pay rent. It was a lot. It always has been."

When I pictured living a life like Milo's, I felt lucky for the first time to be at Richter. I had time to do homework. I had time to hang out with Amy. I got to eat family dinners. I was able to keep the money I made from helping with funerals. But it still didn't make me want to stay here. I still felt the urgency to leave, to be as far from Richter and Somerton as possible.

"I wish that wasn't all my life had been," Milo said.

I felt that tightness. "I'm so sorry."

"I really don't want your pity. That's not why I told you."

"No, sorry, I didn't mean it like that." I pulled my legs toward my chest.

"I know." Milo sighed. "I've had to deal with too many people feeling bad for my family. And now it's going to be worse, since I'm dead and all."

I kept my lips pressed closed because I didn't want to say the wrong thing again.

"Somerton swallowed me whole, Georgia," he said. "You're lucky, though. You still have a chance."

I closed my eyes and took a deep breath, trying to ignore the feeling that the walls of Richter were pressing in on me, that the fibers from the carpet were slowly growing longer to wrap around my ankles and wrists, that I would someday be one of the bodies prostrate on the metal embalming table.

When I managed to send the thoughts away, I opened my eyes to see Milo's head in his arms and his shoulders shaking.

I couldn't hug him or even put my hand on his shoulder. Even if I could, I was probably the least qualified person to comfort him. All I could offer him right now was privacy. I stood up and headed to my door, making sure to quietly close it behind me.

CHAPTER 11

The last invitation I'd received was for Eileen's birthday party in seventh grade, right before Grandma died. Amy and I spent hours planning the party with her. She held it at Richter because Eileen always loved the funeral home for some reason, and the night of the party felt infinite, like birthdays were what we lived for. It was one of the only days Richter ever felt full of life. I couldn't wait to invite people to my and Peter's birthday next, and to be invited again, to continue to think of birthdays as little forevers instead of checkpoints marking down our days.

The next invitation I ever received was to Milo's vigil. Everyone was posting about it, sharing the invitation online. I'd gotten a notification at least four separate times from different versions of the event. The school board had organized it, hopefully with the consent of the D'Angelos. A couple of local parents were asking people to donate candles beforehand and to bring flowers and cards for Milo's family.

Amy had accepted their invitation right away. Eileen had just accepted hers, which I got a notification about for some reason. I was sitting at my desk, hovering my mouse over the Accept button, wishing I hadn't been invited in the first place.

"Should I go?" I asked Milo.

"To?" he prompted, and I remembered he wasn't inside my head. He was lying down on my bed, but when he asked, he sat up on the edge. He was still sporting Peter's gray sweatshirt and jeans.

"Your vigil," I said, pushing my laptop so he could see the screen. He leaned forward and rolled his eyes before lolling his head back onto the pillow.

"I won't go if you don't want me to," I said.

"I don't want anyone to go." He kept his finger pointed at the laptop for a few of my breaths and maybe a few of his.

"Okay. I won't go." I closed my laptop.

He didn't directly respond to me, but he got up off the bed. "Who is going?" He knelt down beside my chair and leaned his elbows on the desk. I opened the laptop again and scrolled through the list of guests.

"Sherri Greenwich? Brad Anderson? Eileen Smith?" Every name a question. "I never spoke to these kids. All right, you have to go. You have to tell me what happens, since I can't leave and all."

"Do you want me to record it or something?" I was joking, but Milo's expression told me he was considering my offer. "Do you want me to say anything to your parents? I imagine they'll be there."

Milo's face went blank. He shook his head.

"Okay, I won't."

Amy texted.

Amy: Meet you at the church yeah?

Me: See you at like 5:45?

Amy: *thumbs up emoji*

And yes, they actually typed out the emoji in asterisks instead of sending the emoji.

"Actually," Milo said, "if you do see them, make sure they know I love them. And that I'm sorry."

I desperately wanted to know what that meant, but I wasn't going to prod him any further.

◊

When it was time to leave, I gathered my things and told Milo, "I'll see you after."

"Morty will keep me company." He seemed in good spirits. At least outwardly.

I closed the door behind me and found Mom, Dad, and Peter waiting in the kitchen. None of them were wearing black, but Mom and Dad still looked professional. Dad tried to look presentable and businesslike anytime he was in public because inevitably a ton of people would recognize him and he'd end up talking business.

I suddenly realized I had never been to a vigil before. All my traditional get-togethers over the deceased were limited to funerals. I hadn't even been to a non-Richter funeral. I didn't know what I should be wearing or what to expect.

My heart palpitated when I saw what Peter was wearing. The gray sweatshirt that he hadn't worn in years. The one I had stolen from his closet. The one Milo had been wearing five seconds ago when I left him in my room.

"Do you have multiple of those sweatshirts?" I asked Peter. He knit his brow. "No?"

"Oh," I said, chewing at my lip. It must be like the bowl.

"Ready?" Dad asked us.

The Richter family walked down the steps together. I was the only one who skipped the creaky one.

It was barely 5:30, but it was already getting dark. Dad locked the front door, trapping Milo and his body in Richter without me. I knew I could be away from Milo—we'd proved that when I went to his house. But nevertheless, I felt like some new rule would arise and Milo wouldn't be at Richter when I got back.

"The street parking by the church will probably be a nightmare," Mom said. "Let's just walk."

Mom and Dad walked side by side, leaving Peter and me next to each other behind them. They were discussing some recent communication with the manufacturer that supplied Richter's memorial products, their fingers interlocked. I often wondered about their relationship. They talked more like business partners than a couple but would occasionally offer the other a moment of softness with a kiss or a handhold.

"So, are you or aren't you going to Warren's party Wednesday?" Peter asked quietly, pulling my attention to him.

I had pushed the famous Fall Break Extravaganza out of my head because, well, I didn't care about it. Everyone in the school was going to drive five miles out of town to the giant country McMansion to party like there was no tomorrow while believing they'd live forever. The kids in this godforsaken town needed something exciting to hold on to.

"No," I told Peter.

"I'm going with Eileen. I'll be the designated driver." He smiled weakly and shrugged. Peter had gotten his license as soon as he could this past summer. I, on the other hand, didn't like the idea of controlling a murder machine. Especially now, after Milo. I felt on edge even walking down the sidewalk and was glad that Mom and Dad were in front of us, a double layer of heads to look both ways.

"Very chivalrous of you," I said to Peter. "Hope you have fun."

"Thanks. I hope you have fun staying at home." It sounded condescending, but Peter seemed to mean it.

The vibe between us had definitely changed over the past few weeks. He'd started paying more attention to me, started trying to make conversation, started watching me like he was waiting for something. What was up?

"What are you planning on doing there, if you don't drink?" I asked. "Isn't that what parties are all about?"

"No, there are a lot of kids who go who don't drink or smoke or anything. Mostly it's amusing to watch the slow decline of the species as they become more intoxicated and more chaotic in their decisions. That's mainly why Eileen likes to go. Same reason she loves reality TV, as you know."

"Bleak. But makes sense." He kept bringing her up.

"You should really come with us." He sounded uncharacteristically eager. I didn't often hear him use this tone anymore. At least with me. "We won't stay forever or anything. But don't you want to be witness to the stories that will go down in infamy for the rest of our high school career?"

I shook my head. "I have zero interest in those stories." And I didn't have to tell him I didn't want to hang out with him or Eileen. He should know that.

"Oh, come on. This party is a Somerton tradition. Warren's older brother threw it, and his brother before him, and his brother before him."

"Warren only has one older brother."

Peter and I shared a little laugh, a moment of harmony that reminded me what it felt like to be his twin. To be his friend. But Peter was the popular one. The football player who everyone liked or had a crush on or wanted to be. Who everyone said hi to in the morning, who would no doubt be prom king and valedictorian. Who didn't drink but got respect for his decision instead of being hassled about it. The one with an intense enthusiasm for Richter. The one who could get out but didn't want to.

"Well, if you change your mind . . ."

"Not happening."

Then we were at the church. The street parking was full, as Mom had predicted. People were filing though the large wooden front doors. I could hear an organ playing inside, and I could smell the incense even before we stepped under the vast ceiling. The building had looked pretty small from the outside, but craning my neck, I could have sworn this church was nearly seven stories tall.

With fifteen minutes still before the vigil was set to start, the pews were almost full. The noise of people talking echoed chaotically through the beams of the arched ceiling. I guessed the entire town was squeezed into this church, filling every inch with their bodies.

I saw teachers, classmates, business owners, people who had come to funerals at Richter, and plenty of faces I didn't recognize. This was the only time this exact group of people would exist together in the same room. Whether they had known Milo personally or were here out of obligatory sadness for the tragic death of a teenager, their presence here felt exquisite and wrong. Sure, Milo was a member of the community and should be remembered as such, but how many of these people could actually say more than three general statements about him?

Did I even deserve to be here?

A volunteer handed us large wax candles and told us we would light them toward the end. I held mine tightly, feeling the wax stick to my skin even before it melted.

People continued to shuffle in, sending us down the aisle. We spotted Eileen's family, Eileen's coat strewn across the empty section of the pew where they were sitting. When she saw us, Eileen stood up and stepped into the aisle, waving us down.

Eileen's family had practically become strangers to me. I'd still occasionally see them around town, but the interactions were never more than awkward smiles. Eileen had an older brother, Amani, who was a senior and used to hang out with us when we played at Eileen's. Mrs. Smith ran the local bank while Eileen's dad stayed at home to take care of her younger sister, Tia. She was six now, and I hoped she wasn't like me at six— entirely too aware of mortality. Even if she wasn't, I guessed being at this vigil would change that.

As we all squeezed into the pew, I realized the Smiths' lives and jobs could've changed dramatically in the past few years, and I never would've known.

Dad and Peter sat down first, then Eileen slipped back in ahead of Mom and me so that she'd be sitting next to Peter. I was closest to the aisle, making sure to leave space beside me for Amy when they showed up. Eileen gave Mom a hug, and I was suddenly annoyed that she was on Mom's other side.

"Hey, Georgia." Eileen leaned over to offer me a little wave.

I twitched my hand into an awkward wave back.

I couldn't help but notice she had changed her hair since I'd seen her in algebra on Friday, and it made me remember how she would always ask for my advice before she tried anything new.

"Andrea," Eileen said, turning her attention to Mom, "Peter was telling me that I might be able to help out around Richter a bit?"

Mom's eyes lit up. "Oh, for sure. We'd love that. We could always use some extra hands."

Eileen had always been interested in Richter. It was one of the main reasons we got so close when we were little. Her parents, unlike most of our peers' families, actually let her go play in the creepy funeral home. She wanted to play in Richter. She'd ask Dad questions about being a mortician like it was the coolest job ever. And apparently now I'd have to deal with her coming over more. At least she'd had the sense to keep her distance the past few years.

Funny how the thing that brought us together ended up pulling us apart.

I caught myself staring, thinking too much about how it used to be, so I looked for more people I knew. I spotted plenty of classmates, but I was really searching for Mr. and Mrs. D'Angelo. I eventually spotted them up toward the front. They weren't talking to anyone, just sitting in wait. Maybe they too were here out of obligation and wanted to go home.

Amy showed up a little late, their handsome suit marking them as the best-dressed person here. They squeezed into the pew beside me. "Feels like it's been years. Missed you," they said, leaning their head against my shoulder.

"Missed you," I told them, guilt stirring as I rested my cheek on their head.

"You okay with being here?" they whispered.

"Yeah," I said, and it wasn't a lie. I felt okay being here, and it felt good to feel their hand in mine.

"Everyone, thank you for coming." Principal Wendell had

made his way to the front of the church. "Throughout the service, there will be a collection plate going around. This is not for the church but for the D'Angelo family in this hard time. If you have any money to give, it would be greatly helpful to them in paying for the medical bills. Meanwhile, we'd like to begin with a prayer."

The prayer came and went, the same kind you'd hear at any old Richter service. The entire time my head was down and my eyes were closed, I wondered what Milo was doing at Richter.

I had tried to pray before. Usually during funerals. While the rest of my family kept their chins up, I'd dip mine down and close my eyes. I pictured a man sitting on a cloud, because that's what I thought God was and that's where I thought he lived. I didn't know what I was supposed to do, because I had never been taught. I started by asking God for things that I wanted, and it slowly turned into me asking him questions about the world, until it turned into me telling him that I was scared. I thought I was getting better at praying every time, but each prayer came to no avail. The man on the clouds couldn't listen to everyone at once, and I knew he wasn't listening to me because nothing got better after Grandma died.

The whole time, I'd been pretending. I hadn't actually thought I was talking to anyone. I'd been going through the motions, hoping that I could convince myself it was real. After a while, I stopped trying to force what didn't feel right.

After the prayer, Wendell returned to the podium. "Milo D'Angelo was an incredible boy, a boy whom we were all blessed to know and have in our hearts. He was such a bright young man and an incredible student. He attended Somerton High and lived in this community for five years, since he first moved here in fifth grade."

He'd been the new kid no one paid much attention to, and that never really changed.

"From the moment he started school, he worked incredibly hard. His teachers can attest to that."

But that's not true, I thought. Milo had told me he barely tried at school. He never got good grades because he was working at Lucky's. Why would Wendell lie like that? What was the point?

"Milo fought hard while he was in the hospital, until he took his last breath. Let's remember Milo and honor his memory—as an exemplary student, one of the kindest people we have been blessed to know. A true hero here in Somerton. And may we keep the D'Angelo family in our hearts during this terrible time." He made eye contact with the D'Angelos. "The town is here for you in everything you need. Next, we'd like to play a song in remembrance of Milo, and then some teachers and students will say a few words."

As the organ started playing a song that I recognized but couldn't name, I processed what Wendell said. Exemplary student. Hero. Those words crawled like spindly spiders along my arm and up my neck. Did Wendell really believe those things, or did he just feel obligated to say them? Did he even know anything about Milo, or was he reading off his own version of a what-to-say-when-a-student-dies Mad Lib? He hadn't even mentioned Milo's art.

Maybe a vigil was just another funeral. It wasn't about the dead. It was another way for the living to feel better about themselves.

When Mrs. Berry stepped up, I felt less put off by her grief. Milo was her student, and English teachers probably knew their students better than any other teacher because they get to peek inside their mind through writing. Unless Milo never turned anything in. Or maybe her class was the only one he'd tried in. I didn't know.

When Berry finished and Warren Erikson took the podium, I was prepared to tune him out. He was student body president and varsity quarterback, and he always gave speeches at student gatherings, where I had learned to ignore him. Even Peter, the person who liked everyone, wasn't a fan.

"Man," Warren began, looking up to the ceiling. "You took our friend too soon." It was impossible not to roll my eyes. Amy produced an audible scoff. Out of the corner of my eye, I saw Peter make a gentle gagging face at Eileen, who pressed her lips together.

I knew all the speakers were trying to be nice. They were trying to honor Milo's memory—that's what you were supposed to do. But it all felt so wrong. How can you honor someone's memory with lies? I thought about Milo's parents. Having to listen to people pretend to know your son better than you did must be a special kind of pain.

Behind me, I heard someone start laughing loudly. My head shot around, but no one in the pews had an expression to match that haunting sound. The sound stopped, and I settled back against the bench.

"You okay?" Amy whispered.

"I just thought I heard someone laughing," I said.

"Jesus. I didn't hear it."

A few more lines into Warren's bogus speech, I heard a bloodcurdling scream echo through the church. It sounded like someone in pain, like they had been stabbed in the stomach.

I practically leapt from my seat, looking for the source.

No one else reacted like I did. Warren didn't stop talking.

Heads faced forward. I swiveled around, gripping the back of the bench, ignoring the confused looks of the people sitting behind me.

Although I thought I would find him hovering at the back of the church, I eventually saw Milo near the dais, standing over his parents. He was clutching his hair in his hands. His chest heaved with a sob.

I instantly stood. Milo spotted me.

This time, Warren did pause. People reacted with looks and whispers, directed at me instead of Milo, because no one knew a ghost was attending his own vigil. Amy grabbed my hand. Mom and Dad were telling me to sit down. Eileen said something that I didn't register. Warren awkwardly kept talking while people were trying to decide who to pay attention to.

Milo ran down the aisle, past me, and pushed the main doors open. He left.

I was struck with the panic of Milo being so far from Richter. By Milo roaming free. I didn't know where he was going, and I couldn't let him risk this.

I stepped over Amy, their hand trying to catch mine, and ran for the doors, leaving everyone to wonder what the frantic daughter of the undertaker was doing. I had no time to think about what was left behind. I had to chase down what was in front of me.

Out in darkness, I shouted for him. I searched for a familiar shadow but saw nothing in the dull gleam of the street lamps. I didn't care if anyone heard me calling for a dead boy.

I ran.

I didn't have my key to the front door, so when I got back to Richter, I dashed around back, typed in the code to the garage, and rushed past the hearses to get inside.

"MILO!" I shouted. I ran up to my room, checked Peter's room, the bathroom. I even ran down to the embalming room. The house returned my pleas with silence.

I sat down on the couch in the front room, out of breath, my head in my hands. The spirals started twisting inward. Milo could be anywhere, he could be gone. I didn't know the rules. If he was too far from himself for too long, or too far from me, maybe he wouldn't be able to return. His soul might be lost or fade into oblivion, and I would've cursed him to the exact fate that I had cursed Grandma with.

I cried, feeling the darkness of Richter pressing in on me, the walls collapsing, holding me down to this floor, crushing my chest and never letting me get out.

Until I realized where he was.

CHAPTER 12

I ran to the garage, grabbed my bike, and rode. When I saw the porch light to the D'Angelo house, I skidded to a halt and jumped off my bike, dropping it onto the grass.

Milo was sitting on the front lawn, staring at the house. He had his legs crossed and his arms rested on his knees like he was meditating.

"The door was locked," he said, not turning to me. "Can't get in. Can't open the window. Just waiting for them to get home." I could hear the layer of his voice that told me he was still crying.

The porch light illuminated him against the browning grass, but he looked more like a ghost than ever in the fog. If I blinked too many times, I could have blinked him away.

"I'm fine," he started before I could ask. "As fine as I can be. I'm still here, aren't I? I can be away from my body or whatever, Georgia. I risked it and I figured out that I can. We're learning the rules together." He still wouldn't turn to look at me.

"Come back," I told him.

"You can go back." It was almost a command. "I needed to see them. I needed to see my home."

"I'm sorry," I said, unmoving.

"Fuck this!" he shouted up toward the sky. "FUCK!" It rang in the air like his scream had in the church. "I can't get into my house. I can't see my parents. They can't see me. I can't talk to them. I had to stand there and stare right at the pain on their faces and they had no idea I was so close. This is so fucking unfair! I didn't deserve this!" He slammed his fist against the ground, but the grass muted any satisfying thud it could have made.

I moved toward him. "Milo, please."

"Just go away!" He turned to look at me, and his face was terrifying. All of his anger radiated out at me. I began to cry too.

"You did this," he said. "And you have the ability to end it."

"Then I will!" I cried. "I'll end this for you."

"But that's just it!" He jumped up from the grass, and I instinctively took a step back from him, even though I knew he wouldn't hurt me. Couldn't, even if he tried. "I don't want you to send me away. I want this to be over, and I also can't fathom the idea of disappearing forever. I need both and can't have either."

"I'm sorry" was all I could say. I was trying to stay quiet. I didn't want neighbors peeking out windows to stare at what looked like a girl having a breakdown in the dead kid's yard.

Milo crumpled to the ground and went back to crying. I took a seat on the grass with him, staring up at the house. The structure was perfectly stable, but I knew the house was falling apart.

"I don't want to be remembered like that," he said.

"I know." I started picking at the grass, pulling as much from the ground as possible before tossing a blade away and trying again.

"None of that was for me. That was all for their own benefit. Their own comfort. God, my parents."

The vigil was going to be over soon, which meant Milo's parents would be heading home. I checked my phone to see the time and saw texts from my parents, Amy, and Peter. They were all worried, wondering what had happened. Amy said they didn't want to leave and be rude but that they were really concerned and I needed to call them immediately. So instead, I pocketed my phone.

"Georgia?"

I thought it was Milo at first before registering that it was a woman's voice. Both Milo and I shot up from the ground and turned to find Mr. and Mrs. D'Angelo standing on the sidewalk.

"I'm so sorry," I said again, scanning the yard for where I had dropped my bike. "This is so inappropriate, I'll leave—"

"It's good to see you." Milo's mom held out a hand.

"Dad?" Milo stood right in front of his father. Mr. D'Angelo stared straight through his son toward me.

"I thought I had scared you off," Mrs. D'Angelo said. "Thank you for coming again."

I was stunned she didn't find my presence creepy at all.

"Why are you here?" Mr. D'Angelo asked the rational question. "We saw you run out."

I gulped. "I got really upset, I had to leave. I was being irrational, and I came here and . . . I wanted to think about him being alive again. This seemed like an easy place to imagine that." The words slipped out effortlessly, though I felt their wrongness as soon as I'd said them.

Milo tilted his head at me like he was trying to figure out if I was lying.

"That's kind of funny because for us, this is the one place

where it's the hardest to do that." Mrs. D'Angelo looked at her feet, as if she could hide the tears streaming down her face. I wondered if she thought it would be better to hide her pain from now on. "Would you like to stay?"

I looked to Milo for an answer, and he nodded, his eyes fixed on his parents.

"I would," I said, wanting to perfectly emulate Milo's nod in my words.

As they walked toward the house, toward him, he invited them to him with his arms held out.

And as they walked, they moved right through him.

Milo turned to follow his parents, broken from their momentary connection. He reached out for them as they stepped farther away from his fingertips.

I trailed Mr. and Mrs. D'Angelo and let the door linger open long enough for Milo to enter with us.

It was darker inside than it was under the sky. The place still smelled of cigarette smoke. Mr. D'Angelo flicked on a light, and Milo gazed around his home. He stepped around the flowers and stood in the center of the living room, his eyes on his parents, who had their eyes on me.

"We didn't realize Milo had so many friends," Mrs. D'Angelo said with a sad smile.

"I didn't," Milo said as I said, "I didn't either."

Milo shook his head and took a seat on the couch.

"Do you know much about his friendship with Warren? The student body president, yes?"

I folded my arms across my chest like that would barricade me from their questions. "Not really," I said.

Milo was sitting, watching. I looked at him for advice, but he didn't offer anything.

"Would you like something to drink?" Mrs. D'Angelo asked.

"No, that's okay, I really should be going." I'd wanted to come in, and then when I was inside, I knew I needed to leave. It was the same feeling as the last time I had been here.

I raised my brows at Milo enough so that he would notice but his parents wouldn't. Milo stood from the couch. But instead of joining me, ready to leave, he turned and disappeared down the hallway.

"You don't have to go." Mrs. D'Angelo's face was pained again. Mr. D'Angelo stepped toward his wife and put his hand on her shoulder.

"I . . ." I tried to see Milo down the hall, but he was just out of my view. "Do you mind if I use the bathroom?"

"Not at all. Second door on the right." Mrs. D'Angelo pointed toward the same hallway Milo had gone down. I said a quick thanks and tried not to rush to follow their dead son.

I turned on the bathroom light and closed the door to make it look like I was in there, but then I went to the door with the sign that read *MILO'S ROOM, KEEP OUT.*

Milo was standing in the middle of his old bedroom. It was about the same size as mine, and the walls were painted navy blue. Clothes were strewn across the floor, covering the carpet. Graphic novels and comics were stacked on shelves, on his desk, on the dresser. Papers—Milo's drawings—were taped all over the wall across from his bed. I stepped closer, my eyes locked on one comic-style sketch of a dragon-like creature.

"Is this a Vagabond?" It had a long swooping tail that wrapped its entire rainbow-scaled body, and its talons gripped the rooftop it was sitting on.

"Yeah." Milo nodded. "It's eerie to be in here. It's exactly how I left it. It has all my stuff but it's so empty."

This space felt like a representation of who Milo was. All the things strewn across the room were his. He'd touched them when he was alive, breathed into them. Now everything looked like it was waiting for him to come back. And even when he was back, it all still waited to be used.

His sketches created an entire universe in this small room. He'd said he wanted everyone to see his drawings, but this world would never leave his wall. I scanned across them all. There were more Vagabonds of all colors, and I wondered if the different colors correlated with the different dimensions they were from. And there were knights and princesses in the same comic style, including a few images that looked like self-portraits, as if he'd been drawing himself into his world. Every sketch was signed *MiloD'Milo.*

"Georgia, I think—"

Milo was interrupted by his mother's entrance. He froze, but I immediately moved toward the door. She'd be horrified by me barging into her dead son's room.

"I'm so sorry . . ."

Mrs. D'Angelo shook her head. "I want you to stop apologizing. We're grieving. There's no place for being sorry for that." She took a deep breath. "Can you tell me more about him? Like, what did he enjoy doing? What did he think?"

Those were very good questions, questions that I also wanted answers to. I thought about offering up my honest answer: that I didn't know, and no one else did either because Milo didn't have any friends. But the look on her face made me say, "He was a really good person. He loved his art."

Milo stepped toward his mom. She had no idea that he stood so close, but it made me want to leave them alone.

"What did you two do together?" she asked.

I bit my lip. "We talked . . ."

"What about?" She moved closer to me while Milo inched closer to her.

"His art, mostly."

She turned to the wall, admiring all the drawings. "Did he ever talk about us?"

"He loved you guys more than anything."

"He told you that? When?"

"Um . . . recently." I turned to Milo, hoping he'd tell me what else to say. When he didn't react, I blurted out, "I really need to go," and rushed past her down the hallway. I hoped Milo would follow me, but I needed to leave no matter what. I wasn't supposed to be there, doing this to her.

"Please, Georgia. Please don't leave again so soon."

But I was stellar at making an exit. It was what I did.

Milo followed his mother out without reacting to what was happening between his mom and me.

I begged him to follow me without saying a word, so that I could leave and he would be with me. He shook his head. I felt the water forming at the corner of my eyes. I almost asked him out loud. Mr. D'Angelo appeared from the kitchen to see what was going on.

"I'm staying," Milo said.

"Mi—" I started to say to him, but I caught myself: "My parents are waiting." And yet I hesitated. It felt like there were two Georgias: one fighting to extricate herself from this situation and one who was desperate to mold it into something more meaningful.

"I'll come back," I told them. The only thing I could think to tell them. "I'll be back. Tomorrow." Because Milo would be here.

"Thank you," Mrs. D'Angelo breathed.

I eyed Milo as I walked toward the door. He stayed firmly planted. He wasn't going to leave his parents, and I wasn't sure what would happen if he stayed here.

Mrs. D'Angelo didn't feel when Milo tried to grab her hand. Mother and son standing next to each other, a lifetime apart.

Mr. D'Angelo followed me out to the porch door. "You got her to step in his room," he said. "She hasn't done that yet."

I couldn't respond.

"We will see you tomorrow, then."

I managed to nod before I stepped out into the gleam of the moon. I grabbed my bike from the grass and left Milo behind. As I rode, the chilly breeze dried the tears on my face, stinging my cheeks until it felt like a permanent burn. I welcomed the pain because feeling that was easier.

CHAPTER 13

The yard of Richter was once our playground. In decent weather, Eileen, Peter, Amy, and I used to hang out outside if Mom and Dad were busy, especially when clients were onsite and Mom thought we were being too loud up in the apartment. That is, until I started to realize that Richter was a killer of fun, and not only for funeral guests.

On one of the last days we all hung out together, I discovered a part of the house I'd never known existed.

Grandma had just died, so I was reluctant to be around the group. Mom forced me to try. She said it would take my mind off things, but I didn't want to take my mind off things. Dad had said the same thing when he taught me how to embalm a body, and not only did that *not* take my mind off Grandma but it brought Oscar into the mix.

To appease Mom, I joined the others on the lawn. Eileen suggested we play truth or dare. Everyone groaned. I definitely didn't want to do that.

The first time we'd played truth or dare, back in sixth grade, the truths started off pretty boring. *Do you have any secrets? Do you dislike anyone in our grade?* But when they started moving toward relationships and sex, I got less bored and more uncomfortable. Peter had started talking about all the girls he'd kissed (which I didn't think was even true), and Amy started googling pictures of celebrities they found attractive, and a lot of details were shared that I still don't enjoy thinking about. I suddenly felt really nervous and I couldn't sit still and any movement made my stomach queasy. For the first time, I registered that the one thing everyone was becoming obsessed with was the last thing I wanted to think about.

I told Amy about it later, and they said I might be ace. After some research and time and a lot of talking with Amy, I realized that felt exactly right. Amy agreed not to mention that stuff around me anymore. I didn't tell Peter or Eileen because I worried they'd make jokes, and I didn't tell Mom or Dad because I didn't want them to tell me I was too young to know what I was talking about.

So when Eileen brought up truth or dare again, Amy said, "It's boring and childish," while leaning back down in the grass to emphasize their disinterest. I was glad they'd shot it down so I didn't have to.

It had been a while since we could all agree on what to do. Playing outside was becoming less fun—*playing* at all seemed to be off the table. Someone would want to watch YouTube videos while someone else wanted to go see a movie or talk about dating, and I didn't like any of it. I missed being able to run around Richter and go on bike rides and film movie trailers. And yet the thought of doing any of that only sank me closer toward the grass.

"I think I'm going to go inside," I told them. I was bored and tired of trying.

"Wait, no," Eileen said quickly. "Okay, let's do something Georgia wants to do." She reminded me of Mom, plotting to keep me busy and make me happy.

"What do you want to do?" Peter asked me, going along with Eileen's scheme.

The idea of going to my bed and lying down became more appealing with every passing moment.

"We will do anything you want us to do," Amy added.

"We will," Eileen confirmed.

I sighed and tried to keep from rolling my eyes. "Fine. Let's play hide-and-seek." I wanted to hide where none of them would be able to find me. And if I got credit for hanging out in the process, that was a bonus.

"Okay, if truth or dare is too childish, then come on," Peter said. He had a point.

Eileen gave him a look. "I like hide-and-seek. I wish older kids would play it more because it's actually fun."

Peter sighed. "Whatever."

"I'll be It," said Amy, and they went inside to count.

I wasn't actually trying that hard, and I couldn't seem to move quickly because I was weighed down with the thoughts I'd been having since Grandma's death. I couldn't go inside without Mom seeing and berating me for ignoring my friends, so I ended up at the opening behind the bush in Richter's garden—the crawlspace underneath the porch. I'd never noticed it before, or if I had I'd forgotten. It seemed as good a spot to hide as any, so I crawled in.

The wood paneling instantly muffled the sounds around me, making me more aware of the rest of my senses. I was pressed against dirt on my left side and wood on my right. It was a tight fit, but once I was all the way under the porch I was able to roll over on my back. The smell of the dirt beneath me was musty and warm, and I was staring at the swirling pattern on the wood panels. I was breathing heavily, but when Amy stepped out of the house, I tried to release each exhale as slowly as possible.

I peered up through the slits in the planks, seeing Amy's shape against the whiteness of Richter's siding. I grew more and more aware of the sound of my breath in my head, of the different sizes of dirt clots pressing into my back, of my nose's closeness to the wood, and of how I barely had any mobility in my limbs.

I was underground. That's the thought that made me start to panic. Sweat formed at my palms and my forehead. I didn't want to move because then I'd be back with the others and I'd have to pretend I was okay—or that I wanted to be okay. I preferred to stay under the porch. When four feet came pounding up the steps and stomped on the wood above me, I held my breath because I didn't want to be heard. But the heat, the tightness, the dirt, the wood were becoming too much, and I could feel my breath faltering.

The wood seemed to bow beneath their footsteps. I was suffocating and burning alive from the heat. I was inhaling dirt and melting into the ground. The tears fell, hot as coal, and I heard them drip onto the dirt. My chest tightened. I was convinced that the tightness meant I was having a heart attack. I wasn't even sure if I was old enough to have one, but I really thought I was dying.

"Help!" I shouted, scrunching my eyes closed, hoping that when I opened them again this would all be over. I clawed at the wood above me, as if I could dig my nails right through to fresh air.

No one came. I couldn't open my eyes to see where anyone was.

I kept crying, and I think I started screaming, and I was

definitely writhing and pounding at the wood above me, but I couldn't break free.

Finally, I felt two hands grasp my legs, and I was slowly dragged out, my arm scraping the side of the bush. I lay there, squinting in the brightness, gulping in breaths that still didn't feel like enough.

Dad stood over me, his brow furrowed. All he said was, "Georgia Richter, what were you doing?"

"Playing hide-and-seek," Eileen said. Everyone was standing behind Dad, bearing witness to the scene. It was like Peter standing at the top of the stairs watching me crying on the floor of the embalming room. I was just some spectacle to be gawked at.

Dad led me into the house to clean up since there was dirt all over my hands, legs, and hair.

"No more hiding under there," Mom told me as she used a wet cloth to clean the scrape on my arm.

Later, Peter and Eileen knocked on the door to my room to see if I was okay. They asked if there was anything they could do, and they kept saying it was no big deal and stuff like that happened all the time, but I wasn't okay and they didn't get it and it felt patronizing and I wanted them to stop. I screamed at them to go away. Eventually, Amy came in without saying a word, and they crawled into bed with me. We cuddled silently because that was what I needed.

◊

When I got back from the D'Angelos', Mom and Dad were sitting at the kitchen table in our apartment. There wasn't anything in front of them—no food, no paperwork—which suggested they had been waiting for me to walk through the door.

"There you are," said Mom.

"What *was* that?" Dad's head rested against the tips of his fingers like he was nursing a headache. He didn't look up at me. Mom had her knuckles at her mouth, and her eyes were full of worry.

"I just got really upset. I needed to leave."

"You caused a scene, G," Mom said, disappointment outweighing the worry. "That was a vigil for a young boy. You should know appropriate behavior in situations like that."

Dad interrupted her. "You were disrespectful. You represent Richter Funeral Home as much as your mother and me. Behavior like this reflects poorly on us and could impact your future in this town."

"I know!" I snapped, the veins in my neck tightening. I hated when he spoke like that. "I'm sorry, but I needed to not be there. I'm going to my room."

"Wait," Dad said. I stopped, but before he could go on any further about what a disappointment I was, Mom spoke.

"You knew him, didn't you?" Her words were softer now.

"I'm going to my room," I repeated.

"Were you friends?"

I didn't answer.

"Georgia, we didn't realize." Mom stood up to come toward me, but I bolted, ran past Peter's open door—confirming he had been listening to the whole thing—and slammed mine behind me.

I'd hoped Milo would be waiting for me in my room. When he wasn't, I felt a little bit more numb. Morty hopped up on my lap. Mom didn't try to come in.

I thought maybe he would show up in the morning, but he didn't. All the terrible possibilities seemed to be winning.

I sat on the couch and scrolled through my phone for most of the morning, growing more dazed with every post until it hardly felt like feeling at all. Peter came out to the kitchen every so often to grab another snack, but I barely even registered him in my peripheral vision.

Milo was gone. I'd let him leave. Now the air around me was entirely empty, and the closest connection I had to him was the hunk of meat two floors below. He would end up like Grandma's ghost and I'd have another layer of guilt to live with forever.

I looked up Milo's profile again. I just wanted to see his picture. I checked to see if he had any other social media—a Twitter or an Instagram. A quick search of his name came up blank. I tried searching the Following and Followers lists of kids from school. No luck. I reread his obituary. I checked to see if the police had found the person who'd hit him. The investigation was ongoing with no further leads. Somerton didn't have many security cameras around town, so I wondered if they would ever be able to find them.

I looked up the statistic Milo mentioned, and he was right. The percentage of unsolved hit-and-runs was terrifyingly high. As if death didn't already have enough unknowns.

Then I thought of Milo's room. All the drawings that he so desperately wanted to share with the world. And I remembered the way he'd signed each drawing.

I pulled up Instagram and typed *MiloD'Milo* into the

search bar. An account appeared. The avatar was an anime character that I didn't recognize. When I clicked on it, it led me to a page with around two hundred followers. The bio said, *I draw stuff.* Every post was a drawing, each signed *MiloD'Milo* in the corner. They were the same drawings he had plastered to his wall at home. The few captions were straightforward, just descriptions of the drawings. His words weren't giving me much information at all. Everything needed to be extrapolated from the art.

He had tons of pictures of his Vagabonds in the style I'd seen in his room but also drawings of nature and of faces I didn't recognize. I knew very little about art, but even I could tell his use of shapes and lighting and color was special. As I scrolled down and back up through his feed, I could see how much he'd developed those skills over time. The lines became clearer, the style slowly coalesced into something consistent and recognizable as his.

There was one drawing in particular that enticed me to click on it. It was a realistic sketch of a middle-aged white man with a scruffy beard. I thought it might be his dad, but the features didn't quite match up. There was no description.

I clicked my phone off and closed my eyes. Mr. and Mrs. D'Angelo had said I could come back. I could go get him. I would bring him back, and I would end it.

As I was about to get up, the door swung open and Amy walked in.

"Hey," I said, sitting up on the couch.

Amy crossed their arms over their chest. "Did you throw your phone in a lake somewhere? Did you physically rip it in half and stomp on it until it shattered into thousands of pieces? Did you incinerate it with a corpse? Because I swear to God,

I can't keep doing this." They threw out their hands to emphasize their anger.

I took a deep breath. "Amy, I don't—"

"Of course you don't. Because it's always about you!" They were practically shouting, and I wanted them to lower their voice because I knew Peter was still in the apartment. "What the hell was that last night? You scared me and then never responded to my texts or calls. You straight *freaked out* and I was worried. And I see your phone is totally fine. Your phone is always totally fine because every time I see you, you're on your phone."

"I'm sorry. I forgot to text back."

"Yeah. You keep forgetting to text back. I get you need space sometimes. I know that when you start to get anxious and depressed, you like to be alone. But this," they drew several vigorous circles in the air, their finger aimed at me, "is not okay by me."

I knew it was all true, all fair. Amy was my best friend and they were the last person on my mind right now. But I didn't know how to tell them what was going on, and I definitely didn't want to with Peter so close. "You're right. I'm sorry. My brain has been a mess," was all I could say.

Amy took a deep breath and nodded. "I know. I'm sorry for getting heated, but I will not stand for you shoving me out too. You've done that to enough people."

They might as well have punched me.

"I miss when you used to send me funny posts, or voice notes that were excruciatingly long. I miss when you asked how my day was or reached out even at all. This needs to go both ways," they said.

What I didn't say was that they should be glad I wasn't

burdening them with everything going on. In a way I was doing them a favor by shutting them out instead of forcing them to deal with the trouble of being my friend. If I dumped all my issues on them, I would only make them feel worse.

Instead, I said again, "I'm sorry." Because saying all that would be a burden in and of itself.

Amy gave another huff, but their posture relaxed. "Well, you can make it up to me," they said.

"Okay," I sighed.

"That sounds enthusiastic."

"I will do whatever. I'll make it up to you."

A mischievous smile spread across their face. I couldn't take it back.

"Warren's party. Tomorrow night."

CHAPTER 14

My agreeing to go to the party also included my consent for Amy to choose what I wore. They knew more about fashion than I did, which was obvious if you looked at the two of us standing next to each other. It was even more obvious when you stepped into their giant walk-in closet.

I went over to their place because my closet only had black funeral dresses and T-shirts for the non-funeral days. I also wanted to get out of Richter since I'd spent all of yesterday and most of today worrying about Milo, and Amy's house was always a safe space. It was much bigger than our apartment, and it was emptier. In a good way. Fewer bodies, dead and alive. Amy's parents were divorced, and their dad lived abroad, so it was just Amy and their mom here.

"I'm going to embrace your whole emo vibe but make it fashionable," they said, flipping through the items in their closet like we were out shopping. Amy would pull out an item and examine it with a pursed lip before shaking their head and returning it to its place. Finally, Amy pulled out one of their pairs of torn black high-waisted jeans. "This is so you."

I took the pants from them and closely examined the size of the rips. "I can fit my whole arm through this one," I said and did it to prove my point.

"The bigger the better. Plus, with those, you can still stick to a T-shirt—just do a French tuck and it'll look purposeful," they said.

"You've never worn these. You never would wear these. Why do you even have them?"

"You have to be prepared for anything. I've saved these jeans for this exact moment."

"For the moment I agree to come to Warren's party after an argument, so I have to wear whatever you tell me to?"

"That was literally the exact scenario. I've actually been planning this for weeks."

I laughed. "Fine." I had given up all control, but it was a relief to be at Amy's house having fun with them, to give my mind a reason to stop thinking about Milo or Richter for once.

"I don't even know what you're supposed to do at these parties," I admitted, jumping into Amy's jeans. I literally had to do several hops to get them on me. Amy's hips were about as wide as mine, but my butt made the last few tugs a struggle. The jeans rode up on me and instantly made me feel self-conscious. The skin on my left leg was entirely visible through the giant hole.

"Get into drunken fights," Amy said.

"Definitely not."

"Fine. No fights. We'll just smoke some weed instead." Amy shrugged.

"Amy!"

"I'm kidding! I know you don't smoke. We can just go and hang out. Watch how ridiculous people get the drunker they get. Last year it was a blast." That was exactly what Peter had said.

"I don't even know what pot smells like," I told them.

Amy laughed. "Oh, you'll know after tonight." Amy had been to a few more parties than me in their lifetime. Which meant Amy had been to three and I had been to none. Amy was sociable enough that they could easily fit in with any group, so they had other friends from school who would fulfill their wilder side when needed. Even though I couldn't do that, they always returned to me. Sometimes I wondered why they bothered.

I stepped in front of the mirror to examine myself. I decided to scrunch up my hair into a messy bun to match the grunge look Amy was going for.

Amy was wearing a flowery dress over a pair of jeans, but their look was punctuated with a hair clip resting right above their undercut. They came up to the mirror and stood next to me, grabbing my hand.

We looked like polar opposites, but our clasped hands connected us through one line of energy.

"Who gets to wear the Docs?" Amy asked, looking at me in the mirror.

"I'll wear my own shoes," I told them. They gave my hand a squeeze, and I leaned down to put on my sneakers.

Amy's mom drove us to the party. She told us to be safe and to call her when we were ready to be picked up. I always appreciated Mrs. Chen's trust in her child. When Amy came out as nonbinary, Mrs. Chen was kind of confused, and she struggled a bit with understanding why Amy wasn't a girl but still liked to look traditionally feminine. Amy told her that understanding someone's gender is a lot easier when you stop trying so hard to understand it. Sometimes Mrs. Chen still slipped up on pronouns, but she corrected herself before Amy had to.

I often dreamed of having a mom more like Mrs. Chen.

She had a normal job, never talked incessantly about whether her child would ever date, and certainly didn't expect Amy to take over any family legacy. Mrs. Chen didn't force Amy to be anything they didn't want to be.

"Have fun," Mrs. Chen said as we got out of the car. Amy kissed her on the cheek and waved as she drove away.

"I love your mom," I said.

"Me too," they said. "Okay, let's do this."

There was already music blaring from Warren's McMansion. It was up on a small hill, reminding me a bit of the way Richter loomed over Main Street. Except Warren's family came from old money and his father was a lawyer in the town over. Much more prestigious than an undertaker.

The driveway had a gate, but it had been propped open so anyone could enter. As we walked up the gravel driveway toward the house, I became aware of the sheer number of kids standing around. I'd always thought parties were exaggerated and faked in movies, but this was exactly like what you'd see in a classic '90s teen comedy. There weren't this many people in Somerton.

The closer we got to the door, the more I realized how little I wanted to be there. The noise was already starting to overwhelm me, and I was seeing too many faces of people I recognized from school. All those faces reminded me of the one that was missing.

Walking inside the house was like walking inside a museum. There were actual Greco-Roman columns holding the ceiling up. I could hardly believe someone could be rich enough to own a house like this. The floors were marble tile that reflected the light from the many, too many, chandeliers.

"I'm literally walking on money," Amy said. "You know

142

when people use pennies to make flooring? They used one-hundred-dollar bills."

Amy led me through the foyer toward one of the many living rooms. Guests were scattered around, some dancing to the trap music pounding through the walls, some drinking from red plastic cups, some leaning against the couches talking. Some of these people had graduated years ago. I couldn't see why anyone would want to come back to a high school party.

"Smell that?" Amy shouted excitedly over the music. I took a sniff of the air and was instantly struck by a sweaty skunk smell.

"Gross," I responded, spotting the people smoking a joint on the couch. Other people around us were vaping, puffing the clouds in each other's faces like it was the funniest thing in the world. The smell, the noise, the smoke, and the number of bodies around me made my pulse race.

"Okay, you're not digging this?" Amy asked. I shook my head, not able to fully form any words. "Let's go out back." They grabbed my hand.

In the yard, there were more people and less music, which helped my pulse slow.

We found a spot on the edge of a raised garden bed. I leaned over, resting my hands on my legs, and took a few deep breaths. Amy rubbed their hand in circles on my back. People probably thought I was about to barf from drinking too much, but I was really about to pass out from another sudden reminder that I was going to die.

It would hit me when I was alone because my thoughts had too much space, it would hit me when I was having fun with Amy because I'd remember nothing could last, and it would hit me in giant crowds because I'd look around and remember we'd all just be bodies one day. I looked up and saw a senior named Alex from school, and I instantly wondered how he would die. Disgusted at the thought, I smacked my forehead to try and get it out.

"Hey, hey." Amy grabbed my hand to keep me from hitting myself again. "We're going to leave. Sorry for making you do this."

And then I remembered why I had done this. My brain constantly ruined things for Amy, and I didn't want to keep letting that happen.

"No. I want to stay," I lied and took a deep breath. "I'm okay."

Just then, some kid I didn't know poked his head out the sliding door and shouted, "Warren is about to make a speech!"

People started shuffling back inside. Amy looked at me, their way of asking what I wanted. I could see what they wanted. Warren was probably about to make one of those infamous memories, and Amy was keen to witness it.

"Let's go," I said.

We followed the crowd back into the foyer where everyone was cramped together. Warren stood on the second-floor balcony, leaning over the railing, looking down on everyone.

People started chanting "Speech, speech, speech," even Amy.

"Thanks for coming, everyone!" Warren shouted. "It's a pleasure hosting you tonight."

I could smell the booze on people's breaths as they let out a shout of approval.

"This is the first party without our classmate Milo D'Angelo, and I wanted to take a moment to honor his memory."

The crowd turned more subdued. Amy instantly grabbed my hand, and I squeezed back.

"It's really not a party without him, but let's make this one count in his honor!" Warren started chugging his drink, and everyone followed suit. When he finished, he crumpled the cup and threw it over the railing with a loud whoop that instantly got the crowd cheering again. Their sadness only lasted for a blip.

Milo would have never come to this party. Technically everyone was invited, but he certainly wouldn't have felt welcome.

"We can leave," Amy said for the millionth time.

But I turned to them, feeling my blood boiling, and said, "I want a drink."

People say that it helps you loosen up. Takes away your inhibitions. Makes things feel freer. And I was feeling so stuck in my head that I thought it was worth a try.

Amy found me a beer. I took a gulp, trying not to smell it as I raised the can to my lips. I pushed past the repugnancy of it and started to chug.

"Slow down, cowboy," Amy said. I didn't listen. I didn't want to slow down. I didn't want to think about any of this right now. I didn't want to be here or back at Richter or worry about where Milo was or remember that someday, at any moment, it could be me. I wanted a moment of relief.

When I finished the beer and slammed it down on the counter, I waited to feel anything. I didn't feel anything.

"You do have a wild side!" Amy said, sounding impressed.

In response, I grabbed for another drink.

I had about five beers within the hour. Amy was still nursing their first. Eventually I started to feel a little dizzy. When I'd move my head, it took a couple of seconds for my eyes to catch up to me. It was when I started slurring my words that I could really tell I was drunk.

It still wasn't working, though. Drinking was supposed to make me forget about my worries, but it was making them infinitely worse. As I watched everyone letting their inhibitions go, I clung even more tightly to mine. I didn't like not being able to focus my thoughts, I didn't like not being able to walk straight.

While I was trying to keep myself from falling over, Amy was flirting with some girl in the corner. They were sharing a Juul or something, but I couldn't focus on her face to see who it was, and I couldn't stop thinking about dying for long enough to really try. Then I felt the sudden and horrible certainty that I needed to throw up. Not the anxiety-induced queasiness from before but actual, gurgling nausea.

I pushed past a bunch of people and ran upstairs. Even though everyone around me was at least as drunk as I was, I didn't want a ton of people to see me vomit.

The bathroom door was locked. I groaned. Then, through the haze, I remembered I was in a house with six living rooms, so it probably had at least another five bathrooms. I ran to the end of the hall—which only made my nausea worse—threw a door open, and discovered I was standing in a bedroom. I cursed my garbage luck, almost ready to let it happen here, but as my vision focused for a moment, I saw two people lying on the bed. I closed my eyes before properly registering what I'd walked in on.

"Georgia?"

The sound of my name made me open my eyes. Both Peter and Eileen shot up from the bed and stared at me.

"Oh my god," I said, my sickness changing from nausea to a type of disgust. I didn't want to think about what I was seeing, and I thanked my drunkenness for keeping me from fully absorbing it.

"Georgia." Eileen pushed herself off the bed to come toward me.

My head was spinning. I needed to leave.

"Please wait a minute," Eileen begged.

I turned and started down the hallway, until I felt Eileen's hand on my shoulder. Judging by how steady she was on her feet, she was completely sober. "We wanted to tell you, Georgia. You were the first person we wanted to tell. But you were the only person we felt like we couldn't tell."

I was staring at the floor to stay balanced. My mind was swirling from more than the beer now.

Eileen let out a big sigh, as if she were releasing three years of pent-up feelings. "I've had so many moments in my life that I wanted to share with you. That I wanted to share with Amy. But you were always so cold. And I wanted to apologize for what happened, you know? But you never would let me, and at a certain point I had to give up. Like, I can't be there for someone who doesn't want me there. It took me awhile to realize that. But I thought maybe now . . . maybe since years have gone by, we could talk. But every time I see you, you're still cold."

This was all happening quickly, and I couldn't process it through the alcohol. I needed her to stop talking.

"I'm happy for you two," I said. "I have to go." I turned and stumbled downstairs to find Amy. My body had swallowed the nausea and replaced it with a crushing feeling. Walking down the steps made me sober up momentarily. Amy was still standing in the corner flirting with that girl. Peter had Eileen, Amy had the mystery girl, and I was drunk and alone. Depressing, honestly.

I stumbled out to the front lawn, sat down by the side of the house where I hoped no one could find me, and vomited the entire night's worth of alcohol. I instantly felt a sense of relief and scooted away from where my insides now lay outside so I could peacefully rest my head in the grass and look up at the stars.

I could walk out on others, but I couldn't walk out on my own brain. Especially when it was shouting, full volume, all of my fears.

Everything stopped spinning when I rested my eyes on a single light. I tried to quiet my brain and focus on that star, shining brighter than the glow-in-the-dark ones attached to my ceiling. I wondered how far away it was, how long its light had traveled before it hit my eyes. I thought about what lay behind the star or behind the smaller star next to it or another star behind that one. I wondered if I was being watched by something within the stars and hoped that they would guide me, help me, tell me how to make it all go away. I closed my eyes and tried to find the stars against the backs of my eyelids, but all I found was Grandma and Oscar and Betty and Milo.

I must've been lying in the grass for quite a while, letting my body sober up. People were leaving the party. When I checked my phone, I vaguely registered the many texts from Amy but mostly noticed it was almost two in the morning.

I closed my eyes again and listened to the feet shuffle against the grass as people left. I wanted to fall asleep, to forget, but I remembered that sleep is just practice for death and I wanted to stay awake all night. I clutched my phone and tried to breathe through the thoughts.

"Need a ride home?" It was Peter. He was peering over me, hands in his pockets, the light from the moon forming a halo around his curls.

"I thought maybe I'd just stay here for the rest of forever," I told him, tracing the constellations around his head, drawing them with my finger.

"That's not productive." He held out his hand.

I grabbed it, and he pulled me up. My head spun, and I could tell I wasn't fully sober yet. But being still had helped.

"Aren't you taking other people home?" I asked him.

"Eileen didn't drink. She took the rest of our group home."

We made our way down the hill and along the gravel path. I could walk without stumbling. Peter matched my pace.

"How much did you drink?" he asked.

I shrugged. I didn't need to invite more judgment from him by giving him specifics.

We reached the end of the driveway and walked down the road a ways until I saw the tan hearse beneath a streetlamp. Peter unlocked it, and we both ducked our heads under the carpeted ceiling. Out of instinct, I checked the back of the hearse. It had become a habit ever since the time Dad picked me up from school after a death call, with an occupied box in the back.

"I'm not going to drive to Warren's party with a body," Peter said.

I slumped against the leather seat, relieved both that the back was empty and that I didn't have to keep my balance anymore. The world stopped swaying around me. Plus, it was somewhat comforting to be away from that party and in a car I knew so well.

I let my eyes flutter shut as Peter started the car.

"About earlier," Peter began, and my eyes shot open. "With Eileen . . ."

"We don't need to talk about that."

"We do, though. We don't talk enough, so we should talk about this."

I gulped. "Do Mom and Dad know?"

"Yeah. They've known for a while," he said.

The words *a while* hit me. This had been going on for longer than just tonight. It meant this big thing had happened in Peter's life and I hadn't known about it. I instantly felt oblivious for not realizing. The two of them were always hanging out, always giggling. God, I was so stuck in my own brain.

"How long is a while?" I asked, afraid of the answer. I could see the silhouette of his face, his gaze fixed on the road ahead, his hands firmly planted at ten and two.

"About two months officially. But it's been building for a couple of years now," he said.

"Damn." I watched the trees brush past my window.

"We weren't trying to keep it a secret from you. We just didn't know how to bring it up with you. We tried. We've been trying, I mean. To connect with you again. But you're always ignoring us and brushing us off. So we thought maybe you wouldn't even care." Suddenly Peter's recent attempts at conversation and the awkward smiles from Eileen made a lot more sense.

"Why would you think I wouldn't care?" I asked.

"I don't know, G. You got so distant from us. It seemed pretty clear that you wanted nothing to do with us. What were we supposed to think?"

My throat tightened.

"I've tried to talk to you," he said. "And every time, you shut me out. We really did want to share this with you. But not when you still clearly hate us."

Tears rolled down my cheek. I wiped them away quickly so Peter wouldn't see them glisten in the glow of the moon.

"I know you've been going through some stuff," he said. "I know. But I miss you. I miss being more than just your annoying brother. I miss being your friend. Your twin."

I felt my breath shudder. It was true. I'd shut them out. Even after everything happened, I never even let them try to explain. And this was what it had cost me. I'd missed a huge moment in Peter's life.

"I don't hate you," I said, barely above a whisper.

"I'm glad to hear that."

I bit down on my thumb to try to focus away the tears. It wasn't working.

"I'm not trying to make you upset," Peter said, glancing over at me. "I just want to have a relationship with you again. I want to feel like I can tell you when my lifelong crush asks me out."

"She asked you out?"

"Yeah," Peter said, the word coming out in a breathy laugh.

I couldn't help but smile at that, knowing that Eileen wasn't the type to wait around for someone else to make the first move.

We pulled up to Richter, into the garage, and Peter put the car in Park. The garage light illuminated our faces while the engine hummed. I turned to look at my twin, not caring if he saw my puffy eyes and tear-streaked, still slightly drunk face. I realized I hadn't looked at him, really looked at him, in so long. He looked so different than the boy who'd been my best friend. Taller, more mature thanks to a scruffy chin and longer hair that fell in front of his eyes. His eyes still looked like mine, though. That could never change.

"Grandma still hurts," I told him.

"I know. And I know that you knew Milo. I know that hurts too."

When he said Milo's name, it came flooding back like a rush of embalming fluid, tightening my veins. Milo wasn't in the house waiting for me.

"I just want to be friends again. Can we have that?" he asked.

He was dating the person who'd betrayed me, and that was a betrayal in and of itself. But looking at him then with his honest eyes, I knew that we'd both grown. And I wanted to continue knowing him.

So I nodded.

He nodded.

"You going to tell Mom you got super drunk?" he asked.

"No way in hell," I said and opened the car door. "Although I'm more worried about Dad finding out."

"They'll be able to tell when you're hungover in the morning."

I groaned and exited the car. We walked up the steps quietly to not wake our parents. We told each other good night before heading to our respective rooms.

When I entered mine and saw a lump on my bed, my heart leapt—for a second I thought Milo had returned. But it was Amy asleep under my covers. Their mom must have dropped them off, and my parents wouldn't have hesitated to let them in. I changed into pajamas, climbed into bed, and wrapped my arm around them, feeling how safe it was to have them there. I told the thoughts, *Not tonight*, and I let myself drift into momentary oblivion, even if it was practice for the eventual one.

CHAPTER 15

The last time I spoke to Eileen was after the hide-and-seek incident. But that wasn't the last time Amy spoke to her.

It all went down a few weeks afterward. I came to school one morning to find everyone's eyes on me. I'd gotten used to people giving me sympathetic looks because of Grandma, but these stares weren't the same. They were horrified. I rushed to my locker, trying to ignore them. As I packed my books into my bag, Amy came up, their face scrunched.

"What's going on?" I whispered.

"Um . . ." Amy bit their lip, avoiding my eyes. "Nothing."

"Amy," I huffed. It wasn't like them to keep things from me.

"Everyone's saying things. About you."

"What things?" I looked around, meeting students' eyes, trying to figure out what they knew about me that I didn't.

Amy swallowed before they told me. They whispered it, as if the whole school hadn't already heard. I remember a blurriness took over the perimeter of my vision, slowly creeping inward, like a menacing vignette threatening to drown out everything else. I wasn't surprised, though. Because I had always been the weird funeral home girl. No one would have ever said this kind of thing about Peter.

"I heard it from Marvin, and I shut him down," Amy said.

"He didn't start it, though. He said he heard it from . . . someone else."

Amy brought me in for a hug. I let them hold me, but I couldn't hold them back. I couldn't move a muscle. The words were replaying over and over in my head, and the thought of everyone hearing them made my mouth go dry and my blood run hot.

Amy stuck by me as much as they could that day. Whenever we'd have to split, they'd text me from their class to check on me and then meet me outside my class and walk with me. I kept my head down, getting intimately familiar with the school's green tiled floor. I didn't make it halfway through the day before deciding I needed to go home. I couldn't stand to be there anymore.

Amy held my hand as I walked to the office to sign out sick during lunch. That's when we passed Eileen standing with a group of people who I didn't even think she was friends with.

And she was saying it. Gleefully. She was laughing about it.

Amy's hand got so tight in mine that it almost hurt. They didn't look at me, didn't even give me time to stop them. Instead, they released my hand and got right in Eileen's face.

"Shut up!" Amy growled.

Eileen flinched and froze. "Amy—"

"Oh, don't *Amy* me. How dare you spread this stuff? How can you be this cruel?"

"Amy." This time it was me. I didn't want them to cause a big scene. But I couldn't convince my feet to move or my arms to reach out to pull Amy away.

"I got this, G," Amy said, not removing their eyes from Eileen. "You're an awful friend. I didn't want to believe it was you. Everyone I asked said they heard it from you, but I

154

thought no way, Eileen wouldn't do that to Georgia. Eileen wouldn't start a rumor that vile about anyone, let alone her *friend*."

Eileen gulped and looked to me, but I couldn't stand to look at her.

"The fact that you're not even saying anything is repulsive to me," Amy said.

They turned back to me, grabbed my hand, and pulled me toward the office to help sign me out.

We left Eileen crying, the group of girls she'd been standing with trying to comfort her. I didn't even care. I wanted her to cry, because the kind of pain she was feeling wasn't even close to what I was feeling.

I went home. I told Mom and Dad I was sick. I lay in bed entirely under my covers in hopes that they would separate me from the world and that when I eventually emerged, I'd be in some other universe where none of it had happened. Where Grandma hadn't died, where I hadn't woken her and Oscar's ghosts, and where Eileen hadn't said those awful things about me.

I replayed the words I heard Amy whisper, pictured them from Eileen's mouth. I couldn't understand why Eileen would do it. She loved Richter. It didn't make sense. Unless . . . unless that was exactly why she said it. If I was the weird funeral home girl, no one would think to pin that label on her.

Whatever her twisted reason was, it was the deepest betrayal. To take my biggest insecurities and stomp on them for fun. To stab me in the back.

I'd already been pulling away, angry that Eileen was so flippant about my grief, so her saying those things was the perfect reason to just be done with her.

155

That whole week at school, Amy called out anyone who mentioned it. After about a week, it died down and no one cared anymore. But it didn't leave me. I still cared.

And when Peter didn't stop spending time with Eileen, I knew I was done with him too.

◊

Amy and I were still holding each other when we woke up the morning after the party. I felt heavy against them and my sheets, each limb like a brick holding me down. When I tried to lift my brick head, the throbbing began, and I let out a low groan.

"I know that sound," Amy said, rolling over to look at me. I had my hands over my eyes, blocking the stream of light from the window. "You got real drunk."

I groaned again in response.

"Good question. I don't know why people drink either," Amy said. That made me laugh, which made my head throb, which made me groan again. It was a vicious cycle. I wondered if *this* was what it felt like to die.

"Peter texted me when he found you on the lawn," Amy added. "I rushed over to be here when you got home, but your bed is just so comfortable I passed out." They fluffed their pillow. "What compelled you to get so drunk anyway? You went from hating being there to plastered in a matter of minutes."

Staring at my ceiling stars, I remembered lying in the grass and looking at the endless sky. "Just wondered what it was like," I lied.

"And now you know what it is like and plan on never doing it again, I assume."

156

"Sounds about right."

Amy helped me out of bed. Standing up actually helped a bit, and once I'd gotten dressed, my limbs felt like flesh again.

We were both sitting on my bed, scrolling through our phones, when last night officially came back to me. I hadn't blacked out, but the night did seem a mess. Warren's speech. Peter and Eileen. Eileen. Peter. The grass. Stars. Thoughts that I tried to keep away but that crept in regardless.

I held my thumb over the messaging app on my phone and looked up at Amy like they could tell what I was about to do, but they were scrolling away on their own phone, oblivious. So I clicked on the app and typed in Eileen's name.

The last text I had received from her was from three years ago. It was her asking if Amy and I were going to the football game that night. I'd never responded.

It took me forever to send six little words. I questioned it, regretted it before it happened, told myself not to do it. But remembering how hurt I'd felt last night convinced me to hit Send.

Me: Did you have fun last night?

She had her read receipts on, so I instantly saw when she read it. She kept typing, and the bubble would appear, making my heart race, and then she stopped typing, making the bubble disappear and my heart race even more. I checked to make sure Amy still wasn't watching.

Eileen: It was okay. Honestly, I'm not sure why it's apparently THE party of the century or anything, but it wasn't terrible. Did you?

Me: I got really drunk. I was pretty drunk when I walked in on you. Sorry I didn't stay.

Eileen: Omg I didn't realize. It's okay.

I was surprised that all the swaying hadn't tipped her off. I took a deep breath, inhaling what Peter and Amy said about isolating them.

Me: Sorry for shutting you out.

Eileen: Thanks for saying that.

I didn't know how to respond. Eileen did before I had to.

Eileen: I'm coming over tonight to help out with the Hoagman visitation. Is that okay?

Me: Not my place to keep you out of Richter.

Eileen: Can we talk then though?

Me: Yeah.

Our text conversation ended there. In less than five minutes, we'd spoken more to each other than we had the whole time since Grandma died.

"I'm starving," Amy said. "Plus, food will help your hangover."

I'd been so distracted with thoughts of last night that I hadn't been processing the dull pain grabbing my head like a pair of hands slowly squeezing an orange.

As we walked to the kitchen, Amy said, "So, last night . . ."

Peter was sitting at the table.

"Hey," I said to him as Amy opened a cabinet in search of food.

He looked up from his phone and smiled at me. Not one of his sad, I-feel-bad-for-you smiles. One that felt real. "How do you feel?" he said dryly.

"Shut up."

"What, you didn't hear the groans through the wall?" Amy asked.

Peter got up from the table. "Eileen just said you texted."

I winced, glancing at Amy.

"Thank you for that. She said she's excited to see you tonight." He pocketed his phone and headed downstairs.

Amy turned to me, mouth agape, one hand still holding a cabinet door. "Eileen? Texted? SEEING YOU?"

I groaned, this time not from the hangover, and explained everything that had happened in the past twelve hours.

"Dating," Amy mused. "Not surprised. They're so handsy with each other, makes me wanna vomit." Then they took a seat at the table with a *humph*, their posture pointing away from me.

"What's that huff for?"

"I don't know, G," they sighed. "Just, why would you want to be friends with her again?"

"I don't know if I want to be friends again. But when Peter told me they were dating . . . I realized I've missed this huge thing in my brother's life. And like, boy did I miss it. Like you said, they're not exactly subtle."

Amy raised their brows and nodded.

"And what you said about isolating myself really hit me. Peter said the same thing last night. Eileen said it. I know I do that. I know I need to stop doing that."

"But she really hurt you."

"Yeah." I wasn't denying that. But I knew it wasn't the only reason I'd pushed her away. By the time Eileen started the rumor, we hadn't all hung out together in weeks. We hadn't even spoken. "I was already feeling distant from her. Pulling away from her, I guess. So when she started saying that stuff about me, it was the last straw, but it wasn't the only reason we stopped being friends. I was responsible for some of it too."

Amy sighed and looked up to the ceiling like they were trying to help process the thoughts by rolling them around their brain.

"Why are you so mad? You're the one who told me I need to stop pushing people away," I said.

Amy shook their head and pursed their lips. I could tell they were trying to fight something back.

"What is it?"

Amy stood up abruptly. "It honestly kind of feels like you're working harder to fix your friendship with Eileen than with me."

"What? No."

"That's what it feels like. Because here you are giving me this spiel about how you feel you've wronged Eileen and I don't ever get that kind of thing?"

"Amy, I—" I genuinely didn't have words. I knew I had been distant, but I had gone to the party, I'd made an effort, and they hadn't even hung out with me that much once we were there. I didn't understand why they were this upset now.

"You're allowed to be friends with Eileen again," Amy said, but it didn't sound convincing. "That's your prerogative."

"I'm not saying I'm going to be her friend." I was completely lost on how the conversation had crumbled so quickly. Amy's lips were pursed, like they were waiting for me to say more.

When the words didn't come, they said, "I'm going to go."

"Whoa, now you're going to walk out on me? Isn't that extremely hypocritical right now?" I got up from my seat, ready to chase them down the stairs and through Richter, but they held up their hand to stop me.

"Please, G, I need a little space."

I sighed. I couldn't fight that when it was exactly what I asked for so often. "Okay," I said and let them leave.

I sat back down at the table feeling helpless. Milo had left.

Amy had left. At least I had Peter and Eileen? I placed my forehead down on the table and groaned.

A few minutes later, Mom peeked her head in. "Georgia," she said, "there's someone here to see you downstairs."

For a second I thought maybe Amy had come back, but they would have walked back upstairs. And if Eileen was here already, she would have also come upstairs.

I followed Mom down to the entryway, where I found Mrs. D'Angelo. My breath caught, and I instantly checked to see if Milo had followed her here.

"Thank you, Andrea," Mrs. D'Angelo said. My mom headed toward the office, leaving me alone with Milo's mom. I stood awkwardly, not sure what to do with my hands or how close to get to her. Mrs. D'Angelo didn't look as if she'd been crying recently. Her posture was slightly straighter.

"I'm really sorry to stop by like this," she said. "You didn't come when you said you would, and I wanted to make sure everything was okay. I wanted to make sure I hadn't scared you off. Again." She gave a little laugh, but it felt forced.

I started to chew on the inside of my cheek, waiting to find the right words or for the right words to find me. I almost hoped she would invite me back over again so that I could try and find Milo. So that I could bring him back.

"I understand we're all grieving." She dropped her eyes to the floor.

"Mrs. D'Angelo . . ." I was about to tell her that I couldn't. That she should go home and stop thinking about me. That I couldn't teach her anything about her son. The person she raised, loved, and cared for until a drunk driver slammed into him when he was walking home from work didn't know me, and I didn't know him.

But when that image flashed in my brain, I couldn't help but replay it. And at that moment, it seemed like Mr. and Mrs. D'Angelo might be the only two people who found that image more devastating—more frightening—than I did.

Now I was the one sobbing in front of her in my house. I felt the panic in my throat and the back of my head and in the tingle of my palms. I was a hot mess.

"Oh, sweetie," she said and brought me into a hug. It was wrong and I felt disgusting, but I welcomed that disgust to distract me from my death thoughts. I didn't wrap my arms around her, but neither did I push her away.

When I finally caught a breath, I pulled back and saw that she was crying too.

"I miss him so much," she said.

That made me cry harder. Because she didn't understand. Because her pain and my pain were different, and she didn't know, and I didn't have the heart to tell her because some repulsive part of me needed her.

"The night before Milo's funeral, his father and I are going to go to the Field Museum in Chicago. It was Milo's favorite place in the world. We could only go so often because of money and time." I could tell she was trying to speak without releasing any howling sobs. "We thought it would be a really nice way to celebrate him. And we were wondering if you would like to join us. It'll be a bit of a road trip."

It was an invitation to find Milo. I could see him again. Even though it felt wicked, I couldn't turn it down. If I lost him, I was terrified of where I'd find myself.

"Okay," was all I said.

"Wonderful," she said with a sniffle. "Thank you. Thank you." She grabbed my hand and squeezed, but I kept my fingers limp. She took a few steps toward the door but wouldn't let her gaze fall from me. I wanted her to leave because I felt more tears coming on, and I didn't want her to try to comfort me again with another hug. And yet I wanted her to stay here until Milo came to find her.

When she finally closed the door, I started to cry even harder. I turned to go to my room, but Mom stepped out of the office and intercepted me.

"Georgia?" Mom held her hands to my elbows, dipping her head to catch my eyes. "Oh, honey. If you want to talk about it—"

I batted her hands away and stepped around her. Mom looked betrayed. I'd never seen a look in her eyes like that before. It didn't stop me from leaving her, hands at her side, standing in the hallway as I walked up the stairs.

CHAPTER 16

The visitation that night was going to be a big one. It was for a local doctor named Bart Hoagman who'd died from complications with cancer. Mom said people from all over town would be attending, and yet I still hadn't heard as much about Bart as I had about Milo. There was no vigil for Bart. No party in his honor. People are less sad when it's expected. Sometimes people are even relieved.

When Eileen arrived to help set up, Mom came out of the office and gave her a hug. "I'm so happy you're helping out!" Her enthusiasm radiated through the room.

"Thanks for letting me," Eileen said. "It means a lot that you trust me this much."

"Of course. You're basically family."

Eileen had been a part of our lives for a long time, but labeling her as family seemed fast and invasive to me. But that was Mom's way. And Eileen didn't act weirded out by it.

Peter was in the chapel arranging chairs, and I continued bringing the bouquets of flowers from the storage closet to the visitation room. Mom went back into the office, and Eileen approached me.

"How's your head?" she asked. "Peter said you had a rough morning."

"Better now." I grabbed a bouquet of white roses to transport.

Eileen grabbed another bouquet and followed me. She knew her way around Richter.

"It was awful this morning, but now it just feels like a tension headache," I continued.

"Good."

"Yeah. Took some ibuprofen."

We loaded a few more flowers. Both of us knew it was awkward. We didn't know how to talk to each other anymore. I wasn't about to be the first one to bring up the elephant in the room.

"Okay. So. I just want to say . . ." Eileen paused.

I'd been adjusting the painting of Tuscan hills above the bier where Dad would put Bart's coffin. I turned, giving her my attention.

"I'm sorry I didn't tell you about Peter and me. Like I was trying to say last night, I wanted to. But I sort of thought you hated me."

I took a breath. "I definitely never hated you." Even if sometimes it felt like I did.

"And I know that you were grieving, back when everything fell apart. I wanted to be there for you. Amy got to be there, and that kind of sucked." She tucked a strand of curls behind her ear. "Then you basically stopped talking to me, and then the rumor thing and Amy getting really mad—and it all got so messy."

"Yeah. It was definitely a mess." The rumor had been simmering in the back of my head for years, something I knew but tried not to think about too hard. Returning to that place was scary. But if I wanted to know Peter and Eileen again, if I wanted to make any kind of fresh start with them, we were going to have to talk about it.

"I really want to apologize for that," Eileen said. "Like fully apologize. I was hurt that you'd cut me off, and I guess I wanted you to hurt too. And there was also a piece of it that came from, I don't know, being listened to. I've spent my whole life feeling like an outsider in school, and when I said that stuff about you, people paid attention. For a second, I felt like I fit. And I really needed that. I didn't have you anymore and I knew losing you would mean losing Amy too. But none of that is a good excuse. I'm sorry."

That didn't make it hurt any less, but it made a little more sense. I hadn't given as much thought as I should have to the ways Eileen felt out of place in Somerton.

"So, I'm not trying to, like, reopen old wounds. I just want to be able to be friends again and . . . I need to tell you the actual truth about it," she said.

I had no clue what she was talking about. The truth?

Eileen took a breath like she was bracing herself for what she was about to say. I waited, thinking I might need to brace myself too.

"It wasn't me," she said.

"What?"

"I didn't start the rumor. I just repeated it. I still said those things and they were awful and I'm responsible for that. But I wasn't the one who started it."

I didn't know how to react. "You said you started it, though." I tried to recreate the memory in my head, trying to build the timeline, but it was all so fuzzy.

"Not really. When Amy assumed it was me, I didn't tell them otherwise because you were already so mad at me and distant from me. I felt defeated, I guess, like there was no point."

"Then who was it?"

166

"It was Peter." She winced like I was about to shout at her, but I only stared blankly, trying to process. "It didn't seem worthwhile to set the record straight at the time because you were already mad at both of us—you just swapped our roles. And Peter was the one who had to actually live with you, so I figured no good would come of telling the truth. It wouldn't make you forgive me. It would only make things worse for you with Peter, and they were already tense enough."

I felt my blood go hot and my vision blur like the first time I'd heard the rumor, but I couldn't bring the words up. I'd spent so long burying the memory that I couldn't reconstruct what she had said to imagine them coming from Peter's mouth. My entire body shook. If Eileen hadn't registered my swaying the night before, I hoped she couldn't see me quaking with anger now.

"I know you might still resent me, because I should've stood up for you and I didn't. I know I can't undo that. The best I can do is be honest with you. Because I don't want this hanging over us forever."

When I looked at her lately, I didn't think about the nasty things she'd said about me. I thought about how much it hurt that she never took my grief seriously. But now, I felt the same pain I'd felt when it first happened. Except Eileen wasn't the cause of it—not the root cause. She'd still failed me as a friend, but not in the way I'd believed.

"Peter's in the chapel. I have to go grab the brochures for tonight," I said and quickly exited the visitation room. I didn't slow down until I was standing out on the front porch, right on top of my hiding spot, looking at the sign welcoming the town to this establishment. I dialed Amy's number with a shaking thumb.

"Hi," I said, my voice weak.

"Shit," Amy said, hearing it in my voice immediately. They could always tell. "She brought it up again, didn't she? This is why, Georgia! God dammit!"

"Yeah but, Amy . . ." My breath was short and quick, and if I didn't get ahold of it, I could tell it would take control and send me into a panic attack, and I did not need that right now.

"She's not sorry, G. She's still the same person who hurt you. And I told her to never bring it up again—"

"Amy!" I practically shouted, trying to get their attention.

"Whoa, what?"

"Will you please remind me what happened?"

"What?"

"Will you tell me how it all went down again? I can't even remember exactly what she said." It was like the memories were pixelating and I couldn't make any of them out.

"Georgia, I'm not going to do that. You know what happened and I'm not going to relive that for you."

"Please." Now I felt like I was no longer in my own body. I leaned against the railing to catch my balance. "Just tell me. Help me remember." I needed something to ground me.

"Fine, okay. Eileen started this awful rumor and said . . . G, I don't want to . . . Okay. Remember? She told people that you like to sleep in the body freezer in Richter and you were like a puppet master with the bodies and stuff like that. I don't know, it was obviously bullshit! And I screamed at her to shut the fuck up about it."

"Did Eileen ever say she started it?"

"What? Um . . ."

"Amy!"

"I'm thinking! I mean. Yeah. I mean . . . everybody said they heard it from her."

168

Oh my god. I wasn't hot anymore. I was cold. Boiling had turned to ice. My ears were ringing. I suddenly remembered it all, except I saw it in a new light. I pictured Peter staring down at me from the top of the embalming room steps, planning what he was going to tell everyone.

"Middle schoolers are trash," Amy continued. "And Eileen is trash for bringing it up again. Want me to come over? I'm just pinning a pattern. I can come."

"No. It wasn't Eileen. It was Peter."

"Oh my god! That's even worse! Wait, did he tell you that?"

"I . . . I'll call you back. I'm . . . I'm having a panic attack. I'll be okay. I gotta . . . breathe."

"Do you need me to come over? Or keep talking to help you get through it?"

I couldn't even tell them no. My voice caught in my throat as I tried to mumble something into the phone, so I hung up. My hands gripped the deck for support as the burning radiated through my body. I thought about the safety I'd felt in the hearse when Peter drove me home. Because Peter was driving. Because even after everything, I still trusted Peter. My chest tightened. This was definitely a heart attack.

I remembered to breathe. I closed my eyes to keep my head from spinning, and I breathed until the tenseness was gone and I could support myself again. Until the one feeling left in my chest was fury. I shot Amy a quick text letting them know I was okay, and then I headed straight back into Richter and threw the chapel doors open, practically shattering their glass from the impact. The room was ready for people to arrive for the visitation at any minute, and it might not be Bart's funeral we'd be celebrating.

Peter and Eileen were both in there. They jumped when the doors slammed against the wall.

"How dare you!" I shouted at Peter. "And you wanted a relationship again?" My voice was hoarse, cracking with how intensely I was using it. "You *missed* me?"

Peter looked at Eileen as if this was aimed at her, but Eileen wasn't the one I had my eyes locked on.

"You wanted to be my twin again?" I shouted, confirming this was for him and only him.

Peter's face was pale with shock.

"What's going on?" Dad's voice rang out behind me. I glanced back to see my parents standing in the doorway, their expressions resembling Peter's. I ignored them and turned back to Peter.

"You said all that stuff to me last night, acting like I was the one who ruined things between us, like you had nothing to be sorry for." I was crying again, my voice now broken. "You know, it was one thing thinking you didn't care about what Eileen was saying, but come to find you had the malice, the pure loathing to *start* it? And you didn't even have the decency to confess. You let me blame Eileen, thinking I'd never find out. You were supposed to be my best friend!" Peter had known my vulnerability, and he'd weaponized it to make me bleed.

Peter's eyes got wide. He looked at Eileen, whose unwillingness to look back probably told him all he needed to know.

"Georgia, oh my god, I'm so sorry." He practically lunged for me, but I stepped back and held my hands up to keep him away.

I'd expected him to deny it. Maybe even hoped he would. But Eileen had no reason to lie at this point—to throw Peter under the bus after all this time, especially now that they were together. And now that I was replaying it all again, it had never made sense that Eileen had started the rumor. Peter was the one who'd seen me in the basement that night.

Grandma's death was the most painful experience of my life, and Peter had turned it into a joke. I became the weird funeral home girl who slept in the body freezer and played with corpses while he got to be the cool one who'd embalmed a body and knew all the secrets about the dead. I wasn't even able to escape Richter at school after that.

"Forget everything from last night," I growled. "I hate you."

"Whoa!" Dad cut in. He and Mom were still standing on the chapel threshold. "Okay, guys, the visitation is about to start—"

Typical of Dad to attempt to diffuse the situation this way, to force us to act more like coworkers than siblings. I didn't stay to listen. I left Peter standing in the middle of the chapel, Eileen with her hand over her mouth, and both my parents in shock. I stormed back down the hall, threw the front door open, and bolted down the street. I needed to get as far away from Peter as possible.

I found myself at the cemetery. I opened the gate and went straight for Grandma's grave. Usually I'd glance at the familiar names on my way there, but in this moment, she was the only thing on my mind. The flowers on her stone were a few weeks old, so they had wilted atop the granite.

I fell to my knees at her plot, seeing her name carved into stone, feeling her ashes beneath me, realizing this might be all that was left of her. I placed my hands in the browning grass and squeezed. This was the closest I could come to giving her a hug.

"I miss you," I told her. I said it to the stone, to the ground, to the sky, to the air, wherever she could be. "I'm sorry. For what I did. For letting you go." I did it to her. I wouldn't do it again. I needed to stop. But mostly I needed her to be here again.

Only the wind replied, but I imagined that was her sending a response. The closest she could come to hugging me back.

It hurt most when I would remember the things we did and realize they could never happen again. They lived on only in my head, but when I was gone, they'd be gone entirely. No one to keep them.

I sat cross-legged on the plot and told her everything. I liked to come here to tell her about the big changes in my life. I came when I started high school. I told her when I realized that I was ace. I knew she would be proud of me.

Tonight I told her all about Milo, Milo's parents, Peter, Eileen. I poured my heart out onto her grave and hoped it would soak through the dirt and down into her ashes to live with her.

As I told her about Peter starting the rumor, I realized that it sounded so childish. Being upset about something that happened when I was thirteen seemed ridiculous when I said it out loud, but I couldn't help how I felt about it. It had been a deep betrayal. And it reinforced why I'd felt so distant from them in the first place—they didn't understand how much I hurt. Death was easier for them.

When I finally said it all, I laid my head down. The sky was getting dark, so the funeral had to be almost over. I was sure my phone had plenty of messages, but I tried to not think about any of that for a moment. I wanted it to be me and Grandma.

I lay as still as the bodies six feet under. I almost fell asleep—a literal dirt nap—but something stirred inside me, causing me to sit up. Even if I wanted to, I couldn't lie there forever. I had all eternity to sleep in a graveyard.

I couldn't stay. I couldn't go home or to the D'Angelos'. I found myself heading toward downtown. At every corner,

I looked both ways as many times as it took to convince myself it was safe to cross. Even as I rushed through an empty intersection, an image of a car slamming into me played in my head. I wasn't sure I'd ever feel safe again.

Right at the end of the semicircle was Lucky's. I hadn't been there in years to avoid all the memories of sharing strawberry shakes with Grandma. But it was where Milo used to work.

I looked through the window at people having late meals, servers dressed in sky blue gliding past the tables. I pictured Milo wearing that uniform, taking orders, walking to and from this place several times a week, walking home for the last time and not even making it there.

Was that the uniform he had been wearing when he got hit? I pictured the sky blue stained with dark red. Then I took a deep breath and shook my head clear of the image.

He had said this place was like his second home. Maybe he'd wandered over here to haunt it. Maybe I would find him.

I made eye contact with one of the servers, and I could have sworn it was him for a split second. He had the same kind of shaggy hair, but his build was stockier.

I didn't have my wallet with me, but I walked in anyway. Even if I didn't find him here, I could at least be in the same space that he'd been in.

"You can seat yourself," an older man behind the counter informed me. Instead of the blue outfit, he wore a gray polo with *Lucky's* embroidered over his heart.

There were booths and tables, or I could sit at the bar. I felt myself gravitate toward the man in the gray polo. He was stacking cups, his back to me. Our eyes met in the reflection of the metallic wall, and he paused for a beat.

"Can I help you?" He turned to me. When he did, I realized

where I knew him from. His scruffy chin, the cheekbones. He was the man Milo had drawn.

"Are you the owner?" I saw on his tag that his name was Jordan.

"You looking for a job?"

I shook my head.

His voice was gruff when he said, "Then why do you want to know?"

I shrugged, not knowing how to casually bring it up.

"Oh, hold up," he said, and his intense stare turned into surprise. "You're Greg Richter's kid, yeah?"

I had to nod.

"How's he doing?"

I shrugged.

"You don't talk much," he said.

"I actually wanted to ask you something."

He raised his eyebrows expectantly.

"Milo D'Angelo worked here." It ended up not as a question but as a statement that hung in the air he once breathed.

Jordan froze for the length of one of those breaths. His eyes dropped to the floor before he hastily returned to organizing the shelves, except this time his movements seemed less purposeful. "Sure did." He said it quietly. "He worked kitchen."

I'd assumed he had been a server. I'd pictured him wearing that outfit. The blood.

"You knew him?" he asked.

I gave him another nod.

"Close?"

"You could say that." I did know Milo now, so it tasted less like a lie than it had with the D'Angelos. But as Jordan crossed his arms and leaned against the counter with a heavy breath,

I knew it still was dishonest. Jordan and I could both say the same thing and it would have two entirely different meanings.

"He was the hardest-working kid I had here. Night I found out, I went home and cried like he was my own kid. Can't even imagine what the D'Angelos are going through." He shook his head.

"Did you go to the vigil?" I asked. I hadn't known to look for him there.

Jordan paused for another breath. "Nah. Couldn't."

"Were you working?"

"It's complicated." He walked down to the other end of the bar, but I wanted to know what he meant. I got up and followed him down, taking a seat at another stool.

"I'm acquainted with complicated," I said.

He chuckled and started drying a cup that looked perfectly dry to me. "Who are you, anyway? I mean, Greg's kid obviously. What's your name?"

"Georgia Richter," I said.

"Georgia," he repeated. "Yeah, Milo mentioned you."

"He did?"

"Yeah, Milo and I did a lot of talking. He worked with me a lot, so I had time to get to know him pretty good. I feel like I know all the stories from that high school." Jordan gave a little laugh. I wondered if Jordan had heard that middle-school rumor too. If it had spread beyond the walls of the school.

But most of all, I realized Jordan knew Milo. He didn't just work with him. He didn't just exist around him. He knew him.

"Anyway, he said you were one of the good ones. Gave me hope that when my little girl gets old enough to go, maybe it won't be hell for her. That kid gave me a lot of hope about the world."

I didn't know what to say to that, so I asked, "What's complicated about going to the vigil?"

"Well, his parents."

I waited for him to go on. He stared at the wall for a second, his eyes glossy, unblinking. He didn't turn his attention back to me when he started speaking again. It was almost like he was speaking to himself. "Milo probably told you. That he was planning on dropping out to help me run the place. When he told his parents, they were furious. That was the day it happened. He was here so upset. Had the day off but came here after a big fight with them. Then he was going to go home and try to make up."

My heart started pounding. "What?"

"Yeah," he said, breaking out of his trance and looking back at me. "Guess you couldn't have possibly known about the fight. I guess I felt like the D'Angelos would still be mad at me and I probably shouldn't intrude on their grieving like that. Better if I keep to myself."

I was shaking my head like this had to be wrong. But I just hadn't known any of it. "Why was he going to drop out?" He wanted to go to college for art. To become an illustrator.

"Shit, you didn't know that?"

My head froze, mid-shake.

"Paying the bills." Jordan shrugged. "Supporting his family."

I had known that part. I mean, I had known that Milo helped pay the bills because his mom couldn't work. I guess I hadn't really known why. Jordan knew why. Jordan knew him. More than I did. More than his parents did.

I was staring straight ahead, locked on the shake machine across from me, feeling the numbness creep up from my toes.

"I'll get you some food," Jordan said, noticing my stiffness. He went in the back, the kitchen door swinging behind him. I didn't wait for him to bring anything out. I hopped off the bar stool and left.

When I got to the corner where it happened, I stood at the edge of the sidewalk and noticed how normal it looked. I'd expected there to be police tape, blood strewn across the street, or at least a small sign with a cross or flowers or a piece of wood with Milo's initials. But it was just a normal four-way stop where cars came and went, driving right over the concrete on which he had lain dying.

I ran as quickly as I could across the street.

When Richter finally appeared around the trees and other houses, I saw someone sitting on the deck, right above the hiding spot. I thought it was Peter, waiting until I came home to force me to talk to him. His head was in his arms, which were leaning on his knees.

I crossed the street after looking to my left five times and then to my right seven more, even though it was a one-way street. I was ready to fight him. I was ready to yell. I could feel my blood beginning to boil.

"Georgia."

He looked up, and I saw who it was.

"Milo!"

CHAPTER 17

"**H**ey," he said.

He looked different. His features were all the same, and he was still wearing Peter's sweatshirt, but he didn't look as . . . present. As I walked toward him, I thought he would feel more *here*, but the closer I got the farther away from him I felt. I had never seen a ghost look anything less than entirely real, but Milo seemed distant even though we now stood only feet away from each other.

"You came back," I said.

Milo nodded.

"Why?" He'd wanted nothing more than to be with his family, I'd thought.

"You're my way out," he said.

It struck me fully then. He was fading. If not out of reality, then out of himself. He was tired, he was hurt. I could end it.

"You want me to send you away? For good?" I asked.

He nodded wearily. "Seeing my parents was amazing. Being in the house, feeling like I was home. But I have never felt so alone. So . . . the only word I can think of is *sad*. I think that's what true heartbreak feels like. Seeing your family grieving for you and not being able to do anything about it. I couldn't tell them I'm okay. I couldn't let them know I'm here. I tried to haunt them. I tried to move things and drop things or write something in the flour or whatever. But I don't have that kind of power. I guess I'm not that kind of ghost."

I couldn't imagine myself in that position. I was used to feeling helpless, but nothing I felt could compare to what Milo was going through.

"It was too much. I thought that's exactly what I wanted, but I couldn't take it. No human being should experience that. So yeah. I want you to send me back. I want it to end. I can't keep living without being alive."

"You don't want to see your funeral?" I asked. "Isn't that everyone's dream?"

Milo shook his head. "Seeing the vigil was painful enough."

"I was hoping you'd be there," I said.

"I was hoping I would want to be there."

"Don't you want to know who did this to you? Who did this to your parents? Isn't not knowing killing you?" I was desperate to find a reason for him to stay.

"It already killed me, Georgia. It's not important to me. Everything that's important to me is gone, and any last piece of an actual existence inside me is worthless. I've been forced to live in my thoughts for way too long. I want them gone. I want it to be over."

I had no counterargument for that. Instead of getting another chance at life, he'd found himself in an inescapable prison. "I'm sorry for keeping you awake."

"I did kind of beg you to."

"Well, I'm sorry for waking you in the first place." It had been eating me alive for days. He would have never had to experience any of this pain if I hadn't been so focused on my own.

179

Milo didn't say anything, but his face fell, and I guessed that he was as sorry about it as I was.

I led him inside, hoping no one was waiting to ambush me, but Richter was empty after the visitation. My family was probably upstairs. I headed for the basement door before anyone could spot us—me.

It wasn't right to say that Milo and I were safe on the other side of that door because I never felt safe staring down these steep, looming steps. But I did feel something like relief. That we hadn't gotten caught. That this would soon be over for him.

I opened the door to the freezer room. I remembered Milo's drawer.

"Is this what you really want?" I knew his answer.

"It is."

I felt tears welling in my eyes for the hundredth time that day and the millionth time that week. I was so tired of crying. I was tired of feeling like this. Maybe touching him and sending him away would end it all for me too.

"Wait," Milo said.

I turned to him, my hand hovering over the drawer handle.

"Do I have to look?" he asked.

"No," I said.

Milo turned away. I pulled the drawer out, the coldness seeping into the rest of the room, brushing my skin. I pulled enough of the blanket down to reveal his nose. I hadn't yet seen his embalmed features, and although his sculpted smile was still hidden behind the sheet, I knew this body wasn't the same one I'd first touched.

"Goodbye, Milo." I said, like this needed to be some formal moment.

180

Milo breathed in and closed his eyes, preparing himself for whatever would come next. Neither of us could know.

I reached out to touch his body's forehead.

Milo was gone.

But only for a second.

In fact, I wasn't even sure if he'd disappeared at all. Maybe it was only what I'd expected to happen. I blinked, confirming he was in fact still standing before me, even as my finger lingered on his body's cold skin.

It hadn't worked.

"Do it again," he said, his brows knit so tightly that I almost thought he was angry at me.

I had done it exactly right. My skin had met his. He was supposed to be gone.

I tapped the forehead of Milo's dead body and looked at his ghost once again. Nothing happened. I tapped his forehead. His cheek. I placed my entire palm over his face. Nothing.

"I'm sorry. I don't know why it's not working."

Milo's hurt was palpable—in fact, it was the only thing about his spirit self that still felt grounded in reality. The rest of him was faded. Almost like he wasn't in front of me, like if I focused my eyes a little to the left, he wouldn't be in my line of vision at all.

"Try again. Really try," he said, because regardless of how distant he felt, he was still far more present than he wanted to be.

"I *am* really trying." I reached out and touched his hand, thinking another part of the body might work. I didn't even say goodbye again.

"Fuck," he groaned when he was still here. He tugged at his hair. I could tell how tired he was. Tired of being here, tired of asking me to send him away.

"I'm sorry, I don't . . ." It couldn't be because he'd been embalmed; every body I'd touched except Grandma's had been. I wracked my brain for why this was happening. I hardly knew the rules of my own power, and I'd already broken the biggest one.

"So, what? I'm stuck like this forever?" The fear in Milo's eyes radiated out to me and engulfed me in what it would be like to exist eternally in a state of purgatory where only one human could talk to you. And what would happen when I died? No one would know Milo existed still, and he'd be entirely alone until the end of time.

Now I was panicking. What had I done? I'd cursed him to an endless emptiness like Grandma. I was an awful person.

"Try again!"

I'd already touched his dead body more than I'd ever wanted to. It wasn't going to help.

"I swear I'm trying. Maybe—maybe you've been awake too long?"

"What?" Milo shouted. I flinched and glanced toward the stairs, even though no one could hear. Or maybe they could. Maybe all the rules I'd thought I understood were out the window.

"I don't know! I don't know why I can't send you back. But I told you, I've never kept anyone awake for longer than thirty minutes." Except Grandma.

He shook his head and ran up the steps. I was starting to understand what it felt like to be walked out on.

I tossed the sheet back up over the face, closed the drawer, and followed Milo upstairs. I was worried he would leave again. Instead, he slumped up to my room and sat down on my rug.

"This is all my fault," I told him. I'd thought that his arrival at Richter would fix everything. I'd pretended meeting the D'Angelos would fix everything. I'd hoped getting drunk would fix everything. For a brief moment, I'd thought being friends with Eileen and Peter again would fix everything. I was starting to realize nothing was that easy. I couldn't keep alienating people, but I also couldn't invite people in as a way to ignore what was really happening.

Milo sighed. "No. Don't you remember me begging you to keep me awake? The thought of hanging on for even another second was everything. Being faced with your own death? As your own decision? Of course I wasn't going to let you." He took a deep breath, trying to steady himself. "But now, after being with my parents, it hurts too much."

I did remember Milo begging me. It sounded so similar to him begging me to send him back just now. But none of it would've happened if I hadn't woken him up in the first place.

"What do we do now?" he asked.

I honestly had no idea.

"I guess I get to go to my funeral," he said.

"We can try again after the service. Maybe it'll work then? Maybe the universe, I don't know, wants you to be there for it."

"Sure. Maybe."

We sat in silence, but the noise in my head felt like having my headphones on blast. In spite of my guilt, I was glad he was back. I felt less alone, less overwhelmed by thoughts of Peter and Eileen. But his fear and desperation were sinking into my bones, and I felt the dread of a new kind of finality.

"I met Jordan," I said. "He told me you were going to help run Lucky's."

Milo's eyes got wide. "Yep. That was the plan."

"I thought you wanted to be an illustrator."

He scoffed. "That was my *dream*. That wasn't my reality. It wouldn't have provided for my family."

"You could've gotten a scholarship to college," I told him.

"You can't live your life like that. Expecting the best will always lead to disappointment."

"But you were going to drop out? Not even get your high school diploma?"

"I was going to fail out. I wouldn't have made it past sophomore year."

"You wanted to get out of Somerton," I said, my heart sinking.

"There were more pressing issues." He still sounded frustrated, like I didn't understand. "You do what you have to do when your family is struggling."

I'd been to his house. I'd talked to him and his parents. I'd seen his drawings and stalked his Instagram and stood in the exact place where he died. I'd touched his dead body and hugged his mother. But none of that was enough to make me understand what it was like to be him. None of that taught me the complexities of Milo D'Angelo. A person isn't one thing. You can't capture someone in a page of a scrapbook—why even try when you'll always get it wrong?

An unsettling memory poked out from the recesses of my brain—the place I always tried to push the scary thoughts, even though it never had enough adhesive for them to stick. Or I didn't have enough strength to keep them there. "You mentioned hearing the rumors about me in middle school, yeah?"

Milo's lips tightened in answer.

My heart spasmed. "Did you believe it?"

"No, I thought it was middle school kids being middle school kids."

"Do you believe it all now?" I asked. Now that he was a ghost. Now that he knew what I could do.

He chuckled. "I can't believe what you can do, if that's what you're asking. I can't believe any of this is happening."

I'd let it become my normal, but if I really thought about it, I couldn't believe it either.

"You said earlier maybe the universe wants to keep me here. Do you believe in God?" Milo asked.

Deep down, that was the scariest question to try to answer. "My family doesn't go to church," I said.

"That doesn't have much to do with it."

I looked up to my stars, tracing the constellations, imagining something bigger, more than any of us. "I don't think I do. I want to. I think that would make all this a lot easier. But I don't. I can't force myself to."

Milo nodded.

"Do you?" I asked.

"Not a bit," he said, scoffing. "And you're right. That makes it a lot scarier."

I cleared my throat to keep my emotions from overpowering my words. "I've seen so many people come through Richter. Heard so many eulogies. The peace that religion offers the living when someone dies is really beautiful and powerful. I want to feel that. I want to know that my grandma is in a better place, or that people die for a reason, and some greater being is watching out for me. I want to know that when I die, I'll be safe."

"But you don't," he said.

"I can't," I corrected. "I've tried. To fake it, to pretend I believe it, but I just can't. My brain catches myself trying to trick it. Why don't you?"

Milo took a breath. "I find it hard to believe that there's an all-powerful person that allows terrible things to happen to good people, or allows people to hurt other people in horrible

185

ways, or allows their followers to completely misunderstand and misrepresent their word to the point of cruelty. At least, if there is a God who allows all that to happen, they aren't worth worshipping. If there is a God, they allowed my mom to get sick. They let us struggle to live paycheck to paycheck. They let me die. They left my parents alone. If that's part of their plan, they're just a dick. God is supposedly all-loving, but they do a pretty good job of discriminating."

The pain that wrote his words punctuated every syllable. What happened to him wasn't fair, and it definitely didn't feel like a piece of some bigger plan. It was one person making one decision that changed the lives of the D'Angelo family forever.

It was chance.

And that meant it could happen to anyone at any moment. Chance could happen to me.

"People can't stand to believe they won't exist," Milo went on. "All people have ever known is consciousness, so I think that's all they can believe started it all. I don't know what's going to happen to me after you send me back. If you even can send me back. But I know I don't want to spend eternity with a God that did this to my family. I hope I disappear. Like I'm sleeping, sans dreams."

Disappearing was the worst possible outcome for me, though. I knew that if that was what death was like, I wouldn't care since I wouldn't be alive to care. That made rational sense. But until not caring, I cared so much that it suffocated me, completely entrapping me in the thought of my consciousness irrevocably disappearing into oblivion.

I felt my pulse start to race, and I wanted to change the subject. I wanted to ask him about his mom—what had happened, why she couldn't work. But I knew it wasn't my business. The complexities of his life were his to keep and his to tell. So instead I said, "Your parents invited me to go to the Field Museum tomorrow."

"I love the Field Museum." An inkling of a smile found its way to his face.

"Why don't you come?"

"I don't think—"

"You're here, right? Something about the universe is keeping you here—God, chance, whatever it is. You should come. Enjoy your favorite place one more time. Plus, it feels kind of awkward going with your parents."

"Why did you agree to go?"

"I think because I missed you," I said, looking down to my hands.

"Oh," he said, probably trying to unravel what that meant. I was still trying to unravel it too.

"They won't know I'm there," Milo said.

"Even if they don't know, you still will be. And that's really special."

"Yeah." Milo nodded. "So long as there aren't any awesome interactive displays I'll be missing out on, I'll go."

We shared a laugh that felt like a hand reaching down into the darkness to help me up.

CHAPTER 18

Once again, I'd been so preoccupied with Milo, I'd forgotten to let Amy know I was okay. Well, I wasn't exactly okay, but last they'd heard from me, I was in the middle of a meltdown. Now I was dealing with a quieter, subtle panic following me around like a shadow.

The next day, as always, they were the one to reach out to me. Milo was taking a walk. He said he needed to clear his head, but his absence left my head swollen with worry.

Amy: How are you doing? Have you talked to Peter?

Me: I'm okay. Sorry for not texting. And no. I've been avoiding him.

Amy: Yeah I get that. Let's hang out tonight I miss you.

Me: I can't. Sorry.

My phone rang.

I picked up because I didn't have an excuse not to. They knew my phone was in my hand.

"Is there a funeral tonight?" Amy asked. They sounded like they already knew the answer.

"No," I said. I tried to keep it simple. Maybe they wouldn't ask what I was doing. I couldn't possibly explain it to them of all people. I could let my parents and Peter think I knew Milo. I could even let Milo's parents think it. But Amy knew the truth.

"You're hanging out with Eileen, aren't you?"

"No, I swear," I said.

"Uh-uh. I can hear you're hiding something from me. Stop doing that."

"I swear I'm not hanging out with Eileen."

"Then what's going on?"

"I'm going to the Field Museum, okay?"

"What, with your family?"

I gulped.

I could've said yes, and I probably could've gotten away with it. But I was so sick of lying, especially to Amy. "With Milo D'Angelo's parents."

"I have no words. Wait, yes I do. What. The. Hell?"

"It's such a long story—"

"Please, begin at any time. I can't wait to hear this."

I knew they wouldn't understand. But what was there to understand? I was tricking a dead kid's parents into thinking we'd been friends.

Except that now I did know Milo. I knew his dreams and his fears. We'd laughed and cried together. Wasn't that what friendship was?

As Amy waited, listening to my radio silence that had been getting louder by the day, I knew what friendship really was. I wasn't giving it to Amy.

It had to start with honesty. "Milo's parents think I knew him."

"Did you?" They sounded horrified, like they were suddenly unlocking this whole other life I had. There was a whole piece of me they didn't know about, but it wasn't what they were thinking.

"Not really. I'm just trying to do a good thing for them. I'm trying to help them."

189

"By lying to them?"

"I'm not really lying, I'm—"

"Wait. So you've been spending all this time pretending you were friends with the dead kid, while ignoring your actual best friend? Are you even registering how fucked up that is?"

"I know it sounds bad, but it's complicated—"

"Okay, Georgia." Amy sighed, and the phone turned the noise into a crackle that stung my ear. "I guess text me when you're ready to figure out your shit. Because I'm honestly tired of doing all the work here."

They hung up.

I tried to call them back because I wanted to explain. I wanted to at least try. They didn't pick up. I tried again, and I sent a few texts. No response. This was what they'd felt like this entire week, and I understood how much it hurt.

◊

"Are you sure you want to go?"

The question would have been more appropriate coming out of my mouth, but Milo was the one who asked it as I gathered my things into a purse. His parents were expecting me in fifteen minutes.

"Yeah." I hesitated. I wasn't sure, and I wasn't sure how to justify why I was going anyway. "I mean, you told me that your final wish was to make sure your parents are okay. I feel like this is another chance to help make them okay. One last chance. Or at least remind them there are ways to feel what okay means again. But—what do you think?"

"I think they need this," he said.

Their son was a better judge of what they needed than I was.

I didn't tell my parents where I was going, but they also didn't ask. Mom saw me walk out of Richter. She gave me a sad smile, and I left quickly, waiting for Milo to exit behind me before closing the door.

When we arrived at the D'Angelos' house, Milo's parents were waiting on the porch. Mrs. D'Angelo gave me a sad smile that wasn't too far off from Mom's.

We climbed into the car, Milo and me in the back but only one head in the rearview mirror. Milo didn't wear a seat belt and shrugged.

"I'm already dead."

I buckled mine and pulled it tight to make sure it was secure. I took a few deep breaths and told myself everything was okay.

The drive to the Field Museum was about an hour and a half. I could make it. It wasn't too long. But it left plenty of time for awkward silence.

Milo's parents were mumbling to each other, and Milo and I obviously couldn't have a conversation.

"We could play Twenty Questions," Milo said. "Seriously. You could think of something and gently nod yes or no to my question. Since you can't honor me with your conversation skills."

I nodded subtly so that if one of his parents could see in a mirror, it looked like a head twitch. But before I could come up with a person, place, or thing, Mr. D'Angelo broke the silence.

"The Field Museum was Milo's favorite," he said. "At least, we think it was." His hesitance was sad, but Milo gave an approving look to confirm his father's statement.

"Yeah, he said he loved it," I said, wanting to give them that confirmation that they did know at least one real piece of their son.

"We would go every year for his birthday. We obviously couldn't afford a lot of traveling or fun family activities, but for him, we wouldn't miss it."

"Why did he love it so much?" I asked, turning to Milo.

Milo waited for his dad to answer first.

"I think it was partly the excitement of feeling like we were splurging a little—we would also get a nice dinner after. Beyond that, though, Milo was fascinated with history, with the idea that we are made up of all that has come before, and museums are a way of honoring that. When Milo was around twelve, he said that museums are kind of like churches in that sense. It's true, isn't it? He was such a bright kid. I remember thinking, dang, he's twelve, and he's saying wiser things than me."

Mrs. D'Angelo placed a hand on her husband's shoulder as I turned to look at Milo.

He was staring straight ahead, his expression blank. He hadn't ever mentioned that he loved history.

"That, and the interactive displays," Mr. D'Angelo said. I chuckled, remembering what Milo had said earlier.

Mrs. D'Angelo started laughing, a genuine belly laugh, and Mr. D'Angelo joined too. I don't think they thought anything was funny. I think they found a moment where it felt okay to laugh, and they embraced it.

"I haven't seen them smile," Milo said, "this whole time. They always give each other these sad smiles to pretend they're okay, but they're not real. That right there, that's what I remember their smiles looking like."

Mrs. D'Angelo ran her hand along her husband's hair before resting it again on his hand.

"That," Milo said, "is the reminder. If only for a moment, it's possible."

I watched them. Her hand on his. Occasionally, they'd turn and look at each other, and Milo was right—their smiles did seem different. They seemed, even if only slightly, stronger.

"We've thought about it," Mrs. D'Angelo said, turning to me. "We wanted to ask you to say a few words tomorrow at Milo's funeral."

My breath caught, and Milo's head lifted.

"We know it's really short notice, and we understand you might have to help run everything. But it doesn't have to be long. We just want you to speak from the heart. We're worried that we won't be able to muster anything much more than blubbery sobs."

I looked to Milo for help, but obviously he couldn't do anything. I wanted Mrs. D'Angelo to take it back, because the look of earnest on her face made it impossible for me to imagine saying no.

"I do have to help run things," I said.

"But surely during the service, you'd have time to say a few words. Share a story? Something?"

"We would love it," Mr. D'Angelo emphasized.

Milo wasn't giving me any help. He looked straight ahead, leaving it up to me.

"Okay, sure," I said, hoping that was the right answer, instantly worried it wasn't.

"Thank you," Mrs. D'Angelo repeated, and my shoulders sank back into the seat. I tried to get Milo's attention to ask without words, but he was looking out the window. I had to sit with my decision, knowing it had been mine and only mine.

I spent the rest of the drive staring out at the trees blurring past. When we finally arrived at the museum, I tried not to let the D'Angelos pay for my ticket, but they were adamant.

A dinosaur skeleton greeted us with a smile, welcoming us to its home. Or maybe growling at us for invading its space. I wasn't really good at reading people—or dinosaurs. I kept glancing between the skeleton and the illustration of what it would have looked like with skin and meat and consciousness. Voices echoed around the atrium, kids tried to reach up and touch the dinosaur, and families gathered together to fit into a photo. This was a new group of people that would never be in the same place at the same time—that would never again exist in exactly the same way.

"Where would you like to go first?" Mr. D'Angelo asked, looking at the pamphlet as we wandered toward the middle of the atrium.

I remembered their laughter and their gentle smiles in the car. It was a moment of peace, and they'd found it together. I remembered that our pain was different, and healing from theirs wasn't the same as healing from mine.

"I thought maybe I'd let you explore," I said. "We could meet up later."

"No, Georgia, we brought you, we'd love to explore with you," Mr. D'Angelo said.

"I know. And thank you. Um. But I want you two to have this time. I can meet you back here at five."

Mrs. D'Angelo looked disappointed, but she nodded and said, "Okay." We began exploring in opposite directions. I think she had learned to stop fighting me, and I think she knew I was right. At the core, I was an interloper.

Milo decided to stay with me. Being alone with his parents was too painful.

"Do you think you're the best one to give my eulogy?" he asked right away. "Since you didn't know me?"

I bit my lip. "I know you now, don't I?"

"Do you?" he asked.

I couldn't read his tone. Was he annoyed at me? Angry? I hoped he was just joking, but I felt a seriousness in the question.

I decided to change the subject. "What's your favorite part of this place?" I asked.

"It's this way." He didn't even need a map. He started speed-walking. No one could see him to yell at him, but I would get in trouble if I walked at that pace.

"Slow down!" I yelled. No one batted an eye. It felt good to be able to talk to him without raising concern.

Milo led me to a taxidermy exhibit.

"This is what happens when a zoo turns to history," he said. We stood in a darkened room full of glass cases displaying all types of animals. There were smaller dioramas full of birds, and larger ones with mammals climbing makeshift cliffs. Images of the sky were plastered against the back walls of the displays, or fake snow covered the ground, all to make it look more authentic. But no matter where you turned, there was a preserved body striking a pose.

The sight of the animals didn't faze me. I was used to that stiffness, those empty stares. I leaned over the rail of one of the larger displays, with lions and bears climbing a mountain, and birds hanging from the ceiling, stuck in midflight. That's how so many things die—midflight.

My focus shifted from the birds inside the case to my reflection on the glass. It felt like the first time I had really looked at myself in so long. Although my image wasn't perfectly clear,

I saw how tired I looked. And how perfectly my face rested between the birds and the top of the mountain.

"I always loved this room," Milo said, coming up beside me. He had no reflection. "I loved getting to see all the animals, especially the extinct ones. I thought it was so cool they get to be forever. I always imagined they were still in there, though. That after the museum closed it was like *Toy Story* or *Night at the Museum*, and they partied until they had to go back to their places for work the next day. I loved imagining that. Except that's not how it is at all."

Not at all.

"It's different now," he said. "Knowing that's happening to my body makes it different."

When I was in elementary school, kids called Dad a human taxidermist. I hated when they did because that dehumanized his work, made it sound like a joke. It wasn't until Dad taught me how to embalm a body, until I saw him prod and poke a person like they were meat, until I learned their blood drained into the sewer and was nothing more than waste that I thought maybe those kids were right.

"That's life, though," he said. "We're just meat in the end." I turned to him, afraid he could read my mind. "We think we're more than meat. We aren't. Nothing is. We're just narcissists."

I couldn't tell if it was pessimism or realism. I couldn't tell if the "we" meant everyone, or just the two very scared teenagers standing in front of a taxidermy exhibit talking about death.

"I have one other thing I want to show you," he said. The next thing I knew we were heading to the Egypt exhibit and my focus shifted to not losing him in the crowd. It was darker than the taxidermy room, and I started to feel more claustrophobic as the walls grew taller around me. We didn't stop to look at any of the descriptions or displays. Milo took me right to a glass case in the center of the room with a fragment of an ancient scroll. We leaned over the case together.

"Some hieroglyphics?" I asked, confused as to why he thought I'd want to see it.

He pointed to the description. It was a scene from *The Book of the Dead*.

"I didn't realize the Field Museum had this," I said.

"It's a copy of a scene," he said. "I think the original's mostly at the British Museum, or it travels or something. That's not the point. Do you know what the book is?"

"We learned about it in school," I said. "Didn't pharaohs get buried with it to go to the afterlife?"

"Yeah. They wrote spells to give to the dead so that they could live forever."

"Okay," I said. "Nice. So, why did you want to show me this?"

Milo shrugged and turned away from the case. "Never mind, Georgia."

"Whoa, wait, what?" Two seconds ago, Milo had been eager to bring me here, but now he was ready to move on. I didn't get it. "You said you wanted to show me this. Why?"

Milo shrugged. "Never mind. Want to go look at mummies?"

"Milo!" But he was already on his way down the dark hallway that led to the rest of the exhibit. I took another look at the page. I couldn't make sense of the hieroglyphics, obviously, so I couldn't figure out what Milo had been getting at. I decided he was just being weird, and the dark was starting to creep me out, so I followed him.

We spent the rest of the afternoon wandering the museum. We saw mummies, we stepped inside an earth lodge, and we saw a ridiculous number of artifacts that were thousands of years old. With each exhibit, I started to realize how right Milo was. People are just meat. There were no human beings preserved here (okay, besides the mummies). Instead, the museum was populated with what people made. Because while consciousness fades, we can still leave things behind. Ideas, artifacts, stories.

The whole time, I contemplated what I'd say at his funeral tomorrow.

We met up with Milo's parents at the end of the day. They asked me what I'd seen, and it felt like the entire museum. They said they'd taken it slow, stopping by some of the spots Milo loved, but we'd never overlapped.

"We could get dinner," Mr. D'Angelo suggested.

I bit my lip, trying to imagine having to make conversation through a whole meal, wanting to keep myself out of their space. "It's getting late," I said. "My parents will probably want me home." I felt bad for ruining their tradition.

Mrs. D'Angelo said she completely understood, so we went to the car to head back to Somerton. The sun had already set, and the city lights waved goodbye. When we finally made it to the country roads that would take us the rest of the way home, I felt myself settle into my seat. We all knew what tomorrow morning meant, but none of us wanted to talk about it. I'd wake up and set up the chairs, put on a pair of Mary Janes, grab a black dress, and hand out pamphlets as people walked in. I'd watch person after person enter and sit down. No matter how well they knew Milo, they would be there to honor his memory. I'd get up in front of everyone and say . . . something. I only had a few more hours to figure it out.

Just then, the car lurched as Mr. D'Angelo yelled. I instinctively gripped the seat, trying to steady myself. The car swerved, then skidded to a halt, throwing all of us forward. My face almost slammed against the seat in front of me, and my heart was beating as powerfully as the collision. Time stopped for a moment. Maybe my ears were ringing, but I was definitely alive. I made sure to check that several times.

"Everyone okay?" Mr. D'Angelo asked when the car settled.

"Fine," Mrs. D'Angelo said.

"I'm okay," I said, confirming one more time that my heart still beat.

"Me too," Milo said, looking as if he hadn't moved an inch.

"There was a deer. I'm sorry—this car can barely make it to Chicago, let alone survive hitting a deer. I panicked and swerved. I'm sorry."

The airbags hadn't even deployed. I wasn't sure if that was because the impact wasn't that bad or because the car wasn't that safe. I touched my face and my legs to ensure everything was in one piece. I kept my hand on my heart to feel it, convinced it would stop at any second. Mr. and Mrs. D'Angelo hugged.

I looked out the window into the darkness, realizing we were half in a shallow ditch. Nothing had flipped. Nothing was smoking or broken.

This was the closest I had ever come to being in a car accident. Or maybe this was my first car accident.

"I'm going to get out and make sure everything is okay. See if the deer is okay."

As Mr. D'Angelo exited the car, I realized that no life had flashed before my eyes. All I'd felt in that moment was pure terror, pure instinct to hang on and make it through.

"Everything's fine," he said, returning to the car. Everything was fine. I didn't even feel desperate to get out of the car and walk the rest of the way home. I wasn't afraid to be there. Instead, I wanted to get home even faster.

When we finally reached the D'Angelos' house, I got out of the car and stepped into fresh air. I made sure to savor that first breath in my lungs. For the first time in a while, I was thankful I was alive instead of thinking about the moment I'd die.

Something about that feeling made the words come out.

"I have to tell you something," I said to the D'Angelos as they were heading toward their front steps. Milo was standing off to the side, watching.

"Yes?" Mrs. D'Angelo asked, clutching her bag tightly again.

"I haven't been entirely honest."

Mrs. D'Angelo tilted her head, her eyes wide. I saw Milo in them. Mr. D'Angelo waited.

"Milo and I . . . knew each other. But I didn't know him the way you think I did. The way I've let you believe I did."

Neither of them moved. The thudding of my heart made the air vibrate between us. I was unsteady. I knew I couldn't confess completely, because I still wasn't sure what was even true at this point, but I knew I'd let these interactions go beyond what was fair.

"I thought I was his closest friend. I thought it was my job to make sure you were okay. I didn't lie when I said we talked about his art. We talked about a lot of things, but I wasn't the person closest to him when he was alive, and I'm sorry for letting you think that."

Understandably, they both looked confused.

"You . . . knew him but you didn't?" Mrs. D'Angelo asked.

"I guess that is what I'm saying."

Mrs. D'Angelo shook her head. She didn't look mad or even upset at all. She looked like her son's funeral was tomorrow and she didn't have the capacity to hold anything else right now. She turned without another word and headed into the house, dropping the weight I'd put on her.

Mr. D'Angelo stayed.

"I'm sorry," I said, ready to feel his wrath. Ready for him to finally scream at me, tell me to go home and leave them alone and not to dare show my face at his son's funeral. But instead, he scratched his beard and gave me a sad smile.

"We know Milo didn't have a lot of friends," he said. "No matter how close you and he really were, I think he was still very lucky to know you."

I turned to look at Milo, remembering he was here, watching all of this. I could hardly land my focus on him now because of how distant he looked. He'd barely spoken during the ride home, almost like he hadn't been there at all. Like after the museum, he was fading even more. His focus wasn't landing on anything either—his eyes were trailing the grass, then looking up to the stars. I wasn't sure if he was even listening.

"I won't speak tomorrow," I said.

"I would still like you to."

It felt like he hadn't understood what I was saying. I was confessing this strange, wrong truth to him, and it was like nothing had changed.

"But what about Mrs. D'Angelo?"

"I think she'll feel the same as I do. Look, Georgia, I get that you weren't Milo's best friend in the entire world," he said. "But you know a piece of him we didn't get to see. No matter how small you think that piece is, it's still special to us, and it hurts that we never knew it." His expression changed to the same exhaustion I'd seen on Mrs. D'Angelo. He was ready to release the weight of me too. "We'll see you tomorrow."

I watched him go into the house without a backward glance.

"Was that okay? Was that right?" I asked Milo.

"All the living do is lie to each other about death to make them feel better anyway," he said. His use of *them* struck me. Of course I knew he was dead, but that word intensified the contrast between his ghostliness and my living, breathing self.

"Ready to head back to Richter?" he asked.

"You can head back. I have to go do something," I said.

He didn't ask any questions. He started walking in a straight line toward Richter, toward his irreversible fate.

If there was anything I could do to make things right, it would start with this.

I ran toward the town square until I reached the door to Lucky's. It was locked. I pounded on the glass, knocking the bells against the frame to create a clatter of unpleasant sounds.

Jordan was standing behind the counter. "We're closed!" he yelled without looking up when I pounded on the door harder.

"Please!" I shouted at him, rattling the unsteady metal handles.

"Georgia Richter?" He squinted through the glass and must've seen my desperation. He finally trudged over to open the door. "You didn't stick around for your meal yesterday."

"I know," I said. "I'm sorry if I was rude. But I have to tell you something now."

"What?" He sounded concerned, a fair reaction to a heavily breathing teenager you just met coming to pound on your business door past closing time.

"You have to come to the funeral tomorrow."

"Georgia, I don't think—"

"You have to." I said it as sternly as I could.

"It's not as simple as—"

"Put all that aside. Milo would have wanted you there."

"I'll think about it," he said.

"You'll regret it if you don't," was all I said before turning back into the night to run my next errand.

◊

Mrs. Chen opened her front door, frightened by my urgent knocking.

"Is Amy here?"

"They're upstairs. What is wrong?" she asked, leading me in. I insisted I was fine, though I don't think she believed me. If anything, I was finally feeling a moment of clarity.

I ran up the steps and found Amy sitting cross-legged on their bed. They looked like they were sketching some new design, but I was more preoccupied with the way they locked eyes on me, removed their headphones, and flared their nostrils.

"I'm sorry," I said. "I need to use your printer and your Photoshop."

"Whoa, whoa, whoa. We have to talk first." Amy pointed to the bed. "Sit, Richter."

I took a seat on the edge of the bed while they leaned toward me. They pressed their fingers into a diamond and brought them to rest at their mouth.

"I was trying to explain and you hung up on me," I said, trying to rush it all out hoping to move past this conversation quickly.

203

"Unbelievable," they scoffed. And then they took a shuddery breath. "We're not talking about whatever your thing is with Milo's family right now. We're talking about the fact that you keep ignoring me. I have repeatedly communicated to you that I need you to talk to me, to be there for me, and every time you say you'll be there again, you're gone five seconds later because you need to wallow or whatever. You never respond to my texts anymore, you're hardly present when you're with me—which isn't often. And you always need something from me. I want to be there for you. I honestly do. But I have been there for you through everything, and it really feels like you can never be there for me. It's not even that I need support or anything. I literally just want you to pay attention to me, like at all. Then the second Eileen comes crawling back, you're ready to hop right into reconciling with her. It's not fair, Georgia. So that's what we're going to talk about right now." Amy said it sternly but calmly, and every word was filled with hurt, emanating from a wound I'd made.

I didn't speak right away. I sat with their words and my mistakes, and I didn't try and explain or justify. They were right. It was the cycle of Georgia Richter. It was me not recognizing what was right in front of me, hiding in that place where no one could find me, and not appreciating the person who was always there.

Amy patiently waited while I formed a response. And that was just it. Amy was patient. Even after they'd expressed a pain from deep inside themself, after I'd hurt them repeatedly and deserved to be screamed at, they spoke calmly. They gave me time. They treated me with a kindness I hadn't earned.

"*I'm sorry* isn't even close to enough," I finally said, feeling at a loss for words.

"It's not," Amy said. "Because you've apologized before. I want to see action, you know? You keep saying you're sorry, and I believe you are. But things don't change until they actually change."

"You're right, Amy. And I don't want to make excuses for myself."

"Good. Then don't."

I looked at them, seeing a distance between us that existed even when we held hands or hugged or cuddled. I saw the damage I'd caused. But most of all, I saw that line of energy that always connected us through everything.

"I appreciate you," I told them.

Amy's shoulders dropped, a tenseness finally loosening.

"I wouldn't be where I am without you. You have supported me in everything I do. You're my safety net. And you're my balancing pole and you're the tightrope and you're the audience cheering me on and I'm overusing this metaphor but you know what I mean."

Amy chuckled and shook their head. They were still patient.

"I appreciate you," I repeated because it felt like the most important thing I could say. "I'm sorry for not telling you that enough. For not recognizing what you do for me and only being there when it's convenient for me. I know you want to see change. You will see it. I promise."

"Thank you."

"And I don't value Eileen more than you. I didn't mean for it to seem like I was trying to fix things with her before I fixed things with you. It's not even close to true."

They didn't say anything.

"Can I hug you?" I asked them, needing it.

"Of course. You don't have to ask, G."

"But I didn't know if you didn't want me to or—"

Before I could finish, they wrapped their arms around me. We held on with a tightness that said we needed each other. I could feel the energy between us strengthening as we pulled closer. But there was still that twinge inside me I couldn't make go away, the reason I'd been distant in the first place. I begged it to leave, just for now, to let me have this time with my best friend. But it didn't.

"So, what exactly happened with Peter?" they asked when we released each other.

I told them what Eileen said and about yelling at Peter and going to Grandma's grave but left out the part about Milo.

"Why wouldn't Eileen tell us it was Peter who started everything?" Amy asked.

"She said we were going to hate them both anyway and finding out it was him would've made everything worse. Plus, we really never tried to listen to them."

"They didn't try that hard to explain."

"I think we all sort of gave up on each other."

Each of us could have done better. But Eileen was trying now, so the least I could do was try too, right? Except I needed to try with Amy first.

"So, are you friends with Eileen again?" Amy asked hesitantly.

"I don't know where we stand. I mean, just because Peter started it doesn't mean she wasn't wrong for spreading it." I sighed. "I don't know. It was seventh grade."

Amy rested their cheek on their hand and nodded.

"You're my priority," I said. "You come first right now." Almost. There was still a haze, and although I was starting to break free of it, I needed to do one more thing.

"Okay," Amy said. "I believe you. Now why are you in such desperate need of my Photoshop skills?"

"It has to do with Milo," I said, wanting to tread lightly on that subject.

"Ah, yeah. I also am going to need a better explanation for that," they said.

"I knew Milo a little," I said. "We had classes and stuff. And when he showed up at Richter, I felt like it was my responsibility to make sure his parents were okay because, well, Milo didn't have any real friends. And I let them think I was who they wanted me to be more than who I am."

"That makes no sense," Amy said.

I wanted to explain why the situation was even more complicated, but I wasn't ready to drop the ghost bombshell. "I'm going to make it up to them."

"With Photoshop?"

I explained my idea.

"Okay. Fine. I'll help."

After gathering everything I needed, we agreed to finish our conversation tomorrow when my brain would be less clouded from clarity. When I could remove the final block between us.

Back at Richter, I assumed I'd find Milo upstairs in my room. My door was open, and when I stepped in expecting to see him, I instead found Mom sitting on my bed.

"What is this?" Mom asked, not looking up. I froze, staring at the pink binder in her hands, watching as she turned another page.

CHAPTER 19

"Why are you in my room?"

Mom met my eyes, still clutching my scrapbook. "I'm sorry. I've been really worried about you. You left and haven't been responding to my texts."

"That doesn't mean you can go through my stuff!" I ripped the scrapbook from her hands and tossed it onto my desk. After Peter, this was another betrayal of trust.

"I shouldn't have," she said, lowering her head.

"Yeah," I shot back and folded my arms across my chest.

"I wasn't digging through your things. It was sitting open on your bed. I thought it was an art project, and I was curious . . ."

That didn't make any sense since I kept it tucked away under my bed. There was no way it could have been sitting out. She had the audacity to lie to my face.

"G, what is that?"

"None of your business!" I shouted.

Mom hardly reacted. "Practically every person who has come through here in the past three years is in that book. Their photos, their obituaries, little details. Your grandma—"

"Stop!" It was mortifying to hear her say it out loud.

"Why do you keep that stuff?"

208

"I don't know," I said. All I wanted was for her leave and for this moment to be over. My chest started heaving. It felt like the start of another panic attack, but even if I tried to shut it away, tell the thoughts *not now*, they wouldn't listen. I wracked my brain, trying to remember if I'd ever written about talking to the ghosts in there, but I never had.

"Is this about Milo?" Mom asked.

"No," I said. "Not entirely."

"Your grandma. Is it about her?"

"No." I clenched my jaw, angry at her for bringing Grandma into this.

"Then what is it about?"

"Everything!" It slipped out, my whole body tensing when it did. "All of this! Living here in this suffocating house!" Saying it was like releasing a monster that had been caged in my brain. And then I decided to say it, the heart of the monster. "Living here terrifies me."

Mom nodded like it suddenly all made sense, but there was no way it could. I took a seat next to her. I'd thought it was just Grandma, that I was learning to grieve for the first time. Then Oscar and the others . . . It all started to build and they all started to haunt me. It was about all of them, about everyone who came through Richter, about every celebrity death I read about online, about the constant fear that it could be me and the constant reminder that it inevitably *would* be me. There was no escaping it.

I burst into tears and buried my face in Mom's shoulder. I wasn't even trying to be quiet. Mom wrapped me in her arms and pulled me close. It reminded me of when Milo's mom had hugged me, but this hug didn't feel wrong. It felt safe. I finally felt safe.

"I know Grandma's death was hard," she said. "I didn't realize it turned into this. I'm so sorry. We tried to help teach you to grieve—"

"You tried to help?" I was staring angrily at her through my tears, but I wanted to laugh. "Mom, Dad tried to *help* by showing me how to embalm a body. I was grieving my dead grandma, and Dad told me all about how he cut her open and sucked the blood from her and stuck her full of chemicals. He was totally fine with doing that to his own mother. That was supposed to help me?"

"No." Mom shook her head. "No, Georgia. You don't understand. Your grandmother wanted to be embalmed and have her funeral at Richter because she didn't trust anyone else to do it. Your father was fulfilling her final wish, sweetie. But doing it practically killed him. When his mom died, he was so upset he almost died with her."

That didn't make any sense because Dad had barely grieved. He didn't even cry at her funeral.

"He didn't want to show weakness in front of the whole town. He has some issues trying to keep up this strong appearance to everyone around him. To be the tough one. People grieve in different ways, and his way was to dig himself further into Richter. That doesn't mean it was easy for him."

"But he always makes jokes about dead people like it *is* easy. Like it means nothing."

"God, I know. Those jokes get old. But that's his way of handling tough situations. You think it's easy for your dad to see dead body after dead body, grieving families, corpses in horrific shape, to see his friends and family on that embalming table, or young children? He makes jokes because he has to stay strong for clients, and for you. Those jokes are how he copes, how he makes one of the hardest jobs something a little lighter. Some directors develop addictions to alcohol or drugs because of how hard it can be, so we can be thankful that hasn't happened with him. He tried to help you cope in the same way he does, but that clearly didn't work for you. I'm sorry it just made it worse."

He'd made it seem like it meant nothing to handle corpses. I'd resented him every day for showing me what he did to Oscar, to Grandma. But Mom's words shined an entirely new light. Of course he hurt when Grandma died. He just didn't show us.

"So why does he do it? If it's so hard?" I asked, trying to make sense of it.

"See, your grandfather put everything he had into this funeral home. So much so that he didn't have time for your dad and his brother. Michael resented this place so much that he eventually left, cut everyone out. But your father's reaction was to prove that he could do it. That he was worthy of this place and of your grandfather. And he does this work because it's one of the most rewarding things in the world. To help grieving families, to offer support and comfort in the wake of the most terrible situation a family can face. This business isn't about the dead, Georgia."

I pictured Mom in client meetings, talking with people like Mrs. D'Angelo. She always put their comfort first, and not just in an obligatory customer-service way. She genuinely cared about helping them through. I remembered what it felt like the first time I sat down with Milo's parents. I'd been at such a loss, but Mom dealt with that kind of situation all the time, and she was good at it.

"Sweetheart, why didn't you tell me this was bothering you?"

I leaned away from her and tried to catch my breath. "How can I tell you?" It came out through hiccups. "This is our entire life, we live here, and this is your and Dad's job and it's my job and Peter loves it and I'm expected to run Richter someday with him. How could I tell you I'm scared and I hate it and I don't want to?"

Mom shook her head. She ran a hand over her forehead like she was pressing her thoughts into place. "You don't have to run Richter," she said. She laughed. "Not one bit."

"But you and Dad always talk about when Peter and I take over . . ."

"We shouldn't talk like that. Your dad went the complete opposite direction of how his father treated him about this place. He wanted so badly for you to believe you can do it that he forgot the key piece of it all: only if you want to. You have no obligation to take over this business."

"But you and Dad want us to, and Peter wants to. And now Peter has this perfect girlfriend and I never want that and I'm nothing like you want me to be and I never will be and I'm a disappointment to you." I started sobbing again.

"No." Mom shook her head. "No. Don't even say that."

I stood from the bed and started pacing, my shoulders heaving with every staggered breath. I couldn't handle that it was all tumbling out. Mom stood with me and grabbed my shoulders to steady me, to calm me down, but I couldn't catch my breath.

"You are not a disappointment at all, Georgia. You do not have to run Richter. You never have to get married or have a partner if you don't want. I'm so sorry I've made you feel that pressure, but no, stop, look at me. I want you to live the life that is true to you. Your uncle didn't want to run this place. Hell, I didn't want to run this goddamn place." Mom laughed, throwing her arms out. It felt rebellious of her to refer to Richter that way.

I wiped my nose on my sleeve and laughed shakily. "What do you mean?"

"You think I grew up dreaming of marrying a mortician? Yeah, every little girl's dream. I've known your father since we were in fourth grade, but we fell in love in high school, and he and Richter Funeral Home were kind of a package deal. I made sacrifices, came back to Somerton after college, and here we are."

I hadn't known that. "Was it worth it?"

"Honestly, it was. I've grown to love this place. It's home. Plus, I have you and your brother, don't I?"

I smiled and sniffled. She brought me into another hug. We rocked back and forth for a few minutes.

"I'm sorry that we work you so hard here. We have pressured you into this. And your friend died, and we've been so focused on work that we haven't been there for you. I'm so sorry."

"It's okay. But Mom . . ." I pulled away from her. "I do think I need a break from funerals for a while."

Mom nodded. "Okay."

I felt another pressure release, wave goodbye, and exit out my window, even if only for a bit. I'd take any amount of relief.

"But I guess my question is, what do you want?" Mom added. "If you don't know, that's okay. I just feel like I don't know you. I don't know what you want or need, and I want to know." Our faces were still red and wet, but her tone was more conversational now.

I breathed out, hoping the ghosts would leave with my breath. Except they didn't, and that was exactly it. I held so tightly to those ghosts. I wanted to fight for their lives. I wanted to keep them around because they all deserved more time. But I always met them too late.

"Maybe I want to be a nurse." It felt right to say it, even though the idea was as new to me as it was to Mom. If I couldn't fight for lives after death, then maybe I could before.

"I love that," Mom said, running her hand over my hair.

"I do care about Richter," I said. "I care about what you do. I just don't want to do this part of the process. I know you said it's about the living, not the dead. But I think I want to work with people, try to help them heal, help them feel safe when they're sick, and maybe make it less scary for them when they have to die."

"That's why I'm not disappointed in you, Georgia," Mom said, smiling. "That right there is why I'm so proud of you. How much you care about people. You always have, since you were little."

I bit my lip, feeling like that wasn't true at all, especially considering what had happened with Amy. She had to say that because she was my mom. Maybe she was right, though; maybe I'd see it when I wasn't shaded by my spirals and fears.

"You know what we are going to do this weekend?" Mom got a bright smile on her face. "Research nursing schools. See what we need to do to get you into a good one."

"Mom, I'm a sophomore." I rolled my eyes.

"It's never too early to dream," she said.

"I don't even know yet." I took a deep breath to wash away all the tension and gave her one more hug. Her hugs were contagious. Once I started getting them, I didn't want to stop. "I'm glad we got to talk."

"Me too." Mom smiled. "I'm sorry for looking at the binder. I didn't snoop through your stuff to find it. It really was open on the bed." This time I believed her, but I still didn't know how it could have been left out. I hadn't touched it in a week.

"And you definitely don't have to work Milo's funeral tomorrow. You should be able to attend it."

"Thanks. And also, there's something I'd like to do for Milo . . ." I explained my plan, and she was on board.

Then she said, "I'll let you rest." I looked over at my clock and realized it was almost midnight. "I love you."

"I love you too."

"Oh, and G." She paused at the door frame. "You get to decide what kind of a relationship you have with your brother. That's not my place. I just want you to consider that it happened in seventh grade. Think about how much things have changed since then."

When Mom left, I pondered her words. I couldn't push past the anger I felt toward Peter. But instead of wallowing in that feeling, I decided to turn it into something productive. I started looking up nursing schools. There were amazing programs all over the country, most of them way out of our price range and all of them extremely competitive, but at least they were far from Somerton. I knew I would have to make sure my grades were perfect and my SAT scores the next year were top-notch. I started a list of things to do, of ways I could start studying and practicing now.

"Hey."

Milo was sitting on my bed behind me.

"Hey!" I said, closing my laptop. "Where were you?"

"Just waiting."

"What does that mean?"

"What are you going to say for my eulogy?" he asked.

"I thought it could be a surprise," I said.

I looked at him, seeing that detachment I'd noticed before. The flicker of his person without a glitch in his existence. He was there, but I could see how he wasn't there at all.

"I'm going to walk around some more," he said.

I didn't even see him leave. He was just gone. When I got up and opened my door, he was walking toward the stairwell leading down to Richter. I blinked to make sure it was real, and I still saw him.

Peter sat at the dining room table with a direct view of me standing in my doorway. He smiled at me softly, an invitation or apology, but after talking with Mom, I didn't have the energy to talk to him. So I went back in my room and stayed up late into the night.

I wrote Milo's eulogy, the words appearing on the page because they were mine. I hoped they were close to what Milo would say. When I finished, I folded the paper and let myself believe this was good enough.

Getting the words out created space inside me. For me. So I filled it by researching schools, watching YouTube videos of nursing students answering frequently asked questions and day-in-the-life vlogs. My searches and my new-tab clicks weren't fueled by anxiety like they so often were but instead by warmth and purpose.

CHAPTER 20

Waking up the morning of Milo's funeral felt like having another hangover. As soon as I caught sight of the ceiling stars, I wanted to go back to sleep and forget everything. Sleep at night felt like practice for death, but sometimes during the day it felt like freedom. I probably would have rolled over and closed my eyes again, except I hadn't woken myself up.

"Come on!" Milo leaned over my bed. "Get up. It's the big day. Lots to do. People to see. Places to go. Don't make me start singing. That might kill you too."

"Ugh," I said, throwing a pillow over my head.

"I'm excited."

"No you're not." I pulled the pillow down to shoot him a look. "Two days ago you were begging me to send you back."

Milo shrugged as if that moment meant nothing to him now. "I'm looking forward to your eulogy. I mean, my eulogy. Written by you."

"I really hope it does you justice." I looked over to the folder on my desk to make sure it was still there. It was, right next to where I'd thrown my scrapbook.

It was only 8:00 a.m., but the service was scheduled to start at noon with the viewing an hour before.

"I should probably go down and help set up," I said.

"Are you working my funeral?"

"No, Mom said I didn't have to. But there's a lot to set up since this funeral is going to be bigger than usual. I thought I should help with that part at least."

"Is that what you're wearing?" Milo asked, seeing the black dress draped across my chair. "I like it."

"It has pockets, so it's my favorite."

Milo placed a shaky hand over his heart. "Pockets! Well, only dresses with pockets are worthy of my funeral."

It hit me that I didn't know what would happen to him after today. I'd have one more chance to send him back after the service. What if that didn't work? Would he haunt Richter forever? Would I have cursed him to that life?

"I think I'll take a walk," he said. I could tell he hadn't actually meant it when he said he was excited. His hands gave it away. At this point, taking a walk was probably the most exciting thing he could do as a ghost.

Milo left without another word. I didn't stop him. He needed to be alone. I slipped on a pair of jeans and a sweater to go downstairs.

Mom was in the front room with her folder that held all the lists and papers she needed for today to run smoothly. A florist was hauling bouquets of white roses through to the front room. No fake ones from Richter's storage closet this time. Milo got real flowers.

Mom looked up at me over her glasses and smiled. "You okay?"

I nodded and looked around. "Where are Dad and Peter?" I asked her, wanting to avoid wherever Peter was and go wherever Dad was.

"Pete's in the chapel setting up the extra chairs, and your dad . . ." Mom trailed off, so I knew what that meant.

It was finally Milo's turn to be pulled from the freezer, dolled up, and placed in a casket, ready for his final resting place. Frustration crept up my spine, but I stopped it by reminding myself what Mom told me the previous night. Dad did what he did because he cared.

I decided not to go to the embalming room.

"Why don't you go help Peter?" Mom suggested, adjusting her folder like she had to cross her children's reconciliation off one of her lists.

"I don't want to talk to him."

"He really wants to talk to you."

I looked at the ceiling to avoid her eyes.

"Think about how good it felt to talk with me last night."

I didn't move from my spot.

"I'm not going to force you to," Mom continued, "but I think you'll regret it if you don't."

I didn't respond, just fidgeted in my skin for a few moments, debating the pros and cons. I could swallow my own pride and recognize that what happened was years ago and he was sorry and we could work on it, or I could let this grudge simmer inside me, boiling into an endless hatred. I knew what would satisfy the vindictive bit of me, but I didn't let that part win.

I walked down the hall toward the chapel, over the red stale carpet that I'd first learned to walk on. The hallway felt longer than usual, like maybe if I kept walking, I'd never reach the end. Richter would go on forever and I'd never find another door to escape. I'd be trapped, and the inevitable oblivion would consume me right here on these red fibers. Except I did come to the end of the hall, and I did reach Peter, and there was an end to Richter's walls.

Peter was unfolding the white resin chairs and setting them up in rows behind the benches, which placed him right in front of me when I walked through the doors. They hadn't broken from my slam, but I did see a crack along one of the glass panes. It felt good to leave a mark on Richter like that.

I walked over to a stack of chairs on the wall and grabbed as many as I could muster. I unfolded one and slammed it down in the row. Peter jumped.

"I want to talk," I said.

"Good, because I do too."

"Then you can start. I want to hear you explain." I folded my arms over my chest, abandoning the chairs.

"Fair enough," Peter agreed. "I'm so sorry for what I did. It was after Grandma died, obviously, and it was after you stopped hanging out with me and Eileen. You got really close with Amy and started to completely ignore us. And I know you were upset and hurt, I recognized that then and I understand it now, but when I was thirteen, your distance hurt like hell. You were my best friend. We grew up doing everything together and then suddenly you didn't care about me anymore. I was angry. I was so so angry and more hurt and even more immature. I wanted to get back at you."

"Well, you really did."

"I know. I can't believe I did it. I wish I could take it back."

"You can't."

"At least no one remembers anymore. The story died down really quickly."

"That doesn't change that you did it."

"I know it doesn't. I'm sorry that I made everyone think that stuff about you."

I threw my arms out to my side. "I don't even care about what the rumor said, Pete."

Peter paused. "Then why are you still mad?"

"I care that you so easily turned my grief into a joke. You thought so little of it that you figured it would make a funny story for a week and then *die down*."

Peter dropped his head. I could feel his shame radiating through the chapel.

"And you let Eileen take the blame. That was really awful of you."

Peter gulped. "Yeah. I thought that if you found out it was me, I'd lose you entirely. Which I did anyway, I guess. But that was never what I wanted. I guess I'd thought hurting you like you'd hurt me would make us even somehow, and then we could go back to normal. When the whole thing blew up and I saw how upset you were, I got scared."

"That's not an excuse. It was cruel to do to Eileen."

"You're right. We've talked about it. She knows I regret it."

I didn't know how to feel. Everything he was saying should have made me angrier at him, but in the way he wrung his hands and his shoulders drooped with remorse, I could still see my twin.

"But I'm glad you had Amy still," Peter said. "They are a good friend. I'm glad you chose someone who really cares about you and would never hurt you like I did."

"Chose them?"

"Well, yeah. I mean, you completely chose Amy over us. Even before the rumor stuff."

"No." I shook my head, trying to recall what was going through the head of thirteen-year-old Georgia. Amy's grandma had died too. They knew what I was going through. Amy and I were feeling different from everyone else. Amy's trajectory lined up with mine.

"You wouldn't be sad with me," I said, only barely audible.

Peter leaned in to hear it better when I said it again.

"You and Eileen wouldn't be sad with me. You always wanted to cheer me up and play games and try to help me ignore my sadness and forget about Grandma. I didn't want that. Amy would be sad with me."

"You wanted someone to wallow with?"

I hated that word, and I hated how people used it against me. Peter said it like it was ridiculous.

"It wasn't that I wanted it. I felt like that was the only thing I could do. It felt unfair to have fun without Grandma." I couldn't help but fall into the darkness, this terror deep inside me. I didn't feel like I could ever be happy, and I resented anyone who could. "Eileen didn't get that, and neither did you because Grandma's death was easy for you."

"Easy?" Peter shook his head. "No. I mean, I wasn't nearly as close with Grandma as you were, but it wasn't easy, G."

"But you also didn't care about Oscar or Jonathan or Betty."

"Who?"

"Exactly. You love Richter. You love embalming bodies and you find it fascinating and you want to run the place one day."

"You're angry at me for wanting to take over the family business? I don't understand."

"No." I laughed because I was frustrated at how hard it was to articulate everything going on in my head. "I'm jealous that you're not terrified of death." I felt the sting of tears, but I wanted to get through one conversation without crying.

"Oh," was all he said.

We both got quiet for a moment, letting the words hang between us.

"I didn't know you were afraid of death," Peter added finally.

"I'm terrified. It's debilitating. I think about it every night and every day, and living here makes it worse. My whole life has been surrounded by death and revolves around death. It literally consumes me, it keeps me from wanting to fall asleep or get in a car and now, with what happened to Milo, walk across the street. And I don't know what will happen to me after I die, and I think about that way too much. I want there to be an afterlife because the thought of not existing is horrifying, and then I think about existing forever and I'm horrified even more because, god, what could I even do with eternity? And then I think everything is okay because I am alive right now and that's good, but someday inevitably I'll have to face it and it could happen at literally any moment."

My breathing got heavy as one of the spirals imprisoned in my brain came coiling out of my mouth. But it felt good for it to live outside me for once.

"Okay, okay." Peter reached out and placed his hand on my shoulder, the only gesture people knew to give a person about to have a panic attack. "Have you told Mom or Dad this?"

"I kind of told Mom last night," I said, but that wasn't really true. So much of the iceberg was still hidden from her. "I just don't get why it doesn't scare you too. Why do you want to live and work here forever?"

"I think it's cool," he said, looking worried that it would only make me feel worse. "I guess I'm not really scared to die. It just feels like part of the process. Yeah, it's weird to think about my body being in someone else's hands without my consciousness and all, but knowing there are people like Dad in the business makes me feel a lot safer."

If only I could see it that way.

"It's not like I'm looking forward to dying, I'm just not scared of it, if that makes sense. Of course I don't want to, but I know it's part of what makes being alive so great. I guess I don't think about it much."

"How can you not think about it when you wake up right in front of it every day?"

Peter shrugged. We were twins, inseparable for thirteen years of our lives, but our brains worked in very different ways. What was to Peter a part of life's process was to me the most terrifying step I would ever take.

"I'm not going to run Richter with you," I told him.

"You don't have to," he said. "I can hire other people when I'm in charge. Actually, Eileen said she might be interested in working here. That's why she's been helping out. Trying to learn the business, see if she's fit for it."

I nodded, remembering what Mom had told me about her and Dad in high school, knowing what that meant for Peter's and Eileen's future, realizing there was so much more to their relationship that I didn't know about. Maybe I was even a little sad that Eileen was going to be what I couldn't in this place.

"Good," I said. "I'm glad about you and Eileen. I'm glad you have someone."

"I don't want to have just her, though. I want to have you as my friend again. Can you forgive me?"

"I think I can," I said. "But I don't think I'll ever stop feeling jealous."

"I'd say that's okay. Will you be my twin again? That's all I want."

"Okay," I said. I still felt hesitant. But I also felt like I could get there. Peter wasn't an enemy.

"Okay." A smile grew across his cheeks. "Now help me finish setting up the chairs."

The rest of the morning was task after task, going through the cookie-cutter process: arranging decorations and flowers, printing the programs, and finally, setting up the easel with the photo of Milo. Mr. and Mrs. D'Angelo had given Richter a new one that wasn't the profile picture used everywhere else. This was a photo Mrs. D'Angelo had taken a few months ago. She told Mom that Milo hadn't wanted her to take it but she was glad she'd insisted because it was the only one she had from this year. Milo was wearing a genuine smile, one of the ones that would accompany his bad jokes. His hair was brushed out of his eyes, and his freckles were prominent across his tan cheeks. I wondered if this picture was more the real Milo than the profile picture. I'd never know.

After the viewing, Milo's coffin would be carried in by the pallbearers—Peter, Dad, Mr. D'Angelo, Milo's grandpa, and his two uncles. It would be placed right in the center of the dais next to his photo, a gold-and-red wreath atop the lid, representing his body at peace.

I stood up on the dais right next to the photo of Milo, staring out at the many seats. I'd been in this room alone so many times, touching the bodies to wake them and hear their stories, but it was different now. Purple and white flowers lined the pink walls, and petals lined the dais. I was glad I'd helped set up because the arrangement didn't feel as fabricated as usual, at least to me.

I hopped off the dais and made my way toward our second viewing room, which wasn't being used for Milo's visitation. I examined the walls, the space, and the size. It would work. It would work perfectly.

I peeked my head around the corner and saw Peter and Dad rolling Milo's coffin into the first viewing room. The lid was closed, but my heart skipped a beat knowing what lay inside. I waited until they'd settled Milo's coffin on the bier under the dim lights. When they were done, Dad appeared again with the empty rolling table. I went up to him.

"Hey, G," he said.

I wrapped him in a hug. I could feel him tense in surprise, but he quickly reciprocated with a squeeze. I couldn't remember the last time we'd hugged like this, but I thought it had been before Grandma's funeral.

When I pulled away, he maintained his pose out of shock. "What was that for?" he asked.

"Thank you for all your hard work," I said.

Dad smiled, still confused but happy with the surprise. "You're welcome?" It was a question.

"I'm sure it can be taxing sometimes," I said, remembering what Mom explained.

His surprise turned to an emotion I hardly ever saw on his face: gratitude. "I'm sorry for being so hard on you," he replied. I wondered if Mom had told him about our conversation and if that was where this was coming from. Either way, he sounded honest, and I was glad to hear it.

I smiled and then headed upstairs to change into my black dress and grab the folder on my desk. Once again in the Richter household, it was funeral time.

CHAPTER 21

'd just finished setting up in our second visitation room when I heard Milo's parents arrive.

They came thirty minutes before the visitation was scheduled to start in order to finish up some final touches, approve Milo's body, and have some time alone with him before people arrived. Milo still hadn't returned from his walk.

Mom and Dad welcomed them and gave their condolences again. I watched, thinking about what Mom had said the night before. This job wasn't about the dead, it was about the living. I noticed how Mom held Mrs. D'Angelo's hand with the perfect expression of sadness mixed with light, while Dad pressed his hands together in front of him and made conversation more smoothly than a talk show host. They managed to be empathetic about Funeral Day while making people almost forget that was why they were even here. That was Dad's true magic trick, and I allowed myself to actually appreciate it as a kind of magic.

I stood to the side, hands pressed against my thighs beneath the black fabric.

"This is the big finale." I thought it was Mr. D'Angelo at first, but it came from Milo. I spotted him on the other side of the room.

227

Mrs. D'Angelo eventually saw me. She gave me a gentle wave before turning her attention back to Mom. I bit my lip, still terrified of what she thought about me now.

"Thanks for saying something today," Mr. D'Angelo said.

Mom raised a brow and looked to her folder like this time she'd find *Georgia reads eulogy* in the schedule. She knew about my other idea, but I'd forgotten to mention the speech.

I smiled awkwardly at both of them before Dad asked to lead them into the visitation room and make sure everything was to their liking. At least, as much to their liking as Milo's body could be.

I stayed behind, waiting for Amy to arrive. I didn't have my phone with me, so I couldn't ask them how soon they'd be here.

"What happens after this?" Milo asked while we watched our parents walk away together.

"I don't know." I felt the familiar tug of uncertainty.

"No matter what, I can't stay here," Milo said.

I understood that. I couldn't either.

"Well, for now, I guess we can go in the visitation room and wait for people to show up," I suggested.

"I'll follow your lead."

Straight back against the far wall of the visitation room, under a row of low hanging lights, was Milo's open coffin.

There he was, eyes closed, face painted, his hands resting on his heart. He didn't look like the Milo standing beside me. He looked like a wax figure of Milo in a museum. The kind that makes you wonder whether or not it's real. His skin was too drained of color, too tight, his lips lacking plumpness, his cheeks too empty. I looked over at the Milo standing next to me and calculated the differences and looked for the similarities.

I couldn't understand how the Milo beside me had once lived in the one motionless in the coffin.

Even his ghost looked different from the photo of him resting on the dais in the chapel. If I closed my eyes, I wasn't sure which Milo to picture. I couldn't tell which was the real Milo anymore.

"Weird," was all he said.

"I guess you could call it that," I replied quietly.

"Let's stop looking now," he said.

He turned away, but I let my glance linger a little longer. Dad had put Milo in a blue suit that I doubted he ever would have worn when he was alive. It would have been more honest to bury him in his ripped jeans and black hoodie, but no one would want to see that. Next to his coffin was a large basket full of single roses. It was a tradition at so many of our funerals but something I had never participated in. When Grandma died, I hadn't wanted to put a rose on her because it felt like throwing dirt on her grave—like I was only helping her die, pushing her away from me. Now, I understood it. I grabbed a red rose out of the basket and placed the first one on Milo's chest. I knew our final goodbye was yet to come, but maybe this would guide us there.

◊

People arrived quickly. Most came up to the D'Angelos and gave their condolences, then dropped a rose on Milo's chest until he was covered in them, his face still visible. Milo and I stayed to the side. I noticed Peter and Eileen standing together, holding hands. Besides the party, I hadn't seen them act physically intimate in any way. I wondered if they'd been trying to hide it from me or if I really was that thick.

"Everyone seems really sad," Milo said.

"You did die," I noted.

"But, like, is that Madison Andrews? Why would she be crying? We never talked in school."

Why did I cry when I found out, before I woke him up? We never talked in school either.

"I knew it. I knew Warren was going to come." Milo shook his head, but he was laughing. "Oh, Mrs. Berry," he added as she walked in. I couldn't tell if he was happy she was here or not.

"Georgia." Mrs. D'Angelo waved me over, her face completely covered in tears. I glanced at Milo to make sure it was okay to leave him, but he was perfectly occupied with trying to identify all the guests of his funeral. His mom was holding a handkerchief, dabbing it at her face every other minute. I cautiously stepped over to her and an older woman whose face was also red from crying. "This is my mom."

Milo's grandma held out her hand to me and I took it. I decided to try touching it with my other hand like Mom did, but it felt awkward and I quickly dropped it.

"Nana!" Milo was suddenly behind me.

I was holding her hand, staring into her eyes, and Milo was far away. Every memory of Grandma Richter flooded into my heart. I pictured Grandma attending my funeral and found peace in knowing it didn't have to be that way.

"Thank you for taking care of my daughter before we got here. Thank you for being Milo's friend."

Milo was beside her now. While she kept looking at me, he tried to wrap his arms around her, but of course, his arms swept right through her and brought his hug in on himself. His mouth trembled in a silent sob. Neither of us could hug our grandmothers anymore.

I let go of her hand. "You're welcome." I wasn't as good at talking to the family members of the deceased as Mom and Dad were, but I wanted to try.

By now, the room was filled with people. The turnout was slightly smaller than his vigil and much quieter. The cream curtains and carpet kept the sound from bouncing around like in the church. People were grabbing plastic cups and sipping lemon water.

Thankfully, Amy was one of them. They were wearing a black suit and tie and looked stunning. They were next to their mom and in the middle of chewing on one of the lemons.

"Hey," they said when I walked up. "I peeked in the other room. Looks awesome. I think people will love it."

I took a deep breath, hoping Amy was right. Hoping my idea would do Milo justice. "Thanks."

I said hello to Mrs. Chen and asked if it was okay if I took Amy for a moment. When she nodded, I pulled them aside. I needed to tell them one more time. "Thanks for being honest with me. Thanks for being there when I need it even when I'm terrible."

"You don't have to thank me," they said. "I love you, G. I think I'm going to go put a rose on Milo and say goodbye. It would feel wrong not to." Amy kissed my cheek. "Sit with me during the service?"

"Yeah, for sure."

Amy gave my hand one last squeeze before letting our fingers untwine.

I found my way back to Milo, who had been wandering between people, listening in on conversations. Together we drifted to a corner.

"How're you liking your funeral?" I asked under my breath.

"I'm waiting on the juicy stuff at the ceremony." His tone turned serious as he pressed his thumb and forefinger across his eyebrows. "It feels like being at home did. I can't talk to them. I can't let them know that I'm actually here. All I want is to—"

Milo stopped, eyes wide.

"What?" I turned around in search of whatever had grabbed his attention.

"He came," Milo whispered, as if there was any chance that the man walking through the door could actually hear him.

Jordan was wearing a jacket and a tie. I had weirdly expected him to wear his Lucky's shirt. He stood awkwardly by the entrance, maybe waiting for someone to invite him in, questioning whether or not he should leave.

"He wasn't at my vigil," Milo said. "Sorry—that's my boss, or was my boss, at Lucky's." He was so in awe he'd forgotten that I'd already met Jordan.

Milo was still staring when Jordan approached me.

"Thanks for inviting me," he said, pulling at his tie like it was choking him.

"You invited him?" Milo asked.

I couldn't respond to Milo. "You're welcome," I told Jordan.

"Seriously, if you hadn't, I, er, wouldn't have come. And you're right, I would have regretted it."

"Mr. and Mrs. D'Angelo are over there." I pointed to them in the middle of the room.

I didn't have to tell Jordan anything else. He took a breath and walked across the room. As soon as I saw the conversation begin, I turned my head because I knew it wasn't mine to witness. Milo walked over because it was his.

I found Amy again, and we took a seat on one of the pink couches in the middle of the room. I felt myself wanting to glance over at the D'Angelos. I wanted to know if their talk with Jordan was going well or if I had started a terrible conflict at their only son's funeral, but I kept my focus on Amy.

"I talked to Eileen. I apologized," they said.

"You did?"

Amy nodded, running their hands on their pants to wipe off the sweat. "It was stressful, but I needed to apologize for hating her for something she didn't do instead of just being mad she spread it, you know? We kind of worked it out. Don't worry, though—I still hate Peter."

"Oh, no, I talked to Peter this morning. We're good too."

"G! You have to keep me updated on these things. Now I have to go apologize to Peter for being cold to him while I was standing in front of him making up with his girlfriend? Damn. Make me into the bad guy. What did you say?"

I explained our heart-to-heart.

"Hmm. I'm still mad, but I'm going to be honest. I believe he's sorry. I know how much he loves you."

"I do too." And I did.

Dad announced that it was time for the service and everyone could head to the chapel. On my way out of the visitation room, I turned back to watch as Dad closed the lid on Milo and his flowers, sealing the latches to keep him in. I gulped, hoping I'd be able to get to his body again for one final attempt to send him back. Sudden worry crept in. Maybe it would never work and he'd be a ghost forever.

Amy and I found seats in the middle of the chapel, next to Eileen, with an extra spot for Peter.

I was sure Peter had talked to Eileen this morning, but I needed to say something. Making amends had to be more than just her apologizing.

"Hey, Eileen?"

"Hmm?"

"I'm sorry for making you feel like you didn't fit. And for shutting you out before even trying. I'm going to try more from now on."

"Thank you, Georgia," she said. That was our new beginning.

Barely a week ago, the five people attending Betty's funeral had sat here. This time, the room was full. Milo was sitting on the floor in the aisle, right beside his mom and grandma up front. He had the best seat in the house at his own funeral.

Hugh was the pastor at Milo's family's church, so he stood before the crowd to welcome them. I thought it ironic that Milo's funeral was religious, being led by a pastor who had no idea of Milo's actual beliefs. But it was for his parents.

And so the funeral began.

"Please, may we all rise for a prayer."

Everyone stood, even me. Although lately I'd let these moments pass and my mind wander, this time I decided to send something out into the universe in hopes it would find its home somewhere.

I thought, *I don't know if you're there. But if you are and if you forgive me for all my doubt and whatnot, please bring comfort to Milo's family. Let them find happiness. That's all I ask.* Before the moment was over, I decided to not just pray but to think about Milo. I devoted a moment to letting him be the only thing alive in my brain. I'd had plenty of moments like this, where Milo took over every firing neuron, but this time I let it be peaceful instead of urgent: a reassurance that even if I managed to send him back, he still had a way of living on.

The moment was quick. As I took a seat with the rest of the

congregation, the pallbearers walked down the aisle carrying the coffin while the pianist stationed at the end of the stage played a soft melody. Simultaneously, a slideshow with pictures of Milo scrolled by on the projector screen. Photos of him as a toddler, as a dorky preteen. There was even a photo of our entire soccer team, and I found Amy and myself in the lineup.

When the pictures came to an end and Milo's coffin had been secured on the bier, Hugh began to speak. It was the familiar template again. Kind. Brave. An exemplary student. Somerton's hero. The best son parents could ask for. That was the only one that rang true. I couldn't see Milo's expression to know what he felt about it all.

He told stories he wasn't there for and made assumptions about where Milo was now without knowing he was staring right at him. "Next," Hugh finally said, "Milo's friend Georgia Richter has been asked to say a few words."

I gulped and reached for the folded piece of paper in my pocket. I rose from my seat, thankful I was sitting closest to the aisle. At least I didn't have to stagger along the pew past other people and fall on my face. I could barely stand steadily as it was.

Everyone's eyes were on me, but instead of following me out of the room like at the vigil, they followed me up the stage to the podium where I adjusted the microphone.

"Hi." Great start. I looked down to Milo, who had been crying. He gave me a thumbs up, which was enough for me to take a deep breath, shuffle my paper one last time, and keep going. "I'm Georgia Richter. Um. My family owns this funeral home, and, uh, I, uh, knew Milo. We got to know each other."

Some people looked confused because obviously no one had ever seen us hanging out in school.

235

"Um. Death is confusing for everyone," I said. "No matter what you believe in, no matter how much it scares you or doesn't scare you, it's always confusing. But there's something especially confusing about when someone young dies. Because it's not fair and it feels like the universe has decided to spite us or something. And so, Milo's death is confusing, it's unfair, and it hurts. It hurts us all no matter how much we knew him, because he was young, because he didn't deserve it, because we all know he was a good kid, because we are all afraid."

Milo's mom was shaking, her hand covering her mouth. I tried to tune out the sound of her crying. I wanted her to approve of this. I wanted it to be worthy of Milo.

"So I think sometimes we try to make ourselves feel better by making him out to be something he wasn't. We call him a hero, a great student with so many friends who loved him, the epitome of a sixteen-year-old boy. That makes us feel like he had more than what he got. But I don't think that's fair to Milo."

I felt like I was going astray, like my thesis statement had gotten tangled in a mess of my anxiety and Milo's ghost and his sobbing parents. I was just talking. I wasn't even reading off my paper anymore.

"Milo wasn't a hero. He wasn't that great of a student. He didn't actually have that many friends. He wasn't the epitome of . . . anything. We shouldn't pretend he was something he wasn't to make it easier for us. We should remember him as honestly as we can. A teenage boy who loved his parents more than anything, a person who worked hard at Lucky's, someone who was willing to give up his dreams to help his family. Most importantly, he was an artist."

Milo's lips twitched into a grin.

236

"I didn't actually know Milo that well," I said. "No one did. The only one who truly knew Milo was Milo, but he left us with a way to remember him, to maybe understand who he really was a little better."

Milo now had his hand to his mouth, and Mrs. D'Angelo was looking up, and Amy was nodding encouragingly. I gulped before starting again.

"In our second visitation room, just out of the chapel to your right, you'll find a gallery of Milo's art. He was always sketching. I think that is one thing everyone in this room knew about him. Milo wanted to share his art and never got to. Thanks to the help of my friend Amy, there are copies of Milo's art hung around the room, and I ask that after this you take a walk around and look at his incredible drawings. I've also set up a fund for the D'Angelo family that will be linked on the Richter website. Please admire Milo's art and remember him by it, and if you feel compelled, please donate to help support his loving family. Thanks."

Milo smiled through his tears.

As I made my way down the aisle, Mrs. D'Angelo grabbed my hand.

"He would have loved that," she whispered. "Thank you."

"He did love that," Milo said.

I took a breath of relief and sat down, ready for the end.

CHAPTER 22

After the service, the entire funeral crammed into the visitation room, aka makeshift gallery, to see Milo's art. Amy and I had printed eight-by-eleven images of his Instagram posts. They'd helped me blow them up to the right size in Photoshop, fix any oddities, and print them on their fancy poster printer. There were random sketches, self-portraits, digital art of his Vagabonds, and pages from a comic book work in progress.

"That was a great speech, Georgia," Warren said when we bumped into each other in the gallery.

"Very pretty." Madison Andrews.

"You took a risk there, and I appreciated it." Principal Wendell.

"It'll go to your head," Amy said after the seventh or eighth person complimented my eulogy and the gallery project. We were standing in front of one of Milo's digital drawings, a knight who looked like Milo riding a Vagabond. But as I looked at it, I realized Milo didn't just resemble the knight—he *was* the rider who could move between dimensions.

"If anything, I'm going to try to keep a lot less from going to my head," I said.

"Yeah?"

"Yeah. I mean, that's easy to say and a lot harder to do. But I think I'm going to ask my mom if I can go to therapy."

"G!" Amy almost spilled their cup of lemon water. "That's great. I'm so proud of you! I'd suggest my therapist, but they already know too much about you."

"You talk about me in therapy?"

"Duh."

"Good or bad?"

"Both. Mostly good."

"You can talk to me about things too," I reminded them. "I know I'm not a therapist, but I'm here. I really am here."

"I know." We followed the wall around the room, moving past various clusters of people regarding the prints.

"Hey," I said, "I wanted to ask if you were working on any new sewing projects?"

Amy's eyes lit up. "Um, always! I'm getting really interested in silk organza, but it's tough to work with so it's a learning process. Oh! And there's this internship in Chicago at a design studio for high school students, and I'm going to apply. I have to send in a portfolio. I've never put together a portfolio!"

"That sounds amazing." It *felt* amazing to connect like this—like we used to. "Let me know if you need a model." I struck an awkward pose.

Amy laughed and grabbed my hand as we kept walking together. Closer together than ever before, I thought.

Eventually, people started to exit the visitation room to go to the reception, which was being held at a banquet hall a few miles out of town.

"You going?" Amy asked.

"Actually, I think I'll stay." My attention snagged on Jordan, who was leaning in close to the spread from Milo's comic.

"I have a few more things to do. But you should go, don't worry about me."

Amy nodded and headed out with the crowd.

One of the side tables in the visitation room had little compartments that we usually kept empty, but I had stored away a particular print for Jordan earlier that day.

I grabbed it and held it behind my back. "Hey," I said, joining him in front of the comic.

"He was an amazing artist," Jordan said. I could hear the tightness remaining in his voice. "It's not fair. It's confusing. You were right. That was a good eulogy. I think it kind of horrified a few people, but Milo would have liked it."

"Thanks."

"Thank you." He turned to me. "I meant what I said earlier. I wouldn't have come if you hadn't told me to. I would have stayed away, and then I never would have talked to the D'Angelos like that. They aren't happy with me, but they're glad I came."

I nodded. I didn't ask any further questions about their interaction.

"He was like a son to me. He wasn't my son. But he was damn close."

"I'm sorry you lost him."

Jordan turned to me, pursing his lips to keep from crying, but I could see the shimmer of tears in his eyes.

"I think out of everyone," I said, "you had the best understanding of who Milo D'Angelo really was."

"That kid was still a mystery in so many ways," he said.

"Definitely. I just mean that he trusted you with a lot of himself."

Jordan nodded, looking down at his feet.

"I have something for you." I brought the frame from behind my back and held out the portrait Milo had sketched of Jordan. I'd swiped the frame from a random drawing hanging on the wall of Richter, but no one would notice it was gone, and this was a far more important use for it.

Jordan grabbed the picture, holding it like his life depended on it.

"I found that on his Instagram. I wasn't sure if you had a copy or not, but I thought that you should."

He hugged the frame and threw his head back, trying to keep the tears trapped.

"So, I should go. I just wanted you to have that. Thank you for coming."

I left him alone in the visitation room to give him whatever time he needed. I would never fully understand Jordan's relationship with Milo. I would never know all the things Jordan knew about that mysterious kid who'd walked the halls with me. I didn't need to because that stuff was Jordan's and Milo's to know and no one else's. But it was like Mr. D'Angelo had said—I found solace in knowing a piece of Milo lived in Jordan, a piece of him lived in me, in his parents, and now everyone who enjoyed his art today. It didn't make up a complete picture, and it would never be the same as having Milo here and alive, but at least he wouldn't be entirely gone.

◊

The one moment my brain had been so focused on for an entire week had passed, and I was left to greet the other side with nothing to offer. The end of the funeral made me think more about death than the funeral itself.

But I still had one more task. I still had to try to send Milo back.

The chapel was empty except for me, Milo's body, and his ghost.

He was sitting in the pews looking up at the stained-glass window at the top of the wall. The light from the early setting autumn sun was shining in, perfectly illuminating the coffin and the aisle down to my feet, everything glowing golden.

I took a seat next to him.

"Hey," was all he said, his eyes unwavering, and I instantly worried I hadn't done the right thing after all.

"Was that okay?" I asked and pointed back toward the gallery. "Did I mess up?"

"That was perfect. You fulfilled the final request I didn't even realize I had." He smiled. "Although you said I wasn't a hero and I didn't have any friends. Like, how dare you." Milo held his hand to his chest in feigned offense.

"Yeah, that was totally uncalled for."

"Seriously, though. My parents loved it. That's all that really matters. You said before that you're sorry for waking me up. I was sorry too. I was angry, even. But not anymore. What you did with my art and that speech—you made something so pointless and unfair matter a little more. Thank you."

I couldn't shake the bitter taste on my tongue that had been lingering there the past week. "It still feels wrong. Like I shouldn't have ever knocked on your parents' door. That I shouldn't have ever woken you up."

"Maybe it was wrong. Maybe it was a morally gray thing to do. Maybe you lied and shouldn't have. And maybe it was all a lie at first but isn't one now. Maybe doing the right thing took you a bit to figure it out. Maybe you eventually found it. Maybe you didn't."

242

"Is that supposed to make me feel better? Because damn," I joked, trying to make this moment a bit brighter. But I felt the weight of unknowns in what he was saying. Unknowns not just in death but in every part of how we live.

"Well, you have to decide how you feel, and you have to decide what you're going to do with how you feel. You get to decide what you do and whether or not it's the right thing for you. No one else can."

The sun was shining right in my eyes, but I had only just noticed. Sitting on the bench right then, I felt closer to Milo than I ever had, but I felt a new form of uncertainty.

"Does death make you wise?" I asked as I considered his words.

"No, but I think being a ghost for a week and really contemplating your own death and how that affects those around you beats you down until you see things in a different light."

We sat in silence for a bit.

"I think we're even now," he finally said.

"Even?"

"I did something for you, and you did something for me. That's even."

I could think of a lot of ways Milo had helped me, but I couldn't place the one he was referring to.

He must've seen my confusion because he said, "I left your scrapbook out," as if it were obvious.

"Wh—" My breath caught. "I wouldn't have talked to my mom if she hadn't found it," I finally said, a final brush across the canvas to make it complete.

Milo shook his head. He looked smug, entirely aware of himself.

"Which means I wouldn't have talked to Peter."

Milo nodded, that look still plastered on his face.

"Which means . . ." I knew what it meant, and he did too. That I would have continued to keep everything buried inside me. That the only person who would ever hear about little selected aspects of my life was Amy. That I would continue to shut everyone else out around me until I was left empty.

"How did you even know about the scrapbook?"

Milo tapped his temple with his forefinger. "Like I said, wise."

"You said you *weren't* wise."

"That's what a wise person would say."

I wanted to shove him but knew I couldn't.

"I thought you couldn't make changes like that. How did it stay out on my bed when you moved it?"

"I guess this is one change the universe let me make," he said.

I thanked the universe for the favor.

"Where do we go from here?" he asked.

"You could go to the reception," I suggested.

"No. You know what I mean."

"Well." I gulped. "It's not my choice. What do you want?"

Milo bit his lip and brushed his hair out of his eyes. He looked vastly different from the photo surrounded by flowers. That boy looked less worn down, less tired, more excited.

"I think you're ready," Milo said.

"I'm ready?"

Milo nodded. He didn't look smug this time.

I felt less ready than before. I felt more afraid to see him go, more terrified of what my world would be like without him, more worried about what would happen to him and his parents. Except the fear had manifested into something different.

It was more a fear of missing someone than of running toward oblivion.

"I don't feel ready, though," I said. "I know that's unfair. I know. I'm not trying to keep you here. But I don't know if I'll ever be ready."

"It's something you'll have to accept eventually."

Eventually. It had to happen Eventually. When it would be, I couldn't know. But it would, and I would have to face it then. For now, though, I only needed to come to terms with Eventually.

"It's a good life," he said. "It was short and there were a trillion things I wanted to do that I probably wouldn't have ever done but liked having the option to do. But I'm glad I got what I was given."

"Aren't you mad it wasn't enough? Aren't you scared?"

"Yep. Hard not to be. I'm more scared of what I'll miss out on. I know it's not going to hurt. It's going to hurt less than this does now. But when I think about, you know, the vastness of our universe, and I realize I didn't get to experience even a tiny sliver of existence that human beings are given, I'm terrified and angry about what I didn't get."

"More time," I said. "It's what everyone wants."

"Do you think it's the unknown about death that scares people so much, or is it that we all secretly know and we're too scared to admit it?"

I thought I had an answer for him, but I was too scared to admit it.

Milo inhaled, and he opened his mouth to let the fading sunbeams in. I could swear the sunlight was being inhaled into his lungs, to give him more air and thereby more life, but it was just sunlight. It was only radiation that happened to land in this spot at this time. Anyway, a cloud darkened the beam to remind us we were sitting in a musty small-town funeral home chapel.

"Let's hope this works," Milo said.

I took one last look at his freckles, his brown eyes, his shaggy hair, and tried to reset that as the image I saw of Milo D'Angelo when I closed my eyes. I shoved away all my assumptions, all the unfair images, all the dead ones. *Lucky's. Hard worker. Loved his parents. Artist.* Looking at him, I realized all the things that I'd never know about him. So many neurons danced together to complexly create Milo. A dance that wasn't anyone else's to join, unless invited.

"You're not going to be gone, really," I told him. "It'll still feel like parts of you are here."

"You made sure the me that's left behind is truer to the one in that funeral picture. That's all you."

Milo's casket waited for me while Milo waited for the end. When I was about to start toward the dais and try one last time, a thought occurred to me.

I stayed next to him and held up my hand, my palm to him. He matched my movements because he understood. Milo was more soul than body now.

As our hands inched closer, I knew that this time when I touched him, he would disappear forever.

"Make it a good one, Georgia."

"I will."

We moved our hands to close the distance, and when they collided, I could feel his warm skin against mine for a fragment of a moment. He felt real.

Then the sensation vanished, along with the rest of him.

The room rang silent. The seat beside me empty.

246

I waited to see if he would show up again in a moment. He didn't. He was gone.

The deep loneliness hit when I noticed the curve at the top of coffin, holding his body. The feeling of missing him now permeated the walls of Richter, pressing in on me in a new way. They were pushing my back against the bench and the bench into the floor. My hands clutched at the neck of my dress to get a breath of air. I felt Eventually screaming around me as she turned into Now. I laid my head down on the seat. I let myself cry. I didn't worry about holding anything in or anyone hearing. I let the pain out in my sobs until I was dry.

CHAPTER 23

I stood on the side of the driveway, arms crossed to keep me warm in the bitter morning air, watching as Dad backed the hearse out of the garage. The white curtains were hiding Milo's coffin, which was hiding Milo's body, which was on its way to the crematorium. It wouldn't have to hide much longer.

Dad was almost to the street when a car pulled up. We were both confused when we realized it belonged to the D'Angelos. Milo's parents were supposed to meet Dad at the crematorium, not here. I hadn't seen them since the funeral the day before, and I'd kind of hoped it would stay that way.

Mrs. D'Angelo got out of the car and approached the hearse. Dad rolled down the window so she could speak to him. Judging by her posture, she looked like she had finally gotten a full night's sleep. She was wearing jeans and a jacket and smelled like she had just been smoking. She nodded a few times at Dad through the window, but I couldn't quite make out what they were saying to each other.

Then she turned to look directly at me. "Georgia."

I froze, suddenly afraid she was going to ask me to come along to witness the cremation. My next assumption was that she had taken issue with what I said at Milo's funeral.

"Is everything okay?" I asked hesitantly.

"Everything's okay," she said. "I realized something yesterday, though. I think Milo's father and I need time. This isn't anything against you, we want you to know that. In fact, what you have done for us has helped in ways I don't think we can even understand. We appreciate how hard you've worked to honor Milo's memory. Jordan said you convinced him to come to the funeral. Thank you for that—that would have been important to Milo."

I gulped. She was being too nice after what I'd told her. "It's—it's okay if you're mad at me. For letting you assume Milo and I were closer than we were . . ."

"I'm not angry about that, Georgia. You didn't mean any harm. But I did realize that I've been chasing Milo, and I thought I could chase him through you. I wanted to know everything I could about him, and I thought you could tell me. That's not fair of me to do to you, to make you to feel like you needed to be more than what you are. You don't need an old grieving woman leaning on you. And I think in some ways, it's made it harder for me to work through some things. So, maybe it's best if we don't have contact with you for a while."

I was suddenly more aware of Dad's and Mr. D'Angelo's eyes on me, of the breeze against my cheeks, of the numbness in my fingers, of the slowly changing season.

"I was chasing Milo too," I said.

"I see," she said.

"I think it is best if we have space," I agreed.

"Thank you. Don't be a stranger or anything, though. That's not what we mean."

"I understand."

She nodded again, and she didn't try to hug me. She didn't cry. She pressed her lips together and walked back down the

249

driveway to her car. Her glance didn't even linger.

I awkwardly waved to Mr. D'Angelo when we made eye contact, and he returned the gesture.

I watched them all drive away, taking Milo with them. I watched until the hearse turned the corner, and I was okay knowing that was the last time I would be around him. I was glad to know that I wouldn't be talking to any of the D'Angelos any time soon. Milo wasn't here, but he echoed in the air all over Somerton.

I turned to walk back into Richter, out of the cold, and decided I would be okay if I started calling it home.

◊

Dad returned a few hours later, so I knew it was officially done. He didn't say anything about it. I thought of asking, but I already knew everything I needed to.

Milo's funeral was all cleaned up. His ghost was officially gone, and so was his body. It was all past tense. Now, the only people left in the building were the Richter family. No funeral guests, no ghosts.

Mom said she wanted to make family dinner and she expected us to all join. She made it clear that Dad wasn't to work the rest of the night, I wasn't to go storming off into my room, and Peter wasn't to secretly text Eileen under the table. She started the soup and lit a fire to keep us warm from winter's quick approach. We ate together, and even when funeral business came up as it inevitably did, it didn't feel wrong.

After dinner I went downstairs to collect Milo's prints from the visitation room. I placed them in their folder along with the funeral pamphlet I had saved from that day.

When I checked the fund for the D'Angelos, it had already surpassed the $10,000 goal. People were still donating. I hoped that since the D'Angelos didn't have Milo's income anymore, this would help with everything they were going through.

Back in my room, I grabbed the scrapbook from my desk and sat on my bed under the glow-in-the-dark stars. I remembered leaning down over the glass case to examine the page from *The Book of the Dead*. I understood now why Milo had wanted to show me those pages. I still didn't know how he knew about the scrapbook or managed to move it, but there was a lot I didn't know. At least I recognized what he wanted me to see.

I opened the binder, ready to paste Milo's pamphlet into it and call him page seventy-two. Instead, I flipped to the front and pulled off the picture of Grandma and me making a snowman. I rested the image against my pillow and let the hope that Grandma eventually found peace hold the fear down. If she was still out there, surely she'd have found her way back to Richter somehow. So maybe she really had escaped her abyss. Milo and I had talked about what we did and didn't believe, and even though I might never know what had happened to Grandma, I believed with my entire being that she would forgive me. I deserved to forgive myself too.

I returned my attention to the rest of the pages. One by one, I ripped them out of the binder. I didn't unclamp the rings and slide them out. I needed the satisfaction of removing them with a tear. Grandma's page, Oscar's page, and Betty's page included.

When the binder was empty, I tossed the pages onto the floor, and in their place I slipped the folder with Milo's drawings inside and closed the cover. I took a sharpie and wrote *Milo's art* across the front and slid the binder under my bed.

I might have sent them back, but they were all still ghosts. They still haunted me.

I grabbed the stack of pages from the scrapbook, placing Milo's funeral pamphlet on top of it. I walked out into the living room with the stack under my arm. Mom, Dad, and Peter were sitting on the couch, enjoying the warmth from the fire. Mom was knitting, Dad reading, and Peter scrolling on his phone.

"What's that?" Dad asked me when he saw the pile under my arm. Mom knew right away.

"It's for the fire," I said, kneeling at the brick. I placed the stack of papers right into the flames.

The heat warmed my cheeks, and I kept watching as the pages folded in on themselves, Milo's pamphlet at the center. The light flickered and the smoke stung my eyes, but I stared without a blink as Milo's image melted away. Just like Milo, my ghosts were now just ashes. I couldn't obsess over them forever. I needed to finally set them free. When the pages had been entirely swallowed by the fire, I turned to see my family.

"Can I join you guys?" I asked.

"Of course," Mom said. I took a seat next to her and leaned my head on her shoulder. Through the weaving of yarn and needles, I still watched the flicker of flames.

"Can we hang a few of Milo's drawings downstairs?" I asked. "We have so many of those random paintings. It'd be cool to replace some with something, I don't know, more meaningful."

"I love that idea," Mom said as Morty jumped onto her lap to bat at her knitting. She kissed my head.

"And Pete"—I leaned around Mom's knitting to see him better on the other side—"I thought maybe you, me, Amy, and Eileen could hang out tomorrow? See a movie or something."

"Yeah, definitely," Peter said, a big grin across his face.

"I'll text them right now." I created a group chat for the first time in years and asked if people were free to hang out. Eileen responded first, saying, *I'd love to,* and Amy quickly confirmed they would join. When Peter's thumbs-up emoji appeared on my screen, I couldn't help but smile.

I put my phone away and returned my head to Mom's shoulder, allowing the flames to ripple only in my peripheral vision. Richter was my home, this was my family, and I was free of ghosts.

EPILOGUE

I stood in the back of the chapel in my black dress and black Mary Janes. I was staring at the pamphlet in my hands as the officiant read off his Mad Lib. It all felt so familiar, like I was standing in a dent my Mary Janes had made in this carpet over the years.

I hadn't helped with a funeral in two months. The last time I'd even stepped foot in the chapel was at Milo's funeral. Here I was once again, almost as if I'd never left. No matter how much I wanted to separate myself from this place, it still felt natural to go through the motions I knew so well. The walls couldn't help but feel like home.

In the time I normally would've spent helping with funerals, I'd instead started seeing a therapist, Dr. Katie. She was queer inclusive and specialized in grief counseling, which were pretty much my two criteria. At my first session with her, I'd been hesitant to say anything. But it only took a couple of her prodding questions for my heart to pour out on her office floor. She practically scooped it up and cradled it in her arms that day, inviting her trust to me. By the end of that session, she already knew all about Grandma, Peter and Eileen, Mom, Dad, Amy, Richter, and Milo. Well, mostly about Milo.

I was especially grateful that Dr. Katie helped me learn

254

more about asexuality than I ever knew before. She pointed me toward ace spectrum forums and helped me talk through elements of my identity that I'd never gotten to tell anyone. It felt freeing to sit in that tiny little room on that uncomfortable couch and dig inside my head in less scary ways. To feel validated in ways I never had before.

Now, a picture of Marta, the dead woman, smiled up at me from the pamphlet. The photo was from when she was younger—not much older than me. It was different than the one resting on the easel. That was a more recent photo. In both, she looked so happy.

I felt my heart running circles in my chest at the thought of talking to Marta after the service. It had been two months since I last spoke to a ghost. I wasn't sure I remembered how. What was I going to say?

I still thought about Milo all the time. He didn't haunt me, but he was always with me. Dr. Katie said to fill the emptiness with memories, so that's what I did: memories of our conversations, the moment I first saw his art, meandering around the museum talking about taxidermy. He'd been a friend, if only for a moment.

I tried to let the good memories win when thoughts of dead bodies threatened to consume me.

It wasn't like my death anxiety went away after starting therapy. I didn't think it would ever go away, actually. I still rushed past the embalming room door at night and got anxious in a car. I still fell asleep every night remembering that it's practice for death, jerking awake when the thought became too prominent for me to stay entrapped in the darkness of closed eyes. I still thought of my own death when I remembered Milo's or Grandma's. But I was learning to breathe through it.

To close my eyes again and tell my thoughts, *You're not helping*.

Because I had control. Those thoughts were intruders, and I could tell them to leave where they weren't welcomed. I could use one of my best skills and simply walk away from them. Some nights, they'd even listen to me and stay away. If it got really bad, I'd look up to my glow-in-the-dark stars and think about Eventually and let that settle my nerves. I'd look over to the drawing of Milo riding a Vagabond that hung on my wall, a reminder that so long as I left something good behind, death couldn't take me away entirely. And I still had time.

Marta's funeral was small, but it was full of family. When the service ended, I said goodbye to everyone as they exited the chapel, emulating what Mom and Dad were so good at. It didn't feel as hard anymore.

When the room was completely empty, I closed and locked the door, pulling the curtains over the glass so no one could see in. I double-checked the handle even though I knew it was locked and noticed the crack in the door from when I'd slammed it open. My mark on Richter. Although I was starting to think my mark was even bigger than that.

I turned to face the coffin.

Each step toward the dais was slow. The coffin grew as I approached, but it didn't intimidate me like I'd expected. When I looked over the side to see Marta, I found the resemblance between the photo on the easel and the dead woman surrounded by white cotton clouds. Her skin was much too tight and still and colorless, but her cheeks were the same shape as those in the photo, and her lips looked as if they had smiled hundreds of times. Like they had smiled only recently.

As I stood looking at the woman, I was reminded of Betty. I was reminded of Grandma.

And like always, I looked around the room to make sure no one else was here, to check that I had locked the door and drawn the curtains. Everything was familiar, like a return after a long journey.

I reached over and tapped the woman on her forehead, ready to meet her.

But nothing happened.

I checked the room to find Marta's ghost, but she was nowhere.

I tapped her cheek.

Still nothing.

The dead woman didn't appear next to me. There was not a ghost to be found.

A few months ago, I probably would've started freaking out, wondering what I had done wrong and why it wouldn't work. I waited for my heart to start pounding, for my hands to get sweaty and my thoughts to spiral. But instead, I started laughing.

I threw my hand to my forehead as my laughter echoed through the room. I looked down at Marta's body and whispered, "Thank you."

As I turned around to get Peter and tell him it was time to tear down, I noticed the bench where Milo and I had said our final goodbyes. He was the last one I talked to. The last one I needed to talk to.

I didn't need it anymore. For now, I was all right. I was alive, and that was enough.

AUTHOR'S NOTE

Like Georgia, I first realized I would die when I was six years old. I think we all have that moment of realization—some younger than others—but no matter one's age, it's a terrifying moment to experience.

And like Georgia, by the time I was sixteen, I was consumed by this thought. I didn't know how to break free of the constant fear of this terrible inevitability. I saw death all around me in everything I did, and I couldn't find solace in anything. And then one time, during one of my many panics, I was able to find a moment of peace: an awareness that, all things considered, I could have it much worse. I thought, *At least I don't live in a funeral home where I'm literally surrounded by it every day.*

That's where the story was born—from a scared teenage me who wondered what would happen if someone with my fears literally lived with them. I knew I needed to get my death thoughts out, so I did it in the one productive form I knew.

And, reader, it saved me. It was still utterly terrifying a lot of the time to stare right at my fear on the page in front of me and delve as deep into it as I could, or research all the intricacies of the death industry and learn what happens after death in a practical sense. But in doing that, I learned to understand it all through Georgia's experience. I learned to, in a way, embrace it. It became a cathartic experience to dance with my fear, and now I get to close this book, look at its beautiful cover and say, "That's where you live now." Sure, the death thoughts still often find their way off these pages and sliver back into the crevices of my mind, but I remind them that I've given them a place to live, and they should return to that home now. And maybe that home can be where someone else finds peace from our universal fear.

When I first began the journey to publishing these words, one of my early readers finished the book and told me they needed it. I found a new kind of solace in knowing others could need Georgia's story too. Because we all have that realization. Because it's something we all face and must learn to cope with in our own ways. Whether it's through joking like Georgia's father, taking a businesslike approach like Georgia's mother, not letting it in like her brother, or embracing Eventually like Georgia herself. I hope that if you, like me, have struggled to find your way to cope, Georgia helped you. She helped me. And if not, at the very least, I hope you were entertained. Thank you so much for reading.

ACKNOWLEDGMENTS

In the five years it took to make this book what it is now, so many people played an important role in the journey. Whether they were there at every step of the process or for only a piece of it, I have them to thank. Here it goes . . .

First, I want to thank my incredible agent, Jim McCarthy, for believing in me and in Georgia. You are a mighty advocate. You took such good care of this piece of my soul, and you answered all my questions with lightning speed and complete kindness. I'm so grateful to have you on my team.

To Amy Fitzgerald, my amazing editor. I knew from our first phone call that you were the perfect editor for this story. You knew exactly what I was trying to say, which means you knew exactly how to help make it even better. Thank you for believing in me.

Of course, thank you to my amazing and incredible partner, Carson. I love getting to spend my life with you. Your love and support is such a driving force that I don't know where I'd be without it. Like the dedication says, I've loved you since forever, and I'll love you for forever. Even in whatever comes after.

Thank you to the team at Lerner and Carolrhoda Lab for being a vital piece of bringing this story to life. Special thanks to designer Lindsey Owens, creative director Danielle Carnito, and production designer Erica Johnson. Thanks to expert readers Akelah Adams (through Salt and Sage Books) and Zhui Ning Chang (through Tessera Editorial).

Thanks so much to my blurbers, Saundra Mitchell, and Nita Tyndall.

To all of my early readers, you were the reason I felt confident I could publish. Helen, you're the first one I shared these words with, and that time where it was just us who knew Georgia's story will forever be special. Thank you to Katelyn for your keen copyeditor eye. To Avery for reading this book and telling me "I needed that," because I needed to hear that. And to Gaby, Levi, and Dane for your insights.

To all of my writing friends, I am so glad I get to know you. It's one of the best parts about this job. To Saundra Mitchell for being the first editor of my first ever publication but also for all the wisdom and the laughs and friendship. To Dana Choe Draper for our weekly writing sessions and the excitement for our stories and the brilliant ideas that make me a better writer and person. To Avery Kay for all the FaceTimes and working through story problems together. You're an amazing critique partner. To Jade Adia and Rod Pulido, what a pleasure it's been to have your support throughout this strange and wild debut journey. To Hope Kelham, the most beautiful poet and the best photographer. Thank you for the coffee-shop writing sessions and amazing author pic. To Kaitlyn Hill and Jenna Kilpinen for all the messages and support. To all the 2022 Debuts, I'm so glad I got to share this year with all of your amazing stories. To Jim's Gems—not only do I have the best agent in the world, I have the best agent siblings in the world. And to SubSolidarity, y'all kept me sane during the horror process that is submission, and I'm so lucky to have you all.

Thank you to Mom and Dad for always encouraging my love of writing and letting this dream flourish in the way I needed. I love you guys. Thank you to my in-laws for your constant support and excitement. Thank you to Katelyn, Sophie, and Margaret for being the absolute best sisters I could ever ask for. And Katelyn, thank you for our adventures of all forms.

There are so many other people in my life to thank. Lane for the insight on what it was like growing up in a funeral home. To Avery's dad for all the dad jokes. Katie for crying when you first saw the cover. Grace, Isabelle, Abby, Evan for your friendship.

Thank you to any bookseller or librarian or teacher who pushes this book. You all do incredible things, and this industry thrives because of you.

Finally, my biggest thanks go to you, reader, for picking up this book. I hope you loved it.

QUESTIONS FOR DISCUSSION

1. How does Georgia's anxiety about death affect her thought process and actions in her daily life?

2. Why does Georgia revive and speak to the spirits of the dead? What does she get out of these interactions?

3. Why does Georgia allow Mr. and Mrs. D'Angelo to believe that she was close with Milo? What would you have done in her position?

4. In what ways is Amy a supportive friend to Georgia? In what ways do they set healthy boundaries for themself and express what they need and expect from the friendship?

5. Why do you think Milo wanted to show Georgia the page from *The Book of the Dead* at the Field Museum?

6. Why does Eileen say she spread Peter's rumor about Georgia? Why do you think Eileen might've felt as if she "didn't fit" at her school or in Somerton?

7. What mistakes has Georgia made in her friendships with Eileen, Peter, and Amy? How does she learn from them?

8. Describe Georgia's dad's attitude toward death and his approach to his job. What do you think he and Georgia could learn from each other about coping with death and grief?

9. Many people exaggerate Milo's positive qualities and achievements when memorializing him. How does Georgia find a way to honor Milo's life without embellishing it?

10. Do you think Milo and Georgia could've been friends if Milo had lived? How do you think that friendship would've been different from the one they develop after Milo is dead?

11. Why does Georgia decide to burn her scrapbook?

12. Why do you think Georgia can no longer revive ghosts after Milo's funeral? What else has changed for Georgia?